Carousel

With Music box melody,

And rainbow hue,

Painted horses dance

For you,

Pushing darkness' fears away,

Whilst inside your mind

The monsters lay

In wait.

They appeared overnight. Nobody knew where they had come from, or where they would go, and nobody wanted them here. At least that is what they say now, but then it was a different story. Things are always different with hindsight. People like them are never welcome, Travellers, Gypsies, whoever or whatever they were. This world is theirs as much as yours or mine, although they would argue differently. The world is not theirs, they said, they belong to the world, they are its children, but that does not change people's feelings. People say that it was not the Gypsies they disliked so much. It was what they brought with them.

They did not entice our teenage girls into base desires, they did not steal from our shops and homes, they did not litter the beaches, and they did not even smell. They brought something with them that was far worse than that, far worse than the imagining of small children remembering stories their grandparents had told them. They brought to us ourselves.

You see, evil does not walk the streets, or the fairgrounds and playgrounds in search of victims. Werewolves do not feast on the living, not in England. Witches and shape shifters do not move among us. There is no such thing as magic, there is no such thing as immortality, and there is no dark side, only that created by men in their mercenary hearts. These things cannot exist because if they did the world would not be a sane place, and we need that sanity to prove ourselves sane. Thus have we made the world.

Part One

1989

1. Gypsies

The sun fell from it's perch, leaving only rust behind, flecked with the swirling motions of seagulls. Their calls almost drowned out the gently lapping of waves against harbor walls, but fishing boats, half in and half out of the water heard the lulling of the tide and were caught in its persuasion. They were returning home. Calls echoed around the harbor as mooring ropes thudded against the paved shore. Boots clattered on wooden decks, crates and baskets scraped against concrete. The pleasant odor of water faintly laced with salt was masked, as the crates were unloaded one by one, two by two. Something less subtle filled the air. The day's catch had been good. Mackerel or cod? What's the difference? Can people tell by smell alone? Gregory thought so, he could anyway. Today it was mackerel.

  He sat kicking his feet against the harbor wall three feet or so from the lick of wave against concrete, and watched today's catch unload. What had he done all day? Days were boring without college. It was his final year of sixth form college, and what then? No more lazy days. Holidays and college timetables would merge into office hours and the mortgage trap. There would be no more afternoons in the Happy Trawler.
University?
Possibly, that at least would mean another three or four years

until the dole cue beckoned. The wind shifted direction suddenly, dragging the aroma of mackerel with it. Gregory felt hungry, and it was starting to turn cool out here, so he headed for home. Perhaps he would call into the Happy Trawler first. As Gregory walked in the direction of his favorite pub a seagull, which had been perched beside him fluttered its wings in alarm. It flew up, depositing the discarded remnants of an earlier meal just inches from his feet. Gregory looked up, mouthing abuse then moved on. The bird flew higher, joining its companions circling overhead. There they swam in warm air currents rising from the water, waiting for scraps of fish, or even the occasional pie dinner thrown in a nearby bin. Around and around they glided, dizzy to the eye, whilst underneath, far below, men worked unloading the day's toil. As the men left, leaving their debris behind them gulls swooped low to feed, impatient now as the sky began to lose its rust.

Streetlights flickered dull orange and flooded the harbor and pavements beyond and the sea became gradually calm again, as though it were the men and their boats that had disrupted its peace to begin with. As night became darker and lights stronger the gulls crept away flock by flock to some unknown place and the night was still. All along the coast waves caressed beach, licking the sand clean and giving up their treasures. Cars drifted along the coast road, sometimes in pairs, sometimes in threes, most headed towards the orange glow of Seahaven, caravans pulled by all, some painted some not. The sea did not stir. These visitors were expected, they travelled this way every year or so, abandoned by towns and people along the way. Around hills and through sleeping woods they wound, and around the edge of town. Common gates opened and cars entered, with their caravans, to stake their claim on land for the summer, or as long as they would be allowed. When all had passed the gate swung shut silently. Engines ceased, children slept, men and women put themselves to bed. Perhaps this year would be different. Perhaps they would be left alone. Maybe they would be allowed to stay for the whole summer.

*   *   *   *   *

"Bloody Gypos!"

Martin smirked as his father read the morning edition of the Seahaven Herald and Post.

"Well?" He addressed this at Martin and the rest of the family, "Have you seen this?"

His mother sighed, turning away from the eggs sizzling in pan, "No dear, you haven't let anyone else read it yet."

He looked up at her; glasses perched on the end of his nose.

"They're back again, and after all that trouble last time."

She turned back to the eggs.

Martin shook his head and finished off the last piece of toast on his plate.

"I'm going off to the library, I'll be back around four."

His father grunted.

"OK love, can you collect some groceries from the spar on the way back for me?" His mother asked, without taking her attention away from the cooker.

Martin nodded, "Yeah, no problem."

Anything for an easy life.

On his way out his father chose to throw in the usual remark.

"And get a job while your out."

"Yes dad." He would pick one of those up from the spar as well, in the employment section, between fresh fruit and canned goods.

Martin walked to the library by the harbor front and up one of the little side roads. He liked to watch the fishermen preparing to go out to sea, rigging up the trawlers. Today he was far too late.

The trouble his father had referred to had been in connection with a string of petty thefts last summer, which he knew had been carried out by the Johnson boys, and the sexual enlightenment of a couple of the local girls. Because one of the Gypsy lads had been involved with the latter they had also been blamed for the former. The girls gone to him by their own choice, but the thefts were against the law and the town had needed a scapegoat. Of course the thefts were never really proven, and the Johnson boys had been so scared out of their wits that they had not attempted anything like that since, although everyone in school had known it was them.

Martin kicked a stone out of his path and watched it tumble down a nearby drain. It clattered against the grid bars and fell from sight with a plonk. He walked on. His father was pressing for him to get a temporary job before he went away to Durham in the autumn. He had not decided which college yet, there were three of them after him, but he would make his mind up soon. He did not suppose that it mattered much which one he chose really. He had tried to explain to his parents that Durham was a very prestigious college, but his father had only heard of Oxford and Cambridge, and that was through the fantastic medium of television, and his mother just seemed to nod her head vacantly before asking him what he wanted for supper. She had tried to be sympathetic. She knew he had to study before he went, but he could tell that she was still unsure of the whole thing. What good was it going to do him? Dad would ask him what use archaeology was in the modern world, and she would silently agree, but at least she would let him make up his own mind. He wanted to specialize in mythology, if that was possible. That was something he already knew a little about and found interesting. It was that which led him to the library. It was that which drew his interest, his ambition and it was that which would lead him to places where he didn't want to go.

* * * * *

Travellers' caravans already littered the common, their stalls already up. Ponies grazed, baskets and rugs sat on display stalls and people milled about, everyone looking, none of them buying. Among the travellers mixed a few true Gypsies, darker in complexion, older in the eye. These few watched the newcomers warily, and a few watched the skies. There was a

9

smell of something in the air. A storm? The faint aroma of papyrus dust? Or just the travellers and their old caravans? Gregory could smell it too. That and the mild, sweet smell of candyfloss. He looked around, but none of the stalls sold it.

There was nothing to do here. The stalls had already been set up, no cash to earn, so he wandered around for a while to see what was on offer. A girl winked at him as he approached her stall. Woven rugs of all the colours of the rainbow. He smiled back. "How much?"

She replied with a thick Norfolk accent.

" 'Pends which one, but a tenner for any of 'um to you m'dear"

Her hair hung in rats tails, skin soiled by too much weather, but he still found her attractive, wild. He pulled his pockets inside out and she shrugged, smiling,

"Oh well, never mind love, just be sure and come back when you've got some."

He grinned and moved on.

Someone was watching him, really watching.

He could feel cold eyes on his back, the hairs on his neck standing to attention. He turned in a circle to see if his paranoia was correct.

No one was watching.

Then, at the next stall he saw them.

An elderly man and woman, sitting in front of their caravan, him with a pipe in his mouth, her with nothing. They stared.

The caravan was old, and painted like her face. Gold adorned them both, her hoops and rings, him just the rings, but it was their eyes which drew his attention the most. Like needles, and so old. They burrowed into him. He looked around again, almost spinning this time in search of someone else they might be directed at, but there was no one, and more of them were staring now, their eyes swarming at him like wasps. The eyes told him to go, they demanded that he leave. His head started to spin, and they stared harder. He circled around slowly, suffocating, looking for somewhere to go. The gate, over there. Gregory ran for the gate, clambering through it and out of the common. He did not stop running until he was back in town.

*   *   *   *   *

The stalls stayed open until the sky began to darken, then the travellers packed away and retreated to the sanctuary of their own caravans and trailers. Some of them started a fire in the centre of the common, around which the younger ones gathered, but the Gypsies stayed away. No doubt the police would be round in the morning. Fires were outlawed on common land and beaches; these younger ones had no regard for laws and rules. They were loud drunkards, dirty thieves. The older Gypsies gathered around the oldest caravan. Here they sat in lamplight and discussed older times than these, and grandparents told stories and taught the younger ones of the way, and as they spoke all the while they listened.

*   *   *   *   *

have none of your lip thank you."

The box was quite heavy, and Martin staggered under its weight slightly.

"I don't think they are actual Gypsies Mr. Wilson, I think you'll find that they're mostly travellers. The true Gypsies tend to keep themselves to themselves."

He snorted again, a dog after it's first sniff of pepper.

"Like they did with the Robinson girls last time?"

Martin shrugged, there was no use in arguing, this box was getting heavier and if he did not move soon he would spill the contents all over Mr. Wilson's floor.

"What does the councilor think of all this?"

The councilor was Martin's father.

"The same as the people he is paid to represent I should imagine. Goodbye."

Before Mr. Wilson could ask why councilor Phillips was not doing anything about it Martin was out of the shop. He would be glad when he could step off the train at Durham station and not turn back.

His father was not in when he arrived home. He was at a local council meeting.

"I think it has something to do with the Gypsies." His mother informed him in her tired voice.

He left the shopping on the table, kissed her on the cheek and then ran upstairs.

"What was that for?" She cried after him, a faint smile as evidence of her pride, but he did not answer, he had already shut

14

the door of his room.

There was no space on his desk, so he threw the books on his bed and switched on the sidelight. Twelve books to read, notes to take. As Martin read, and the people of Seahaven talked about Gypsies, about the old days and those yet to come he set off on a sea of discovery. The boat rode the waves and dived deep, his first port of call the beginning. Egypt.

* * * * *

The void was deep and black. It moved, curled in on itself, so none could tell how far, or for how long it stretched, it just was, forever. The blackness within was alive with death, a legion of creatures surfed to it's shores, blending with the night, so it seemed as thought the void itself moved and was bestowed with life and light, black fluorescence. Menes stood before the opening of the void, daring the faceless within to take his claim from him, and under his feet Egypt itched to be born.

"Take back what you gave."

From the void there came no answer, only darkness.

Around him the walking gods bickered, wrapped in their chains.

"Take back what is yours," He said again, calmly this time,

"They are not ours, we no longer want them."

Then an answer came, reverberating in his mind. It buzzed like a crazed insect from ear to ear, and came from within.

"And who do you speak for?"

He raised his voice now, above the buzzing,

"I speak for the land, for my people, and for that which shall be Egypt."

The buzz turned to a chuckle, "But child of mine..."

"I am no longer your child." He raised his hands high, free of any constraints, "I Have shaken off your shackles."

Silence. Then, "But you are still a god."

Menes shook his head, "No, I have chosen life over unlife, I have chosen to lead and not to dominate."

The walking gods rattled their chains, and complained again of their treatment. Menes stood upright and defiant.

"My people no longer want your kind on this earth. They want to prosper and survive."

The blackness rumbled again, "But we give them all they want and all they need we provide."

Menes shook his head sadly, "No. We do not give them dignity, we do not give them purpose, we do not give them will, instead we chain them to ours."

He could feel the void thinking. Legion moved within restlessly. Menes could now begin to feel the weight of his own soul, pressing down on his body as it took new shape.

"We shall see." The buzzing was gone, and the walking gods with it. Now instead of the void he saw open plains. Wheat and grass shoulder high, and an abundance of fruit trees. The water of the Nile laughed and giggled behind him, making its way to the sea, and before him stretched a rich wilderness of greenery and life.

*   *   *   *   *

Martin rubbed his eyes. Outside darkness had closed in,
downstairs he could hear his the muffled voices of his parents.
Evidently his father was back from the council meeting.
"Gypsies. . . . . . . more . . . . . ."
He couldn't hear what they were saying, only the odd word
surfaced from their stifled conversation. Anyway, he thought it
best not to go downstairs until they had finished. His father
would only try and drag him into it all. Instead he ran his fingers
through his record collection. When stylus finally touched on
vinyl it was too loud, so he turned it down. Too late.
"Keep the noise down Martin, for God's sake." Came his father's
voice booming up the stairs.
The old man was not in good humour.
Old man. Perhaps that explained his temper. Does humour die as
the spirit gets older, or is it just the first to go?
Martin brushed the books onto the floor, marking his place in the
one he had been reading, and laid back, his head on the pillow.
A warm breeze washed through the open window, gently
ruffling the curtains and he closed his eyes.
As he drifted into sleep his nostrils twitched. Just the beginning
of a dream. His mum and dad couldn't be eating candyfloss,
could they? He smiled, and was gone. In his dream a scribe sat,
bent over an old, worn desk. He wrote frantically, but Martin
could not see what he was writing.

*   *   *   *   *

Gregory sat in a corner of the lounge, in the Happy Trawler. He felt strange. People had tried to make conversation with him all evening, but he had brushed them off, nodding here and there, and being distant. Half an hour since they had become bored with him and wandered off, so now he was alone.

Perhaps he had imagined it, perhaps not. Had they really been staring? Outside it had started raining. The air was heavy with electricity, a storm brewing. It had been so hot the past few days that this came as no great surprise to anyone, good things never lasted. Inside people drank, sang, played darts, all the usual life went on, only with more vigour because of the rain outside. The place seemed warmer and more homely against the elements, the way it always did in winter when snow and frost lay as treacherous companions on the ground. Gregory sipped at his bitter and scowled. What gave them the right to stare?

What gave them the right to regard him as a stranger? It was his town, he lived here.

Laughter erupted from one of the tables across the way, turning heads wearing smiling faces. On a night like this good humour was contagious. Gregory's face turned a brighter shade of pink. He had thought . . . . . that they had been laughing, yes, but laughing at him. No. They were simply having a good time, along with a good healthy drink or seven. Instead he pointed his face downwards, gazing into his beer, taking in the aroma of alcohol, wood, leather and peanuts. That was the way all good

18

pubs should smell. There had been another smell earlier. Why should a fishing village smell of candyfloss? Fish yes, even ice cream, but candyfloss? Perhaps he was making too much of this along with everything else. This third pint had gone to his head and instead of making him merry it had turned him sour, the way that can sometimes happen. When was the last time he had tasted candyfloss? At the fair last summer, no the summer before. He was sixteen then, and ashamed at wanting it, thought it childish. He would, however, dearly love some now, all sticky on his chin and melting in his mouth. Gregory smiled.

On his way home the rain let up slightly, only a matter of time before the storm now. He could hear the soft rumble of thunder somewhere over the horizon, but saw no lightning.

*　*　*　*　*

Martin awoke during the storm.

A lightning flash blew his eyes open, and thunder shook him from his sleep. The wind had died, curtains unmoved, but the storm was now overhead. He leaped to the window, eyes aflame with light, wanting to feel the electricity tickle his teeth. Outside was pitch and motionless, only the tongues of lightning illuminating the street and town beyond, like strobe lights, or an old, silent film.

2. Martin

The Gypsies left the morning after the storm, before the police turned up to inquire about the night's bonfire. The elders had grown restless during the night, the storm was an ill omen on the first night of their stay, this place was ill fated. A storm could carry off a child on the back of the nightmare it rode, and take that child to hidden, secret places where men were not supposed to go. From them there was no coming back.

Superstition the younger ones called it, nonsense, but they followed nevertheless.

Only the Travellers stayed, and it was they who faced the police. They blamed the Gypsies who had fled in the light of early morning. They were simply here to ply their trades before they moved on, and their trade was not trouble.

The Gypsies had left nothing behind them, only their tyre tracks.

*   *   *   *   *

It awoke with the sun, that feeling of trust, and as the orange light filtered lazily through the blinds of her bedroom window

Sylvia could not help but smile. It came out as a stretched yawn. Her back arched away from the warm sheet beneath, stretching the loose covers under which she lay, then she relaxed. Today was a new day, and a beginning. She could feel it. She sat up in bed, letting the covers fall in a pool around her waist, and reached for the cigarettes on the side table.

Ezekiel, a black cat with coarse, spiky hair and one grey tuft under his chin, leaped up onto the foot of the bed and mewed. Sylvia smiled. Usually she would simply tut and turn away from this obvious cry for attention, today, however, she smiled.

"Yes Ezekiel my dear I'm in a good mood this morning."

Ezekiel approached gingerly. When he was close enough he purred against her face.

"Well I'm happy to hear that, I'm glad to hear that you're in a good mood too."

She lit her cigarette and he jumped from her lap, off the bed. She did not hear him land, but saw his tail flick out of sight around the edge of the doorway. The cat could wait. She was not ready to cook and clean for him yet. Sylvia kicked her legs over the edge of the bed and stood up, stretching. Then she strolled over to the window and threw the curtains back. The sun beamed high in the sky, seagulls circled in the bay below, and the town around that glittered like a jewel with reflections from the water. Yes it was a glorious day.

*　　*　　*　　*　　*

21

As Sylvia Cruz was dressing and telling her cat Ezekiel about the wonders of a new era to be born that day, and P.C. McRae was taking statements from travellers on the common, Martin sat downstairs in the kitchen of number thirty-three Moon Crescent and listened to his mother and father. They were still talking about Gypsies and travellers, and what to do about them. Martin could not really understand what all the fuss was about anyway. Why couldn't they be left alone? He did not, of course ask these questions, he just disagreed silently, the way he had always done.

Perhaps one day he would tell them what he had always thought, but not today. There were more important things to do, like ordering that book.

*   *   *   *   *

All sign of any storm had vanished. Sun smiled through a clear sky, even the muddy earth of the Common had dried to a flaky rock. P.C. McRae examined the tyre tracks left by the departed Gypsies. There was no point in searching for them, it was a minor offence and they were gone now. He did not quite believe the travellers who remained and their stories of how the Gypsies had caused the damage, but that was their story and they had stuck to it throughout the morning. It was too hot to be out in uniform on a day like this. He wiped his brow with the back of his hand, leaving a thin film of dust on his forehead, and then took off his tunic. He stood for a while watching the travellers

22

setting up their stalls as normal. They were pretending not to notice him and the few who did, by accident, glance in his direction smiled. Eventually he walked back through the gates and towards town. Walking steadily down Common Road and into High Street, with his tunic over one shoulder he whistled. It was a tune that just came to mind, from nowhere, but it made him smile.

Santa Clause is coming to town.

*   *   *   *   *

Gregory hated the sunlight. It made him sneeze, and his freckles would peel. So as the morning sun glared through the thin curtains of his bedroom window he pulled the quilt over his head and buried his face in the pillow.

He did not feel very well. His stomach was turning over and something had crawled into his mouth and died during the night. At least, that is what it felt like. Eventually, once the noise from downstairs had died down as people left the house he rolled over and let his legs slide out of bed. Sitting up, he rubbed his eyes furiously and groaned.

Why did he drink so much?

*   *   *   *   *

Menes fell to his knees in front of a broken plough.

Is this what he had brought his people to? Had he led them from slavery into oblivion?

The Nile rich earth had vomited rocks and stones wherever their ploughs had touched. Relentless heat had dried the streams, which once littered this holy land. Houses crumbled as their mortar disintegrate, the parched air drinking every last drop of moisture. Thus the Void had taken back it's own. The Old Gods had reclaimed their gifts and Menes wept.

He wept for his people, for the proud Nile, and for the choice he had made. Perhaps men were not made to serve themselves, but through the tears he could see. There was one among them who could help. His tears formed a pool and in the instant before the greedy earth claimed this moisture he saw a face reflected.

*   *   *   *   *

Martin scribbled his name and telephone number frantically on the order form, as the librarian watched with disinterest.

His fingers felt numb and his mouth dry.

Ideas had started to form in his mind. They had been swimming there a while, incorporeal, but now they had taken shape. They were in the things he had read, over the years, soaking up the knowledge like a hungry sponge. A bit here, a lot there. They had met in his sleep, in his dreams, cross-referencing and discarding all of the useless tales, storing those with some meaning. And now? Now he had a frame.

His forehead was wet. He could feel the cold breeze on his head and face as the library doors opened to let him through into the open air. Had anyone else stumbled across this?

He shook his head, they must have done. The people who wrote those lines, and the parts in between must have known.

Imhotep, Solomon, Galileo, Agrippa, Nostradamus, they all knew something, more than was written. Were there more of them? Aristotle? Newton? DaVinci? Buy piecing together their works he could see the full story, and this last book contained the key. A key to where?

He did not know, but he wanted it, he had to see.

As Martin strode feverishly past the Post Office Sylvia Cruz watched him with some measure of interest. There was something in his face, she thought. Something, which disturbed her slightly, but brought back long forgotten memories of the way she had been a long time ago.

The post box was empty again.

She shrugged and locked it up. It was probably a good thing that there was no mail. She shook her head, no it was not.

"Everything OK Ms. Cruz?"

She looked up, away from the window. "Yes, fine."

A quick smile disarmed the post clerk, who blushed and returned to his rubber-stamping, then she was on her way.

*   *   *   *   *

P.C. McRae walked slowly up Main Street on his rounds. Children skipped around him as he passed, pulling faces when out of sight. He knew they did this, but kids will be kids he thought. He could call in at the florists to see Hannah, that would make the day a little lighter. Hard to figure out though was Hannah. She was a good laugh, but she would clam up whenever things got a bit . . . hot.

She was probably a virgin.

He shrugged. Maybe, maybe not. She was nice though. Good looking. Even better figure, from what he could piece together and make out. (He just had to fill in a few gaps that is all, but more gaps than he cared for.)

Perhaps she was just a little more careful than usual with her virtue. Anyway, a cup of coffee and a friendly chat would be most welcome.

He passed the video shop at the end of the street and glanced in before turning down Hock Road. Poor John did not seem to have much custom these days compared to Videoworld up the street. That was probably due to the selection he kept. John Skene did not keep with sex and violence in the movies. Unfortunately most people who owned video players did. P.C. McRae preferred Videoworld himself, or sometimes Roberts' Newsagents, but only for the under-counter selection. (Strictly for stag nights only of course).

He acknowledged a wave from Mrs. Singer. There was a funny one. He had been along to the Singers' a week or so ago, to take statements about a burglary, and Mrs. Singer had been offering P.C. Dickenson and himself more than a cup of hot coffee. Neither of them had taken her up on her offer there and then, it could have been all in their imagination, but he had wondered about P.C. Dickenson since.

* * * * *

Flowers made her sneeze. Why the hell had she bought a flower shop anyway?

Face it girl, you are too scared to work anywhere else. Hannah blew her nose as quietly as she could and bent back to the task of cutting rose stems. An order of two dozen red and white roses for inter flora. The address on the card said fifteen Rosemount Avenue, but that was Tom's problem. Tom was the delivery boy. The bell above the door tinkled.

Hannah peered out from behind the collapsed bundle of roses at a tall, slim woman. Her face was not in view yet, but she recognised her from town.

"Can I help you?"

The woman turned suddenly, shock apparent on her face.

"Oh, I didn't see you there."

Hannah emerged,

"Sorry, I didn't mean to startle you."

"No harm done." The woman smiled, disarming.

Long, black hair fell in coils about a slim face and pale eyes. A slender hand brushed it back. She was beautiful.

"Anything wrong?"

Hannah could feel herself blushing.

"No, an allergy."

She seemed to find this amusing.

"You wanted some flowers?"

The woman nodded, turning to look at the shop arrangements. Hannah noted that both of her hands were unadorned.

"Your handiwork?"

Hannah nodded, coming out from behind the counter. She felt self conscious in her blue and orange dungarees, unsure of where to put her hands, so she held a bunch of the roses loosely in her left.

"Very nice work."

Hannah found herself smiling,

"Thanks."

"What do you have on offer, relatively cheap I mean?"

Hannah motioned to her left, the roses rustled as she moved her hand so she put them down. The woman was smiling.

"The baskets would probably be the best buy, if it is purely for decoration."

The woman wrinkled her nose up, fingering the flowers delicately.

"Do you have any without the white flowers in?"

Hannah approached.

"No, but I can remove them, or make one up for you if you like."

She nodded, "That would be great. The white flowers wouldn't go . . . with the rest of my furniture, not indoors anyway."

She turned to face Hannah again, "Can I pick them up later?"

Hannah felt eyes sweep in her direction. She had to resist the urge to duck. The doorbell tinkled again and P.C. McRae loomed into the shop.

"Yes," she answered, "we shut at half five."

P.C. McRae nodded to the woman as he entered.

"Good morning Miss Cruz."

She smiled curtly, "That's Ms.", then, "OK I'll drop by before closing. Thanks."

By the time Hannah could reply she had gone.

P.C. McRae took off his helmet, "Did I say something wrong?"

Hannah smiled.

"Would you like tea or coffee Robert?"

*   *   *   *   *

Sylvia Cruz wished, silently of course, that something would happen in this dreary town. Something without her hand in it. Something she could watch. However, it would not happen, some places were doomed to fail.

Now Paris was a different story, had been a different story, but she could not go back, not for a while.

She unlocked the side door of the manse and called for Ezekiel before stepping inside.

Where the hell was that cat?

Ezekiel wound himself around her feet, in his mouth a present.

Sylvia grimaced.

"Well you can keep it, I certainly don't want it."

She went inside, leaving the cat to conclude it's disgusting business on the doorstep. Kicking uncomfortable shoes off in the doorway she entered the kitchen and dumped her shopping bags on a spacious table. She flicked on the television, and then turned her attention to making a pot of tea.

Just in time for Wogan, great.

What a marvelous invention this television was. There was nothing like it for switching off the mind and relieving the boredom, sometimes even the loneliness. Wogan nattered whilst she drank and prepared dinner. At some point Ezekiel strolled in and sat on the window ledge. He was not at all interested in the lives of the stars. He stared blankly out of the window. He infuriated Sylvia like that.

"Well if you're so bored with it all why don't you go outside and find something else to do, or someone else to bother?" she would sometimes say, sometimes scream, but he took no notice. Cats could turn profoundly deaf when it suited them.

Later, with food away and the cat fed, she sat with her feet up in the lounge. She sat surrounded by lush greenery, draping the walls and tables, spilling leaves onto the tiled floor (but not on the rugs heaven forbid), and in the midst of it all a television. Not an ordinary television. A seventy-two inch digital flat screen with Dolby surround nicam stereo. There was no sense in having any less.

Sylvia sat and thought a while. The television's black, unblinking screen stared blankly in return. Ezekiel had gone off again, there was no telling where he would be. No doubt she would have to go out searching for him later. She examined the basket of flowers in front of her. Where was she going to put these? In the kitchen she supposed, or the front hall. There they would catch the light from those splendid stained glass windows. She smiled, sending creases up her face, enhancing the folds under her eyes. The time was half past eleven. Time for the late night horror.

She dimmed the lights to a bare minimum and sank deep into her chair, then let the television work it's special magic.

Erie music weaved from the screen and speakers behind her, around the trees, surrounding her where she sat. Sylvia sank deeper.

A scream, then the title appeared.

Night of witches

She grimaced a little, just a little. After all witch was such an ugly word.

3. A basket of flowers

Hannah fumbled in her bag, searching for the keys to the shop front. Across the road Henrietta of Henrietta's Hats was redecorating her shop window. Apparently there was some kind of special offer on for this month, on straw hats.

The first day of August was upon them.

Finally her fingers latched onto them and she wrestled them free. Sunlight had stirred up the dust inside the shop and it skittered around her as she rushed through to the back, hoping she could remember the code for the alarm. Her fears were allayed however when her fingers seemed to remember it on her behalf. She looked around her at the debris. Rose stems littered the floor, and both tables were covered in a small mountain of cuttings. Residue from her late basket preparation. She had thrown Ms. Cruz's basket together in a matter of fifteen minutes, and was quite proud of the fact, but had overlooked one little thing. The mess she had made in the process.

"Shit!"

The broom leaned against the back wall, accusing her. Hannah snorted. She looked at her watch. Five minutes to go until she should open up shop.

*   *   *   *   *

Gregory sat at the breakfast table shaking. Today was results
day. Today he would find out whether he was joining the dole
queue or going off to college and postponing the inevitable for a
few years. Beans on toast didn't hold it's usual appeal, so he just
stared at it, through it.
"Don't worry, you'll be OK"
His mother placed a mug of steaming coffee next to the
unappetising and now cold plate of beans. His hand grasped it
automatically. He would have to hope for the best and take what
came.

*   *   *   *   *

There was no such problem for Martin. He already knew. He had
known what was going to be on the papers. He convinced
himself that it was a lucky guess, one in a thousand, but he knew
anyway. Whatever he read seemed to stay with him. He could
simply access the information like other people could use a
computer database or flick through the pages of an encyclopedia.
So he sat at the breakfast table and ate a hearty breakfast whilst
his mother looked on with a mixture of pride, awe, and disbelief.
She could not understand how he could not be in the slightest bit
worried. He grinned at her with a mouthful of toast, and she

sighed. In a way it was good that her son could be so bright, but she still could not quite believe that he had sprung from her womb. Had he ever failed anything? She did not think so. Martin scoffed down the last piece of toast and grinned at her again.

"Well, today is the day Mum."

She could not help but smile.

"Good luck."

Before she could say any more he was out of the door.

* * * * *

Gregory's feet were as heavy as lead. They seemed to get heavier still as the school got closer. He had always hated this place; never really felt that he fitted in. The only person that he was remotely friendly with was the Phillips kid, Martin. He suspected that Martin did not have any worries today, so wanted to avoid him if possible.

People were already milling around the entrance, meeting each other and plucking up the courage to enter. Gregory skipped around the side of the building and through the service entrance. It was best to get this over with, before the place got too crowded.

The service hall was cold and dark. No sunlight got in through the back, not into here. Gregory swallowed hard and proceeded past the kitchens, his footfalls echoed around the empty corridor. In his mind he could hear voices. School was in session again

34

and it was almost dinner hour. Pots and pans clattered on kitchen surfaces, chairs scraped over polished wooden floors, students laughed and joked about the dinner duty teacher. Gregory smiled. In a way he would miss this place. Things would not be so relaxed again. The Headmaster's office and the notice board lay ahead. Only a few of his year had actually taken the plunge and entered so far, good. One of them was Martin.

"Hi Greg."

Gregory smiled nervously and nodded, "All right Marty. Don't tell me. Let me see my own first."

Martin winked at him.

Gregory could not look, but he had to. What was Martin so cheerful about? Smug bastard. He read over someone's shoulder. There was his name in black and white, near the bottom of the list, and three letters after it.

C   B   D

He felt a smile spread across his face. It was not brilliant, but it was enough. Next to Martins name there were four neat little As, all but one of them marked with an asterisk. Gregory nodded; today was not such a bad day after all. His eyes lingered on those three little letters that held such significance over his life, until Martin's voice sounded a question in his ear.

"Happy Trawler?"

Gregory nodded, still grinning, "Yeah, Why not?"

*   *   *   *   *

By half past ten Hannah was bored. The cleaning had only taken five minutes, the mess had looked worse than it actually was, and since then there had not really been anything to do. Custom was not too good.

She had wedged the door open to let in some fresh air. There was a faint aroma of candyfloss, which she found quite appealing. Had a fair set up on the Common? No one had mentioned it, and there were no fliers or posters advertising it that she could see, but she would possibly go up and take a look later. Now she stood in the doorway drinking lemonade and watching people pass back and forth. Robert would probably be in again this afternoon for his customary cup of coffee. At least then she would have someone to talk to, even if he could be a bind at times.

Henrietta, of the hats fame had not had much custom this morning either. Hannah sighed. Perhaps she should have left the shop closed today and gone to the common instead, or sat in her garden. On second thoughts maybe not. Clouds were boiling on the horizon and a fresh breeze had picked up. Not quite a wind yet, but a crisp breeze enough to take the warmth out of the air. She looked up; the air was beginning to get quite heavy. Hannah finished off the last of her lemonade and retreated back inside. She left the door open though, because the oncoming rain had not yet masked the pleasant aroma of candyfloss.

*   *   *   *   *

The Happy Trawler was livelier than usual that afternoon. Stan, the landlord, was pleased, although also worried at the distinct oversight on his part. He had only arranged for two of the bar staff to be present so he himself was pulling pints now, which was something he generally tried to avoid. It was not the landlord's job to serve.

Gregory and Martin joined in the general festivities. It seemed that most of their year group had passed and more or less got what they wanted. This had been a good year. Gregory grinned from ear to ear, a feat aided by three and a half pints of fat Stan's finest. Martin and a couple of the others were singing. Well they had started off singing but now they were shouting and the lyrics were becoming more obscene as the alcohol flowed.

Whilst the others shouted, Gregory thought. He could not help but feel uncomfortable. It had even got as bad as to maker him itch. He just felt hot. Lager helped, but not much. He knew that it was some form of claustrophobia, but that was like telling a fish that it could not breath because it's respiratory gaseous exchange could not take place out of water. Knowing did not help. He could also smell candyfloss, and for some reason this upset him.

Martin placed a hand on his shoulder and sat down next to him. "Well, we did it."

Gregory nodded, still grinning, "Yeah."

He grinned, but his stomach was now hurting. He was hungry.

Martin finished off the remainder of his pint. "Another?"

Gregory nodded, and finished his. Before he could put his hand in his pocket to fish for change Martin was half way to the bar. Was the smell of candyfloss getting stronger? Or was it closer? There had been no talk of a fair, no posters. Perhaps it was his imagination. He had not bothered to ask anyone else; it was not the sort of thing people could ask out of the blue. Perhaps Martin would know, as his father was a councilor.

The noise from the bar filtered through him. Sound seemed to dissolve before it reached his ears, and in the emptiness that it left he felt strange. The world did not really exist. It was all a dream. Martin's face loomed into view suddenly and sharply, a tray of lagers in his hands, then the focus went again. Gregory smiled, but could not move. Was the room growing? Everything seemed so slow. His stomach was still aching and his skin itched furiously but he could not scratch. The itch came from within. Someone in the corner of the room laughed wildly. Martin's expression melted, and words dripped from his mouth that Gregory could not understand. They were dissolving before they reached his ears again.

When he awoke he was in hospital.

* * * * *

Sylvia grinned. Ezekiel was scowling again but he was just a cat so what did he know. Rain had started to fall gently against the windows. She sat on the kitchen steps letting the water soak her hair and skin. Ezekiel sat just behind her inside, wary of her perverted behaviour. What else could it be but perverted? Who

38

would actually wants to get wet?

Sylvia tutted, "Ezekiel you have absolutely no sense of adventure or romance."

He did not answer. Instead he licked a paw and began cleaning behind his ears.

"Now that's disgusting."

Ezekiel paid her no attention.

The sun peered through a thin layer of cloud briefly, a promise that it would return. Rainbow weather, Sylvia mused. The resident rooks had taken to their tree top sanctuaries and were holding parliament. Sylvia listened to their cries for order. No doubt Ezekiel would have a few of them for disturbing the peace later on. Outside her herb garden seemed to be flourishing well. All except the rosemary that is. For some reason she did not have the touch with that one. Perhaps the woman in the florist would be able to give her some tips. Yes, she would go down there later and ask. If all else failed she could probably resort to other means, but would prefer not to. She never knew who or what that may attract. Rosemary was not that important anyway, she could get by without it, or buy some from the local supermarket. The rain was slowing now and the sun was getting stronger. She would get her bag and walk into town then. She could do some window shopping, see what was happening in town and ask the flower woman about her rosemary problem. Ezekiel scattered out of the way and glared at her as she strode past. Sylvia paid no attention. She grabbed her bag from the kitchen table and strode back out of the kitchen door, past a disturbed Ezekiel She turned her head and winked at him from the bottom step.

"Look after the house while I'm gone."

The walk into town was a long one, but quite pleasant, so she decided not to drive. In no time she was out of her lane and on the main road into town. It ran along the cliff tops, if one could call them that, and she could see the sea below licking lazily at white sand. Sylvia preferred the caves to the South herself, but the sand had its beauty. The view had a pleasant feel to it and helped her to relax. That is why she had moved here in the first place. Cars passed her on the way and she waved at them, just in case somebody decided to wave back.

Soon she caught sight of the first house, then a petrol station, and then she was walking down High Street. It had all taken twenty minutes.

The first port of call was a newsagent for a copy of this month's Cosmopolitan. A little light reading never did anyone any harm. The woman behind the counter served her with a smile, although Sylvia could see that she was not very happy. She suspected her husband of cheating on her with one of the bar staff of The Nelson. Sylvia smiled back and thanked her for the magazine. She should really stop prying like that, although sometimes she could not help it. Other people's problems were none of her business, but it did liven up the day. It also made conversation easier and made sure that she knew who to keep away from.

Out of the newsagents with her copy of Cosmo under one arm she strolled on down the street. The flower shop was just around

40

the corner, but she would stop off at Henrietta's Hats first.

*   *   *   *   *

Hannah grinned as Sylvia walked through the door. Not only did she get her bag caught up in the door handle, but she was also wearing one of Henrietta's straw hats. Hannah giggled and tried to hide it with a cough. Sylvia smiled back.

"I suppose the hat is a bit over the top, but it's summer, so I thought why not?"

Hannah could not help but laugh now, "I'm sorry it's not even funny, but was it in the sale?"

Sylvia's mouth twitched and she started to laugh. Tears were now rolling down Hannah's cheeks.

"I wouldn't laugh if I were you, ", Sylvia said in between chuckles, "because I bought you one as well."

That was enough for Hannah. She had to sit down before her sides exploded. Her lungs were beginning to ache. Sylvia managed to compose herself.

"No, really I did, as a thank you for putting that basket together so quickly for me, and because I have another favour to ask you."

Hannah nodded, "You shouldn't have, it's my job, but what else can I do for you?"

Sylvia reached into her bag and brought out the second hat. It was a wide brimmed straw bonnet, like her own, with a rounded top and a pale yellow ribbon tied around the inner edge of the brim. She placed it on the table in front of Hannah, who examined it and grinned back at her. Her eyes creased up at the sides when she smiled, and the tips of her teeth showed. Sylvia sat on the edge of the table and looked around the shop at all the displays.

"I was wondering if you knew anything about herbs."

Hannah nodded and looked up at her. When Sylvia looked back at her she had to fight not to look away. Sylvia's eyes were so bright and penetrating, but they held no sharpness, they were simply powerful.

"Yes I know a bit, what's the problem?"

Sylvia took off her straw hat and let her hair fall free down her back.

"Well everything seems to be doing fine except for my rosemary. It doesn't seem to matter what I do, it just seems to die on me."

Hannah frowned and bit into her bottom lip.

"Do you want me to take a look for you?"

Sylvia's face seemed to light up, "Would you? That would be great, when can you come over ?"

Hannah stood up, "Well, tomorrow is Sunday and I won't be opening the shop then, so any time tomorrow."

Sylvia stood and picked her hat up again. She stood about an inch taller than Hannah, though Hannah would have sworn that she was slightly smaller. The effect was that as she stood closer Hannah had to look up to her; Sylvia seemed to tower over her.

"How about in the afternoon some time? That'll give me time to get up."

"OK" Hannah nodded at this.

When Sylvia had gone she sat down again. For some reason she had a fixed time in her mind. Two O'clock, but Sylvia had not set an exact time had she? And how did she know her first name? Hannah frowned; she could not remember Ms. Cruz giving her name.

*   *   *   *   *

Gregory sat up in bed. A burst appendix the doctor had told him, and he could have died. He was a very lucky man.

It had not actually hurt that much. He shook his head, and immediately had to lie down again. He had slept for nine and a half hours after the operation, and had only come around once before. His mother had visited, but no one else. It was Saturday so people were busy. Hospital food was not bad, and breakfast at three in the afternoon was cool.

His dreams had been weird though. Something about candyfloss, and fairgrounds, but they were not nice. For some reason it was all bad, especially the merry-go-round. It span and span and span and would not let you off until you agreed. Agreed to what? Gregory did not know, only that you should not agree under any circumstances, even if it span you until your nose bled and your lungs exploded. There was someone else there, someone who asked the question, to which the answer had to be NO. But he could not see that someone's face.

Gregory shuddered.

Dreams were weird.

*   *   *   *   *

"Sorry. It hasn't come in yet. The British library will not release the original and they have no copies."

Martin could not look at the librarian, lest he got the urge to shout at her.

"Is there no way they can make a copy?"

The librarian shook her head, but as Martin was not looking at her she had to verbalise her response.

"No. Sorry. They say that the manuscript is too old and too valuable to risk moving it or exposing it to bright light, such as a photocopier."

People were now looking over, curious as to what all the fuss was about. Martin held his breath.

"Is there any way at all?"

Again she shook her head.

"Well is there any way of searching for books which may contain extracts of it then?"

She shrugged.

"We can try, but it will take a long time. If there is anything then we may not have it for a few months."

Martin nodded. This at least was better than nothing.

"OK Can we try that then please."

The librarian smiled, out of relief more than genuine happiness.

44

Martin watched as she filled in the necessary form and filed it away.

"I can put the request in first thing on Monday morning for you.

Martin smiled wearily, "Thank you."

* * * * *

Henrietta, of Henrietta's Hats felt strange. As she shut up the shop for the evening she could feel something. She did not really know how else to describe it; she could just simply feel something. It was in the air all around her, someone was watching. She had felt like this all day, but the sensation had intensified as the day went on. Now she could not wait to lock up, get home and lock herself in.

Mr. Roberts of Roberts Newsagents had already closed shop and retreated to the flat above. He felt like being alone. He had also shut the windows to block out that awful music. Why the hell anyone wanted to play merry-go-round music, he did not know. It must be something to do with the raves his nephew was always talking about.

For Gregory things were different. He could smell candyfloss, as could many of the town's people, but for most it was a pleasant smell. Something to remind them of their youth, and the invincibility they had felt.

As the people of Seahaven took to their beds, and the rooks of Sylvia's garden called a recess until the next morning, the wind stirred. Time moved on. One O'clock, Two O'clock, and trees rustled in their beds, the same as they had always done. Sea licked at sand lazily, waiting for the onset of a new day. But the wind stirred again.

Three O'clock.

Dead of night, when everything is silent and the trees sleep. Wind and night made way to the almost silent passage of painted wagons along the coast road. The sea became restless at their passage, but they passed nevertheless. Wagons hissed back at the sea and growled at the wind, a warning for them to make way.

Three O'clock in the morning, when men are at their most vulnerable, when the tide of sleep has drowned us. It is at this hour that they passed through the gates of Seahaven Common, bringing candyfloss with them. Dark silhouettes moved against the night, as darkness itself slept, unhooking trailers and assembling strange machines. They crawled over metal limbs, working silently and swiftly in the darkness. Animals growled and hissed in their cages, and were put at ease by unseen handlers. Tents whispered to the grass of the secrets they would hold. Movement on the Common slowed, and at last ceased. When all was at peace once more, workers safe in their trailers, the machines and tents rested, and at the heart of their camp a carousel slept.

4. Gregory's Pain

Sylvia stirred in her sleep and awoke. Her eyes took a moment
to adjust to the lack of light in the room and she sat up. Ezekiel
purred nervously beside her and she instinctively stroked him.
Something was wrong.

She picked up the clock on her bedside table. A quarter past
three in the morning.

Ezekiel did not like something here. Sylvia could feel it too.
Something strong that she could not see. Something hiding in
the darkness. The sweet candyfloss smell that she had ignored
all week was still heavy in the air, but the wind carried
something else, which she had not noticed before. It was
something not quite as sweet, and the candyfloss was there to
mask it.

*   *   *   *   *

So Imhotep built great temples and palaces, not only for King
Menes, but for the people of Egypt, and a nation was born again.
Menes watched him now at work, preparing plans and laughing

with his fellow builders and architects. Was this man to be the architect of a nation? Was it Imhotep who the people followed, and not Menes the Liberator? Was this another trick played on him by the Old Gods as they watched in glee? Menes crouched low and brushed his hand over the sand at his feet. What difference did it make? His people were now free. Imhotep had built dams and irrigated the fields so that they could eat, and shown them the construction of stone houses so they could have shelter. True, Menes would fade into history and tales, but his people would live on and prosper in this once dry wilderness. Perhaps then the joke would backfire, and the Old Gods would be forced to swallow their words.

Menes was tired. It was difficult for him to get up now, hard to walk. This must be what the new mortals called dying. He smiled. At last he could afford that luxury. His chest burned and itched from the inside, a little discomfort in the grand scheme of things as he prepared to leave this place. Guards were shouting now, but he knew that they would not reach him in time. Imhotep also heard them and bowed his head. Menes laughed out loud as the revelation struck him. This was a luxury that Imhotep would never experience. With his last thought Menes pitied him, and as his laugh's echo faded around the courtyard of the palace so his life departed and travelled once again to the great void.

*　　*　　*　　*　　*

Martin's eyes opened slowly as he awoke from his dream. He had not found sleep easily, so sat up reading all night, or so it had felt. The book lay open on the floor next to his bed, spine up and pages twisted. It must have slipped off when he finally did fall asleep.

A strange dream.

It had been about an Egyptian king, who was not quite human, and an architect, or builder. He had read the name somewhere, but not in connection with King Menes. Imhotep, Martin was sure, came much later in history. His buildings were among the first large stone structures, rather like starting the history of the motorcar with a Porsche 911 turbo.

Martin made a mental note to add Imhotep to the list of people to research more thoroughly.

The sun was not as intrusive as usual this morning, his curtains seemed to be keeping it out, or perhaps it was too early. Martin looked at the clock on his bedside table. A quarter past ten. Then it was not too early for sunlight. He slipped out of bed and shuffled over to the window.

*   *   *   *   *

Sylvia frowned at the world beyond her doorway. The weather was going crazy. It could be sunny and gloriously warm one day, then thunder and lightning could rage across the sky, then it could be like this. A cold dense blanket of fog had fallen over everything. Surely this was abnormal, even for English weather.

49

She could do nothing with this one, it was too wild. She just hoped it would lift of it's own accord by the afternoon when Hannah was due to arrive. She hated it when her view of the bay was disrupted like this.

Ezekiel certainly would not go out in this weather, and would probably be under her feet all day now.

What Sylvia Cruz did not realise was that she had only caught the edge of the fog, being exposed as she was on the cliffs above the bay. The fog was much thicker, much worse in town. Meteorologists were caught by surprise, as usual, and local radio stations had been advising travellers to stay clear of the coastal roads in the Seahaven area since the early hours of the morning. Being a Sunday this had not caused much inconvenience, only to the occasional tourist, or trawler looking for temporary dock. Mainly it had served only to keep the towns people in and visitors out of Seahaven.

John Bradley had not even bothered to open the service station at the southern edge of town, and the Shell garage on the coastal road to the north was open only because Mark Winters did not like the idea of being fired should his boss happen by. He sat in the office with the door firmly closed and portable heater on full blast. There was no way he was going outside in this weather, it was self-service today.

By Mid Day the fog had still not lifted. Hannah was beginning to get a little restless. She supposed that if she drove carefully, very carefully, she could make it over to Sylvia's house. She could, at a push, even walk, although it was a good mile and a

50

half uphill.

She sighed over the top of a steaming cup of coffee. Sylvia probably would not be expecting he anyway, not in this weather, and the journey would be pointless. She could not diagnose herbal problems if she could barely see the plants in question. What the hell, she would go anyway.

There was nothing else to do. Hannah picked up her car keys from the kitchen table and marched out of the back door to her car.

She did not know if this was such a good idea. She could only just see the car in the darkness of her garage, but with the headlights on things would be different, and there wouldn't be much traffic on the roads anyway. Hannah smiled to herself, opened the car door and got in.

The drive was not as bad as she had expected. She had been correct about the traffic, not a single car, other than her own, was on the road. Everyone else was probably far too sensible to risk it. She had kept the car's headlights dipped in order to see anything at all, and it seemed as though the journey took forever. It actually took ten minutes.

Soon enough the turn into Sylvia's driveway appeared to the left, the iron gates made all the more eerie by their curtain of mist. Hannah indicated needlessly and took the turning. This part of the road seemed even more silent than the rest of the journey had been. Everything seemed still and breathless, even her car made less noise, as though it were trying to creep past some sleeping creature, whispering so as not to disturb whatever slept here.

Hannah shook her head. It was all in her imagination. The Manse was very old, and children all over town would dare each other to come up here on Halloween, they always had and probably always would. Hannah grinned, she had done the same when she was in primary school, only it had been a different house in a different town. Sylvia Cruz, of course did nothing to dispel the rumours.

Witch indeed. Hannah could not think of anything more ridiculous now that she had met her properly.

Sylvia watched from her kitchen window as Hannah's car rolled into view. She saw the headlights first, fumbling blindly in the hazy darkness, then the car itself. She could just make out enough to know that the driver was female, and smiled to herself. She reached over and switched the kettle on just as the car's engine ceased.

*   *   *   *   *

The HEAT!

Why was it so hot!

His flesh was burning, and that light, it was too bright to see. His fingernails were melting.

Why doesn't someone turn down the heating?

CHRIST! It was hot, and he wanted to itch all over, what the hell was going on here? He felt so hungry, so FUCKING HUNGRY, how long had it been since breakfast? How long? They were supposed to look after you in hospital weren't they?

And there was that bloody candyfloss smell again. Were they teasing him?

That was it.

He threw back the sheets and swung his legs out of bed. Gregory awoke suddenly as the nurse threw back the curtains. Yellow orange light flooded his room and his eyes swam in moisture. Her face blurred, but he could see a smile wavering in there.

"It's nice to see you awake." She said.

* * * * *

Hannah smiled back at Sylvia over a tall, cold glass of lemon. They sat on the back steps and looked over the bay as the fog began to lift. Sylvia clinked her glass against Hannah's delicately.

"Cheers."

Hannah grinned uncontrollably; Sylvia seemed to have that effect on her. Over the bay the fog lifted and dissipate into thin wisps of smoke. The sea beyond was becoming visible, as though through clouds from a plane as it approaches the runway. Seagulls whirled overhead, dancing on an eternal summer thermal.

"So what about my rosemary then?"

Hannah shrugged.

"I don't know, perhaps you are just unlucky."

She got up and walked over to the herb garden with Sylvia close behind.

"It may be a bit close to the thyme though." Something puzzled her. She pointed to a dark looking plant that crept in the shadows behind the others. "What is this stuff? I haven't seen it before, it looks like a kind of weed."

Sylvia took a large sip of her own lemon,

"Oh, that's hen bane I think."

She took Hannah's arm and turned her around to face the main garden.

"Do you think I could do with some more trees?"

Hannah smiled to herself. She knew when her attention was being diverted. The herb garden was a mess and Sylvia knew it. Those dark plants were weeds. Sylvia probably knew exactly what had to be done, and judging by the rest of the garden she had green fingers. So what had she invited her up here for then?

Sylvia smiled as though she had heard.

Hannah recoiled. No, she could not possibly have heard, it must be her imagination at work again. She had to say something, to change the subject.

"Well, we could replant the rosemary over there, under those trees."

Sylvia seemed to be standing closer now, looking in the direction in which Hannah pointed. Hannah could smell her perfume, and it made her blood flush to the surface, but somehow she didn't mind the close proximity. She did not mind in the slightest. Sylvia smiled and turned to face her again, her face only a breath away.

Hannah held her breath, her hands trembled.

"Would you like some wine?" Sylvia asked, raising one eyebrow comically and retreating a step. Hannah relaxed and smiled back, why not? As though she had heard Sylvia answered her, "Come on then, let's go inside and get some glasses."

*   *   *   *   *

Apparently they would let him go in a day or two, if everything was OK Appendectomy was quite routine nowadays. Gregory was starving. He did not think he had ever been so hungry in his life before. Thank God he would not have to stick to these hospital portions for much longer.

At least, he thought, the aroma of candyfloss had faded.

*   *   *   *   *

By late afternoon, or early evening, whichever you saw it as (Sylvia chose to see it as early evening, naturally), the fog had lifted completely. Where it had been it had left something behind.

V.J. Midnight's Extravaganza!

Carnival of light and dark

Fairground rides

Prizes!

And, the Carousel

(First ride free)

Little Anthony Doyle stood in front of Roberts Newsagents reading the poster as James Roberts himself cursed the vandals, who had posted it there, in his window.

Carousel, first ride free.

Anthony peered in through the window at Mr. Roberts who was rushing towards the door with a bucket of hot, soapy water. He wondered what a carousel was, but it did not really matter, it was free.

He stepped back a pace and watched with interest as Mr. Roberts began to scrub furiously at the offending poster. He scrubbed at the paper, trying to eradicate the words but they would not budge. It must be stuck to his window with some kind of super-glue.

Anthony looked around, turning slowly to take in the whole street. The posters were everywhere.

On lampposts, in shop windows, on vacant walls, even on the side of a van parked at the far end of the street.

Carnival of light and dark.

Fairground rides.

Prizes.

V.J. Midnight's Extravaganza was everywhere, and the first ride was free.

It did not stop in the town centre. The posters trailed up the hill, towards the common, plastered to trees, fences and road signs, and in the distance . . . Was that a big wheel? A rollercoaster? Anthony held his breath and listened. It was faint over the sound

of other people and the rush of blood in his own ears, but was that fairground music? Could he hear the roar of a lion? Could he smell the faint aroma of peanuts and candyfloss?
The trail of brightly coloured posters led to a treasure trove, and Anthony had already decided that he wanted some.

*   *   *   *   *

Martin watched from the lounge window as a group of children wondered past. They seemed to walk, then half run a few paces, then resume their brisk, chaotic walk again, constantly changing the pecking order as they went, so that first one child led the expedition, then another. This change of leadership continued as they made their way up the street and around the corner out of sight.
Martin wondered briefly where they might be going, but the thought soon faded. He wasn't really that interested. There was nothing on the television to interest him this evening either. His mother was in the kitchen, cleaning away the remnants of dinner, his father was attending another town meeting.
Nothing to do.
Martin sighed. He could do nothing on his research until the library chased down the book he had ordered. That withstanding all he had was some mildly interesting reading.
Another group of people scurried past the window.
Out in another room somewhere he could hear his mother humming to herself. He had flicked through the television guide

and had not found anything enticing. All that remained was to read, or perhaps to visit the Happy Trawler. He could really see himself sitting in there alone. It was too late to go and visit Gregory in hospital as well.

More people filtered past the window, this time seven or eight of them, older as well. Martin frowned. Where were they all going? People had been walking past in one direction all evening, ever since it had been clear enough to step outside. Perhaps there was something going on up on the Common. Were the Gypsies still there? He thought that some of them had left but was not sure how many. Was it all of them? Perhaps not. Perhaps there was some sort of show, or the police had been called in or something. There was only one way to find out, and he had nothing else to do anyway.

*   *   *   *   *

Hannah sat with her legs curled up on the large sofa and watched as Sylvia stood, tinkering in the kitchen. She felt quite light headed now, and had not been this relaxed and comfortable in a long time. Greenery bred everywhere here, pouring out from every corner and spare table space in the room. Small plants on tables, large tropical hybrids living in pots on the floor. All seemed to drape over and form a lush carpet of fauna, and this seemed to warm the room in spite of the cold tiled floor at her feet (which she avoided by curling her legs up on the sofa). The room, and indeed what she had seen of the house suited Sylvia.

58

Hannah liked it. The most surprising thing was the enormous television against the far wall. Sylvia did not seem the television watching type. Sylvia was shouting something to her from the kitchen; she was stood in the archway separating the two rooms. Hannah looked over suddenly,

"Sorry, What were you saying?"

A smile spread over Sylvia's face,

"I said do you want it hot and spicy, mild, or somewhere in between?"

Hannah wrinkled her nose up,

"How hot is hot and spicy?"

Sylvia nodded and turned back to the kitchen, "OK I won't make it too hot then."

Hannah turned her attention back to the television. It was not switched on and so a darker image of herself looked back. She glanced at her watch. A quarter past seven. The wine was certainly having an effect, it seemed as though she had only been here a couple of hours, when she had already spent half the day, more or less. She was also beginning to get hungry. Perhaps she should offer to help, speed things up slightly. She uncurled her legs and cautiously tested the floor with her toes, then the soles of her feet. It was surprisingly warm, just right in fact.

As Sylvia worked at the stove, with her back to her Hannah gingerly made her way towards the kitchen, avoiding the plants as she went. In bare feet she did not make a sound.

"There are some plates in the top cupboard on the left there, and cutlery in the drawer below it." Sylvia spoke softly without turning around.

Hannah stopped.

"How do you do that?"

Sylvia stopped what she was doing and turned around, a quizzical expression on her face. Her eyebrows were raised towards the middle of her forehead, eyes wide, so that all the wrinkles and faint lines vanished.

"Do what?"

"You knew where I was and what I was about to say."

Sylvia shrugged.

Hannah reached past her and opened the top cupboard,

"These ones?"

Sylvia nodded, "Do you want to eat outside on the lawn or inside at a table?" Hannah took out two plain white plates, "Outside on the grass if we can. The view from here is fantastic."

She found the cutlery where Sylvia had said it would be and took out spoons, forks and bread knives.

Sylvia placed a lid over the pan she was attending and turned around to face her.

"In that case we will need a ground sheet to sit on."

She pointed to another set of cupboards to the left of the archway.

"You will find table cloths and blankets in there." Then she smiled and raised one eyebrow in the same comical fashion as before. Hannah smiled back and set to the task of finding a suitable ground sheet.

Out in the garden she chose a spot at the far end, away from the house, with a good view of the bay. There was something commanding and satisfying about this view. Perhaps it was the fact that she could see more or less the whole town from here, but the town couldn't see her, no one could. Voyeuristic, perhaps, but so what? She made herself comfortable after laying their places and waited. Presently Sylvia emerged with a large pot under one arm and a plate of sliced French bread in the other.

"Dinner is served Madame."

Hannah eagerly took the pot from her and placed it in the middle of the ground sheet.

"Make yourself at home" She said and patted the ground beside her. Sylvia obliged. Folding her legs underneath her she seemed to glide gracefully to the floor, coming to rest gently by Hannah's side.

"Let's eat."

They both tucked in.

*   *   *   *   *

It was not difficult to discover where everyone was going. All Martin had to do was to follow the posters, like everybody else. There were people behind him now as well, following in groups. The posters led up the lane to the Common. Somewhere at the top somebody was playing music. Coloured lights bleached the sky, depriving the oncoming night.

A fair.

People snaked their way in a semi chaotic order up the hill to the field at the top, where it seemed carnival delights awaited. Martin could smell the popcorn and candyfloss from here. Streams of music flowed into one raging cacophonous river that washed over him as he approached. Wheels span and children screamed. Martin smiled. The louder you scream the faster we go. A childhood memory. He remembered a carousel long ago, and an old man. The louder you scream, the man had said, the faster we go. Martin had screamed his head off.

So he followed the steady flow of people, caught in the current now, to see what the fair had to offer.

V.J. Midnight's Extravaganza!

An unusual name. Martin read the top line of a poster as it floated past.

Carnival of light and dark.

So, something for everyone then. He moved on, letting the current take him forward.

Fairground rides

Then onto the next one,

Prizes!

And finally,

And, the Carousel
(First ride free)

The louder you scream the faster we go. The top of the hill was within reach now, and Martin's feet were no longer on the ground. He was truly being borne by the current, and that current was emptying into the pool at the top of the hill. He briefly wondered if he could swim against the tide and fight his way down the hill, then he was through he gates and into the common. The gates had either been left open or constantly forced open by the tide, which had carried him and everyone else up here. What was the fair called?

Ah yes, V.J. Midnight's Extravaganza carnival of light and dark, a poster informed him so.

Martin stood in the doorway to sensation and breathed in the atmosphere. People toiled around him, shouting, screaming, laughing. Carts roared past on rickety tracks, climbing unfeasibly high and then plummeting to the ground, cheating death to climb again at the last instant. Children giggled as they were hurled around and around. Women shouted and teased, beckoning him to try their stalls. Guns popped, ducks fell, hoops flew, candyfloss span, and clowns frolicked.

Martin dived in.

*   *   *   *   *

Sylvia kept one eye on the lights at the other end of town all the while that Hannah talked. There was a fair, or something like that going on over there, on the Common. She could make out mechanical monsters heaving people into the air. They stood out against the skyline like wheels and instruments of torture. The music must be very loud; it was driving her to despair up here. Hannah was smiling at her now.

"Am I that uninteresting?"

"What?" The question caught her off guard. Her expression must have illustrated this perfectly as Hannah was now desperately trying to conceal, a laugh.

"You've not heard a word I have said for at least the last five minutes have you?" She was smiling

Sylvia thought about feigning innocence, and then decided against it. She smiled back, then sighed. "No."

Hannah started laughing.

"I was distracted by the lights and music over there that's all," Hannah nodded, "Looks like a fair."

She looked directly at Sylvia now. Sylvia tried to focus on what was going on behind her eyes, but could not even get a glimpse of it. The wine must be taking its toll.

"Shall we go over and have a look?"

Sylvia shook her head. Somehow she did not think she would enjoy it this evening. It was something to do with the music. It was up-tempo, but did not seem to meld together properly. It was just noise, and without a cage it raged like a wild beast, not caring what it did or where it went. There was something missing. Besides she had other things on her mind, it had, after all, been a long time.

"No. Let's go inside and finish this bottle."

Hannah smiled. She stood up, the grass rustling beneath her bare feet and offered her a slim, delicate hand. Sylvia took it.

"That sounds like a good idea to me."

* * * * *

Gregory ran and ran.

His feet pounded the earth, cold grass against warm flesh. The blood roared in his ears and his breath quickened as his lungs smarted from the cold, sharp air. He felt good. He had been running now for hours, just running. The hospital had been hot, so he had torn his paper pyjamas free and launched himself out of the window, landing on the grass five stories below. Of course he knew it was just a dream.

Knowing it was a dream made it better, and all the more real. With only the smell of grass and wind in his nostrils Gregory could run tireless and free. Trees could whip at him as he passed but there was no pain. Animals hid and this pleased him. Where he passed and they did not have time to hide they scrambled for cover. All he had to do was reach out, or lunge and they would be his. If he wanted them. Gregory laughed, the sound ripped from him as he ran. It was a primeval sound, the first utterance of man, primitive music.

*　　*　　*　　*　　*

Wheels screeched and turned, carts rumbled past and dust flew all around. Amidst the shouts and the squeals of terror and delight Anthony stood silently watching.

The first ride was free.

At the centre of it all, like the hub of a wheel, stood the carousel. A huge painted castle with colourful horses and all manner of unusual and amazing creatures standing to attention around it. The creatures stood guard whilst the master at their centre slept. He watched in particular a large horse with flared nostrils, which barred the way to its master. The horse glared back at him with one eye, shadows dancing within, cast by the flickering of lights around the fairground.

Other shadows lurked behind the horse, and other creatures. They crept silently and darkly, preparing for their master's awakening, and Anthony too waited. The posters had said that the first ride was free.

He had walked around the fair for a little while, watching the rides and smiling at people as they passed with light in their eyes, but his own eyes had come to rest on the magnificent creature that slept at the centre of the fair. It must have been a thousand years old, with all the cracks and splinters, and yet looked majestic and wild even in the darkness, which yet surrounded it. A small hand painted sign hung around the horse's neck.

Carousel starts at Midnight.

(Sorry for the delay)

Anthony's deep-sea diver's watch reported the time as being eleven forty eight, and it had not been wrong yet. He could wait. His mother would probably have a fit, but at least he had not spent any money, the ride would be free. Midnight was a strange time to start a ride wasn't it? The horse's nostrils flared and it reared slightly, just in the periphery of Anthony's vision. He snapped his attention back to the horse. It had not moved. It stood on three legs, nostrils slightly flared, staring with its one eye. If Anthony stared long enough it would have to move. Surely it could not stay still indefinitely if it were alive, unless it was to move when he blinked.

"Waiting for the first ride are you?"

A silvery voice behind him. Anthony turned around.

A small giant of a man gazed down at him, obscured for a moment by a bright flash of light from the waltzer behind. Then he bent his knees and dropped lower, removing his hat. Silver hair, the colour of the moon fell free, greeting the night as though they were long lost friends.

"V.J. Midnight himself at your service." The man offered Anthony a hand. Anthony tilted his head slightly, considering whether to shake it or not. Mr. Midnight smiled back at him, a grin as wide as oceans, and eyes that contained a thousand glittering prizes. Anthony smiled. He reached out tentatively, just as Mr. Midnight, as quick as thunder, fast as rain retracted his own hand and brushed fingers through silver moon drenched hair. "Too slow!"

Anthony giggled.

Mr. Midnight smiled his huge smile right back at him, his teeth white cliffs holding back the sea.

"How about that free ride then young man?"

Anthony shook his head,

"It isn't Midnight yet, so we can't"

It would not be right.

Mr. Midnight nodded slowly,

"I am sure we can do something about that."

Something told Anthony to look at his watch. It was dead on midnight. Zero zero zero and no seconds. He nodded back, and looked over his shoulder at the horse that awaited him saddled and ready. The hand painted sign had gone.

" It is free isn't it?"

The voice flowed over his shoulder as he stood admiring the splendid horse before him, it's mane ruffled as though from ten thousand windswept journeys.

"It wont cost you a penny."

5. The web of Cornelius

Martin smiled down the telephone. If the woman had been in front of him now he would have kissed her.

"Yes, it arrived this morning." she said, "We close for lunch at Twelve and open again at Two."

There would not be a problem; Martin would be there before Twelve,

"No problem, I'll be there before Twelve, I'll set off straight away."

The librarian said that she would place the book in the library card reserved section under the counter for him. He would have to bring his and another form of identification.

When Martin hung up the phone he was sweating.

*   *   *   *   *

Hannah opened her eyes, in the wake of the morning sun and found that Sylvia had already got up. It could not have been long before as the indentation in the sheets next to her, where Sylvia had been was still warm. She sat up in bed and stretched her arms wide, letting an enormous yawn escape. It spread from her rib cage, around her back and across her shoulders before finally being released. With a sigh of relief she exhaled, finally, and noticed that Sylvia's cat was watching her.

It sat on its hind legs in the archway to the bedroom, just outside on the landing. The sun behind it, shining through its spiky black hair made it look larger than it possibly could be. Cats do not grow that large.

She smiled and called to it.

"Hi cat, c'mon over here."

It sat, hesitantly. She could almost see it puzzling over whether to come over or not, then like a shadow when the sun moves it was gone.

Hannah rubbed the back of her head. They drank a lot of wine last night. She giggled. Her teeth did not feel so good; she would have to borrow a toothbrush.

A little white dressing gown lay at the foot of the bed in a crumpled heap, so she dragged it on and made her way barefoot to the landing and down the stairs. The sun had warmed the wooden floor somewhat, but it was still cold on her feet, so she carefully plotted her way down the stairs on her toes. Sylvia was in the kitchen; Hannah could see her from here. She must have got straight up, as she hadn't yet finished dressing. Hannah noticed bare feet under a flowered dress and smiled.

"Good morning." She yawned.

Sylvia waved, "I was going to bring coffee up. Do you want it down here?"

Hannah shrugged, "Anywhere would be fine by me." At which suggestion Sylvia grinned, "Me too."

Hannah snorted and shook her head, placing her behind squarely on one of the breakfast stools. Sylvia passed her a cup, with nothing in it yet.

"So what time are you working today?"

Hannah wrinkled her nose, "Well I don't have any set time, any time before Twelve really."

Sylvia smiled,

"Well, I'll come with you then," She watched Hannah's face closely, "If that's okay."

Hannah didn't mind at all.

*   *   *   *   *

"Look I'm sorry Mrs. Doyle, but in order for us to file a missing persons report that person must be missing for at least three days." P.C. McRae was beginning to wish he had not offered to fill in for the desk sergeant. Mrs. Doyle looked as though she was about to take a swing at him, so he retreated slightly behind the counter. Her face red and eyes blazing she stared back at him, unblinking.

"He is only ten years old." Her reply came through gritted teeth. Her hands were now both on the counter and she was leaning towards him. He had to say or do something. The little brat had probably gone up to the fair, stayed late and was now too scared to go home to this ogress.

"I'll put a call out to the officers on duty, to see if we can find him."

Mrs. Doyle relaxed slightly, some colour flushing back into her knuckles.

"But I think you should go home Mrs. Doyle."

The wrong thing to say.

Mrs. Doyle shrieked and almost spat at him, then turned on her heels and stormed out of the police station, slamming the door on her way out.

She would find the little brat herself, and when she found him…

Her car keys got caught in the lining of her coat pocket so she yanked them free, tearing some of the fabric. When she found him she would give him a bloody good hiding, teach the little sod a lesson.

Barely avoiding scratching the car door as she fumbled for the lock she could hardly see with the anger she felt. People were beginning to stare, and buzz around like insects hungry for gossip. Mrs. Doyle snarled at a passing car, slammed the car door as she got in and sat in the driver's seat. She left the keys dangling in the ignition and shook. She sat slumped over the steering wheel shaking until tears came.

*   *   *   *   *

Gregory stood at the reception desk. He had been told to sign some release forms here, as he was free to go today. He should not eat too much spicy food for a while, and should increase the dairy products and meat intake of his diet to compensate for the missing appendix. Something to do with getting enough bacteria in his diet to break down cellulose now that he did not have an organ to do it for him. He had shrugged; he did not really like salads that much anyway. They had also given him a course of antibiotics to take, so he was not allowed to drink. The receptionist handed him a pen, once she had finished on the telephone, so he scribbled his name quickly and made his way hastily out of the front door. His mother was there, waiting for him.

"How are you love?" She looked quite anxious, obviously pleased to see him up and about.

Gregory smiled at her, "Hungry." he said.

* * * * *

The Common was bustling with life again, with schools being out for the summer. Every child from town, with a few exceptions was up here, trying their hands at darts, on the shooting range, or simply sitting back in the roller coaster and hoping for the best. Sun glared off giant machine arms as they span and threw people in all directions, music declared the fun to be had by all. Only one machine stood redundant, amidst the turmoil of action and amusement. Hidden away in the centre of all of this stood a worn, faded carousel, unnoticed by the thousands who passed by. If anyone were to stop and closely scrutinise this forgotten ride they may or may not notice one small detail, an oddity. They may, however have given no thought to the fact that one of the parading animals which stood so proudly around the outside of this giant wheel was missing.

*　*　*　*　*

Can you hear them?

Anthony shook his head, he could not. Not very well anyway, just the faint murmuring of his heart.

Listen carefully.

His heart rustled in its cage of bone, and the blood whispered in his ears.

He was beginning to get a little frightened, because it was dark and he should be getting home. The horse felt good beneath him though, and he felt ten feet tall. He was ten feet tall, and Mr. Midnight was riding alongside him.

But he could not hear them.

Yes you can if you listen.

Anthony's horse snorted and picked up pace a little. The wind rushed through his hair, whistling past his ears. Anthony smiled and they spoke to him.

Mr. Midnight said they would and they did. They whispered and shouted and babbled, and no one else seemed to hear them.

Anthony giggled. He couldn't really hear what they were saying, there were too many of them.

Mr. Midnight was now shouting over the din to make himself heard.

Silence!

Again there was quiet, just the rush of blood in his own ears, and the pulse of the horse beneath him. Anthony laughed, he felt like he could ride forever.

* * * * *

Sylvia smiled and listened in the back room as Hannah talked and cut flower stems, letting out the occasional sneeze. Perhaps she would do something about that allergy for her. She felt distant though, as though something else was trying to get her attention, like someone was rooting through her things and she was afraid they would find something.

".........Because otherwise the leaves can burn"

Sylvia smiled and snapped her attention back to Hannah.

Hannah stopped what she was doing.

"You have not really been listening have you?"

Sylvia nodded, " Yes I have." She delved deep, just for a moment,

"You were telling me how I mustn't spray my plants in the summer and get water on the leaves, because they get burnt by the sun, but I can spray them last thing at night once a week, just to keep them moist."

Hannah frowned, "Well I had not said that last bit yet, but I was about to."

"Well there you are then," Sylvia grinned triumphantly, "I listened so well that I guessed what you were about to say next."

Hannah nodded, but she was not quite sure. Sometimes she felt that Sylvia knew what she was going to say before she did, or that Sylvia could just read her thoughts like so many pages of a book, but that was not possible. Mind reading was a cheap trick invented by circus performers.

Sylvia smiled, "Now what about plant food?"

* * * * *

The book was heavy. Martin struggled to hold it under one arm as he hurried down the street. The leather binding perspired under his grasp, threatening to slip away. When he had picked it up the binding had groaned as though being awakened. The librarian had not seemed to want to touch it. Martin smiled uncontrollably; he could smell the old paper. It was not the original parchment, but was a very old copy. Old enough to know, old enough to have seen things. He wondered over the people who had read this book before him, and what they had found hidden within its secret pages.

Not far to go now. He was nearly home. Martin could feel the warm, salty trickle of sweat down his forehead, and the leather was coating his hands with moisture. His house was just around this corner. Once inside he could relax and read in peace. Nothing could happen to the book then. He would be happy once he knew that he could just sit and read it, without having to worry. In the stillness of his room the pages would not blow away, he could take his time and not miss anything. He would go up to his room and lock the door. That way he wouldn't be disturbed. Martin fumbled in his pocket for the keys as his front door moved closer.

The book was too heavy and too slippery, it was going to fall.
He snatched his hand out of his pocket to grasp hold of the book once more.

He would have to balance the book on one knee as he fished his keys out.

The door opened, silencing all thoughts with it.

For a moment Martin stood, balanced on one leg, hand in pocket and book resting on one knee with his other hand on top of it.

Facing him stood his mother, in the way. Martin stared at her, then blinked. He was going to drop this thing any second now.

She stared back and opened her mouth to speak.

Before she could he was inside and half way up the stairs.
"Hi mum."

Before the thump of his footfalls had died he shut the bedroom door behind him.

His mother shouted something up the stairs after him on her way out of the door. He did not really hear, but shouted "Yes Mum" anyway.

The book came to rest solidly on his desktop.

Martin peeled off his jacket and dropped it on the floor of his wardrobe, never taking his eyes off the book. It's dull brown cover lay inanimate and emotionless on the work surface, waiting, its pages ill cut and dog-eared.

How many thousands of people had read this?

Martin sat down and rested his hand on the cover. He felt the
smoothness and the age of the leather, worn beneath a dozen
hundred hands. He was about to be next.

Martin opened up the book and turned the first page.

*   *   *   *   *

The air around the fairground stirred, although hardly noticeable,
and the creature that lay asleep at its centre awoke, but only for a
moment, as though turning in its sleep. The air had a different
smell to it, it was sure, an older smell, all moldy paper and
spices. It vaguely recognised the aroma, but did not know where
from. No matter the memory would come back soon enough.
Darkness spread and once again it slept.

*   *   *   *   *

A little later on that day the voices came back. Anthony sat
quietly on the riverbank and listened to them. They were
soothing, not shouting to be heard like before, but singing, and
all singing the same thing.

He had been sat here throwing pebbles into the almost still
water, watching the ripples spread and float down stream. The
water looked calm and still, but he knew it was moving really.
He had fallen in once, and his dad had to dive in and fish him
out. That was before he went away.

Anthony launched another pebble and watched it glide towards its target. It rose into the sky, getting smaller and smaller, until stopping dead, just for a moment. It hung in the air, suspended for that instant, deciding whether to climb higher, or to dive into the cool water below. Then it dropped, picked up speed and broke thought the shiny skin of water out of sight. Shock waves spread out on all sides, perfect circles, and then were torn apart by the current. The pebble and all sign of it had gone.

Anthony sighed. He wished it was midnight so that he could ride the carousel again. The voices agreed, that would be nice, but first there were things to do, important things. Anthony did not think they were so important, but the voices insisted.

*   *   *   *   *

In the beginning there was the Void, as there had always been before. The Void murmured and land was born, for it's word was bond, but from that land sprung a being, who did not like the chains by which the Void held him, so he broke them. Thus this being took life for his own and embraced death in the same breath, for only those who remain in contact with the void exist in unlife, and only those without life shall not die.

Martin turned the page and looked overleaf. More of the same. He flicked through the pages. There must be something else in here. Some reference to that diagram or something, an explanation.

He sighed He would have to work his way through the text and decipher

The hidden meanings by guesswork, unless he could find that diagram. The copy of it in the other book was too small to read, but he knew it was a key of some sort, it had to be. He could see by glancing through that some of the pages were written in another language, untranslated. That meant that whoever translated the book did not know how to translate these pages, or even worse the rest of the book could just be guesswork.

If he found the key he could start from scratch.

Martin began turning the pages individually. It must be in here somewhere and if it was then he would find it.

*   *   *   *   *

The study room was cold when she walked in, but Sylvia ignored it. She had not really paid much attention to anything all day, there was something else on her mind, niggling at her. She marched straight over to the book cabinet and reached up to the top shelf, unseen above the rest.

After a bit of groping in the dark (she always found it difficult when she could not see what she was getting hold of) she pulled out a small leather bound volume, almost as thick as it was high. She blew dust from its cover and placed it on the table. It had been so long.

She flicked off the catch holding it shut and the book sprang open, scattering a peppering of dust as it did so. Pages flickered slightly and came to rest, the book open with it's spine down on the table. A once familiar odour of musty paper laced the air.

Sylvia sighed; she had no time for memories at the moment. She pulled a book of matches from her pocket and struck one of them against a nearby wall, then she lit one of the candles on the table next to where the book had come to rest.

"OK, show me."

The pages began to turn backwards and forwards, searching. Sylvia thought she would leave the book to it and make a cup of tea. By the time she had made one and fed Ezekiel it should be on the correct page. She was out of practice, so this may take a while.

She strolled back out of the room, leaving the candle lit, and down the hallway towards the kitchen. She was glad that she had not shown Hannah this side of the house. There would only have been questions, which she would rather not answer, especially if Hannah had stumbled across certain things, like her unusual collection of books and ancient relics. Careful with the ancient, some of them were only as old as she was. The kitchen was a little warmer, but she lit the stove and the fire in the lounge anyway. It was going to get a lot cooler later on in the evening. She frowned waiting for the kettle to boil, and stared at the tea bag in her favourite mug. A change in the weather was one thing, but this was ridiculous. There was definitely something amiss here and she could not put her finger on it. All day she had felt as though someone was spying on her, or as though a trespasser was leafing through the pages of her diary.

She had to find out what was at the bottom of all this, even if it did mean resorting to more risky, unsavoury methods. Not that they did anyone any harm, it was just, well they just did not seem right any more. Not after so long. It was like cheating.

The kettle began to boil and Ezekiel was nowhere in sight. He would just have to wait for his supper, or get his own.

She had made her excuses to Hannah earlier, after feeling more and more uncomfortable as the day went on. She had said that she was not feeling very well; it must be the wine they drank. Hannah had nodded, but looked hurt. Sylvia smiled, she would telephone her later. On her way back she had bumped into Martin Phillips. Every time she saw him she was sure she recognised him from somewhere else. Where could she have possibly seen him before?

The kettle switched itself off, and she poured the hot water into her mug, watching it froth up as it met the tea bag. A quick stir and all was done, she kicked off her shoes this time, and marched back out into the study.

The book had finished searching. It lay still on the table where she had left it. Sylvia paused in the doorway.

Did she really want to know?

Dust had settled, but the musty odour of old paper lingered. The lit candle spluttered in the breeze created by the open doorway in which she stood. The book had found it's answer and it was not good. Where was Ezekiel when she needed him? Could she not just ignore whatever was going on and move to another town? Something inside her was telling her No. She couldn't do that. She looked.

The book lay open on a familiar page. The figure at its centre

82

and the symbols surrounding it all too recognisable. No wonder she had felt something was happening, someone was watching her. Looking at the outline of the figure and the weaving of symbols around it was making her nauseous. Sylvia was sure that she would be sick.

As she read the name she began to cry.

*   *   *   *   *

The shop stood utterly empty and devoid of custom, and Hannah quite simply could not understand why. She had not seen a soul all day, and since Sylvia had left she had not uttered a single word, other than to herself or her flowers, which amounted to the same.

It was not just her though. She had hardly seen anyone walk down the street at all. Perhaps they were all at the fair, no that was ridiculous, wasn't it? Hannah gazed out of her window up and down the high street. Not a soul to be seen. Somewhere far away a cry rang out, amidst the faint chime of musical bells. The sound of summers past, of kicking off shoes and racing up to the water's edge. She smiled to herself; perhaps she would visit the fair later, and would ask Sylvia if she wanted to come.

*   *   *   *   *

Gregory sat at the harbour's edge again. He found himself here almost every night; somehow watching the seagulls and listening to the lap of water against concrete soothed him. It made him feel calm again. He had needed that calmness more and more lately, since his dreams had become stranger and stranger. Gregory sighed and gazed down into the murky waters. A crisp packet floated by, followed by a tail of cigarette ends.

For the past week his dreams had been so real, and yet he had known, even as he was having them, that they were not real. What was real any more? He also knew that he liked the dreams he was having. They were better than reality at the moment. He laughed out loud. What was there to do in this place? That was the reason he could not wait to get out, and go off to college somewhere, or get a job in another town. Perhaps then he would not be bored. The local pub was only an attractive alternative up to a point, after that it became a habit.

Why did no one else seem restless? With the exception of Martin, who was in his own little world anyway, everyone else seemed to be quite content just to tick along as they were, having things the same as they had been for generations. Gregory did not particularly want to work on the fishing trawlers thank you very much, or become one of a thousand farm hands for that matter. He stood up and swayed on the edge of the harbour wall. The darkness beyond threw his own dark features back at him. The water stretched forever, always moving, changing everything in its path, feeding on the dead and feeding the living. The strings of his stomach tugged him forward. It would be so easy to step forward and drop into the sea below. So easy not to be found as darkness drew closer. There he would drift for an eternity, still but moving, him and the sea. He resisted and stepped down the other side of the wall, onto the pavement, a mental coin flip.

Over the road the Happy Trawler was throbbing with life, but Gregory was not sure that he felt like it tonight. The open air seemed more appealing, the woods and pastures more tempting. He thought he would go for a walk, and see where he ended up.

*   *   *   *   *

Martin traced the web with his fingertips. It was here at the centre of the book, where it should be. It lay at the centre of the book exactly, reaching out with innumerable strands in all directions, to other pages and beyond. This was it, the key. Each strand of the web was made up of words and older symbols. It seemed to be a hierarchy of some sort. What Martin could not figure out was where that hierarchy started. Was its highest point the singularity in the web's centre or the multitude at its edge? He guessed it must be the centre, on the premise that power and knowledge were a limited commodity, and the more knowledgeable someone got the harder it became for them to find something they did not know, and therefore the harder it became to learn more. This seemed logical, but something else told him no.

It could not be that way.

He frowned, why did he not think so. Martin had learned to always follow his gut feelings, they were usually correct. He stared at the web, first one way and then another, looking at each part in detail. Nothing sprang to mind. Every part of the web seemed to point towards the centre. Or did the web spread out from the centre?

He moved the book to arms length. As the book moved away the web span, very slightly, a clockwise motion. The spiraling arms were moving away from the centre. He smiled.

The web started at the centre, where everything was concentrated and everything was known in minute proportions. It then spread out as that knowledge grew, into specialist areas. The spread would carry on and on and on, to infinity, or eternity if it needed to. That is why the symbols started at the centre and worked their way out, they were reaching into infinity. Martin nodded; they were reaching for the secret of immortality.

He traced the lines again with his fingers, that immortality, or clues of it may be contained within this very book, if he could unlock the code.

*　　*　　*　　*　　*

Anthony trudged down the high street with his hands in his pockets. His left hand held tightly to three round pebbles and juggled them between his fingers. It was now dark, so no one could see him. No one was about as the shops were all closed. Just this one thing to do and then he could go home to his warm bed Mr. Roberts was a mean man. He had tried to stop people going to the fair by peeling off the posters from his window.

Someone should teach him a lesson. Anthony held on tight to the pebbles. Each one had been picked for it's throwable qualities, all three would make excellent missiles in his expert opinion, and Roberts' Newsagent window would make an excellent target, by any standard. He would only be doing what everyone else had felt like doing, and what everyone else wanted to do to the miserable bastard anyway.

Anthony reached the spot and looked left and right. No one was coming. He stood on the other side of the road, so as not to be showered in glass from the window of Roberts Newsagent opposite. He could see the scars where Mr. Roberts had tried to remove the poster, but the words were still clear.

V.J. Midnight's Extravaganza!
Carnival of Light and Dark
Fairground rides
Prizes!
And, the Carousel
(First ride free)

Anthony smiled and fished out the pebbles from his pocket. They really were the perfect shape, how clever he had been to pick these three.

He gripped two of them in his other hand and rolled the third around in his fingers. It felt good, just the correct weight. Then, with one last glance at the window he launched the missile into the air, across the road.

It hurtled towards its target, whistling like Anthony had never heard a stone whistle before. It sounded more like one of those doodle bug bombs from the black and white war films on television.

The pebble rose slightly, and then began to dip in a very narrow arch, the perfect shot. Anthony stood waiting, holding his breath. The pebble whistled and reached its target. It crashed through the window, sending shards of glass flying through the inside of the shop, and falling around the edge of the window. Anthony flinched at the sharp sound the glass made as it broke and then again as it hit the floor and pavement. He had better be going now, before Mr. Robert's woke up.

Then the shop front was engulfed by a ball of flame from within. Anthony stared, open-mouthed as the flames rushed out and licked the outside of the window frame. He felt air rush past him filling the gap left by fire, and then the flames erupted again, this time with more noise. They roared at him and laughed, fed by the in-rushing air.

Anthony ran. What if it had been a doodlebug? He had thrown a doodlebug bomb into Mr. Robert's Shop, and Mr. Roberts was asleep upstairs. The fire laughed and raged behind him as he ran up the street and around the corner, leaving the shop out of sight, but the fire's laughter followed him all the way home.

*   *   *   *   *

Firemen worked into the night, trying to contain the blaze in

Seahaven High Street. Units from three neighbouring towns had been drafted in an attempt to fight the fire from both ends as well as the source, and in twenty two years of service Chief Hawkins had never seen anything like this. He had wrestled with warehouses packed with toxic chemicals, which spewed out smoke that would erode the lungs, trawlers trapped in the harbour, which lurched unpredictably in all directions, and even a petrol station which seemed to have an endless supply of petroleum, but nothing could have prepared him for this.

In virtually no wind at all the fire was spreading at an alarming rate, evenly to both sides of the source, which had been Robert's Newsagent. Although they had been able to reach the fires on either side and slow them down, no one had been able to get near the source. At each attempt the fire would lash out into the street, burning anyone and anything in its way. Hoses simply did no good, as the flames simply raced up the jet of water somehow. Chief Hawkins had thus resorted to containing the fire to the surrounding buildings. They could do no more. He hoped to God that there had been nobody inside.

The fire burned for exactly six hours.

*   *   *   *   *

By Eleven Thirty news of the fire in High street had spread from one end of the town to the other. The flames could be seen from as far away as the common. Faces stared in awe from the top of the Giant Wheel as red haired elves danced and skipped over the rooftops, cackling with glee and inviting them to join. Then the wheel would turn and sight would be lost, to give others the chance, while below them the queue awaited their turn anxiously. An orange glow flickered and wavered over the sky, casting its shadow over all who played and all who watched. The clowns seemed jollier, the tents darker, and the faces of the Gypsies who worked there ruddier. Gregory sat on the gatepost, surveying all that passed before, and behind him. The last time he had been here he had been uncomfortable. The air had been heavy and all eyes had accused him, perhaps because he had been ill. This time the only heaviness the air held was the weight of music and mirth. He gazed in turn at the dizziness of machinery; great whirling cages full of giddy screaming people who would shriek to be let off, then queue and beg to be let on again. Popcorn and candyfloss drifted by in great clouds of vapour leaving trails behind them, each one to the stall where it had originated. Gregory listened over the cacophony of screams, laughter and music to the clicks and whirring of a vast drum of sugar as it span cloud cotton balls for the delight of children and adults alike. He grinned and inhaled the vapours of childhood. Further still in the distance, perhaps at the centre of the fairground wood creaked and groaned to life, something old began to move. Gregory tried to peer past the crowds that gathered, but could not penetrate the confusion, so he listened. There was the groan again, and a faint aroma of old wood. Sandalwood? Rosewood? One aroma flowed into another as though the object were a giant wheel, spinning on its fulcrum.

90

Something else too. Music. Not fairground, walzer noise, but soft belabouring, reaching out over the din, creeping in between the notes of lesser earthly tunes. What music! It was the cries of a thousand years of love and pain, the weeping of the world, and all contained within a note. A tear leaped into the corner of his eye, and Gregory looked away. Again he found himself on a precipice. Sat on the gatepost with one leg in darkness, peace and tranquility, and the other in the chaos of senses. Could he leave now, and never turn back? Could he turn away from that music which made his blood and his bones ache and never know?

Gregory looked back down the hill into Seahaven once more, as lights in a thousand homes flickered out one by one, extinguishing that day for one household at a time. The aroma of candyfloss and the voices of angels begged him not to go. He lifted his leg, heavily onto the top of the gatepost, and swung it down the other side. When he lowered himself to the ground his feet touched the earth of the common. The music begged him, and he followed it inwards.

At the centre of it all, behind the smiles and screams, underneath the aroma of candyfloss, eyes followed him inwards. They watched as Gregory paced in concentric circles around the fairground, heading towards the centre. There was something of a mask to this boy, a more natural being awaiting release. The mouth under these eyes expanded into a broad grin, perhaps it was time they met. Coloured horses stirred beside him, their wooden bodies creaking, all the while Gregory approached. Not

91

to late to turn back boy. Gregory faltered, stopping by a darts stall.

Win a prize with every throw,
no one leaves empty handed.

The horses froze, holding inanimate breath, the air dropped, noises ceased. Eyes continued watching without a sound. It was best to come anyway boy, it is the best way.

Gregory continued his journey inward.

6. A Ride on the Carousel

Laughter rippled in the wind, like butterflies taking to the summer sky, punctuated by the smell and taste of mirth. Swarms of buzzing children span, bouncing off one another and cascading into the next scene, only to rebound again and again on into the night. Adults pretended not to be drawn in, but the urge existed, all felt the pull. To forget their age, to forget their bills, to forget themselves, to abandon themselves to the tide. Few, however could. Where the tide would carry them there was no knowing, and would they drown? Perchance, but what would that mean?

It was the unknown that loomed as a terrible avenger, it was the unknown that would exact revenge for whatever crimes had been committed against one's fellows, and the unknown was a terrible and unremitting nemesis. Only the innocent could play. Only the virtuous were guarded from the unknown, because they knew of nothing that could harm them. To watch the children be taken by giant clumping machinery and be thrown high up into the sky, only to land safely and beg to go again, this time with greater speed was to laugh with the soul and say 'Ha! They have cheated you'. They will go on cheating until that fear creeps up inside of them. They will outwit and despair you and frustrate all that is terrifying to lesser mortals. There is no creature on earth as indestructible and as foolhardy as a ten year old child. The parents watched their children, and others watched them too, and all the while they would be thinking back to a time beyond remembering. How big was the world then, how great was the adventure which the sun would announce each morning? Unfathomable. The night brought only treasures and secrets to be discovered, secrets that would later be hidden again, or forgotten, or disguised. For now though sons and daughters searched out those secrets, and their parents left them well alone. There would be plenty of time for fear later.

The bubbles of laughter washed over Gregory's senses like water dancing over pebbles. As he stood in the midst of chaos he tried to catch each wave as it passed. He would be carried on for a brief moment and then the flow would change direction and he would be lost again. Noise surrounded him, people shouted and cheered, machinery roared. Gregory smiled broadly.

The laughter was contagious. He would challenge even a Dickensian Scrooge to stand in this place and not feel the warmth of that laughter.

In the centre of all of this stood the most magnificent ride he had ever seen. It was not a white knuckle, tooth shattering roller coaster, nor was it a nail biting, goose bump raising screamer of a ghost train. It was simply a merry-go-round. It was old too; he could see that even from this distance, he could smell the spice of seasoned wood. Horses, bears and other stranger animals danced around it's centre piece, all adorned with wondrous colours, tints and hues, some of which he was sure were new. Was it possible to invent a colour that had never been seen before? Shades yes, possibly, but whole colours? It must be the light, playing tricks. Horses tossed their manes which flew in imaginary wind, bears lurched forth, fur rippling over their movement, some yawning, some snarling, and a lone wolf leaped from nowhere into nowhere. Gregory wondered where that wolf was going. Perhaps it did not know itself. Grey fur glistened on it's broad back, playing with passing shadows. It's teeth dripped pure moonstone, as white as pearl, and as dark as blood.

Around it's neck hung a sign, a loose collar, a dog tag. Gregory could not read whatever it said from this distance, although it was written in bold print. Large black spiders webs on a worn, cracked wooden sign. He stepped closer. It was still too far away to read.

Carousel starts at Midnight
(Sorry for the delay)

The wind changed direction and dragged the aroma of spiced wood away. It was once again replaced with that of candyfloss and peanuts. Gregory looked around him. Children still danced and skipped their way around the fair, circling and taunting each other from ride to ride. To his left stood a candyfloss stall, the huge metal drum whirring and turning to spin cotton balls out of sugar spider's webs. The sweet smell beckoned, so Gregory followed.

*   *   *   *   *

As the tears began to dry up Sylvia wiped her eyes and attempted to examine the symbol the book had shown her again.

Yes, It was he, or it. She had never known what to call it. Aleph, she supposed was one of his names, although could never be sure, because the last time he had lied. Bastard.
What the hell did he want this time, had he not humiliated her enough in Paris? She slammed the book shut, sending dust clouds billowing through the air. Ezekiel mewed behind her. "Oh shut up!" She was in no mood for his attention seeking. At least now she was armed with the truth, she would have no more of his nonsense, not in her town. She stamped her way down the hall again, making her presence known to Ezekiel, who already knew she was there. He had no right to show up like this, not after what he had done. Just thinking of him made her blood boil. She could feel her temperature rising and the blood rushing to her face. It was at times like this that she wished she had not decided to take on human attributes. Love and happiness were wonderful feelings to behold, but anger, it had consumed her on the occasions when it had reared its ugly head, and in ten thousand years she could not hope to master it. She just wanted to break something, quite simply destroy anything in her path.

Cups and saucers flew in all directions as the whirlwind of emotion picked up speed, Ezekiel fled. Wise move cat. Sylvia stood in the middle of the vast kitchen floor, at the centre of the hurricane and fumed. Windows shook, cups smashed into a thousand pieces against every wall. Cupboard doors tore themselves off their hinges and threw themselves into the fray, and Sylvia stood in the centre of it all, ranting. What on earth or in hell gave that bastard the right to just turn up unannounced into her town and turn everything upside down for her like this? He would start playing his evil little tricks and soon enough she would have another witch hunt on her hands. They would probably even blame her like they had the last time. She let out a scream of exasperation. She wanted some excitement, but not this. He would ruin everything. She slumped cross legged on the floor and wept. Crockery crashed to the floor around her, the last tinkle of broken china punctuated her weeping with a comma, allowing her a sigh.

She looked around at the chaos that was her kitchen. Broken crockery, cutlery, pots and pans strewn across the landscape like debris on a battlefield. Tiny crystals of glass scattered over the worktops. She had left herself one glass, and one bottle of gin. Everything had been going great last time as well. She had just settled in, had an apartment in the centre of Paris, nearby all the great theatres. She had even collected paintings over the years and had some of the greats displayed in her hallway, from Florence no less. She owned a restaurant and two theatres herself, and the famous Monet had promised her a painting, his next one in fact. She could smell the clean air, and hear the faint bellowing of riverboats as they sounded their horns entering and leaving the city. She would walk the streets early each morning, alive with what she could see. She would applaud the street performers, and had even offered some of them work. She would watch the working girls leaving their hotels after a hard nights work, and smell their perfume as they passed. Then she would sit outside her favourite café, drink orange juice, eat croissants and smoke cigarettes, whilst the rest of the city awoke and came alive. She had read books, seen plays and eaten in the finest restaurants. Twice she had taken a boat trip down the Seine, trailed her hand in the cool water, and listened to the ripple of waves against the bow. She had never been happier.

Then he showed up. It was too good to last and he wanted to share in it. At first he was reasonable, she thought that he simply wanted the same things as her, so she permitted him to stay. It was highly unusual for two of them to live in the same city, let alone the same household, but she let him stay. They visited the theatre together, and ate in the same restaurants; she even helped him buy his first show hall, where he staged an impressive circus, with acts from across the globe, from Tunisia, Arabia and the Russian Steppes. He took to staying out later and later, sometimes would not return to their home at all for several days. When she questioned him he would become irritated and said that she should understand what he was doing. She tried to explain that in the modern world they did not need to do that any more. They could go to restaurants and have the finest foods

98

prepared for them, more exquisite in taste to anything he could otherwise imagine, but he complained that it was not the same. People continued to go missing from the city, and now it was being noticed. She pleaded with him to stop, that he would ruin everything, but he scorned her and called her weak. The humanity that she had adopted had gone to her head. Finally they had argued. She had accused him of being stuck in the old ways. This was not Bulgaria or Romania, nor was it Egypt or Siberia. They were in France now, in the age of scientific discovery, things were different.

The room shook with the anger of the both of them, and people passing in the street had heard. They were followed, she found herself harassed wherever she went, then a body had turned up in the alleyway at the rear of their apartment, drained of blood, some of the internal organs missing.

There would be no sense in staying and protesting her innocence. She had fled as her apartment was burned to the ground. In the guise of night she had taken most of the jewellery and money stored away from him in her theatres and fled to the south. After a while in Sicily rumours of why she was there at all had escalated so she left before any more harm could be done, or before he could find her again. Years of searching brought her to England, where she was unknown, the way she preferred things. Now he was back. Whether he had come looking for her she did not know, but one thing was for certain, they would not both be staying this time.

*   *   *   *   *

Martin closed the book and tossed it onto his bed. There was no use. He could not make head nor tale of it. The most important parts were written in some kind of script that he did not recognise from anywhere, and in some made up language no doubt. Without a proper key he was going to get nowhere with this.

It was as though he author had done this purely to taunt any readers. He had written in several languages. Latin, Greek, Sanskrit, Arabic, and once the reader got past those pieces the language would change again, into some obscure writing which the author had made up himself. The reader would be led on an Odyssey and just as the truth was about to be revealed an unassailable obstacle was thrown in the path. Martin was beginning to think that Agrippa was truly mad, stricken with some form of insanity, like schizophrenia, which scrambled his senses and caused this mismatch of writing and crazy paving of languages. The book had been translated in great chunks only to leave huge gaps. Martin also suspected that the translations were not entirely accurate. The subject matter skipped from one area to anther, sometimes completely unconnected. Perhaps the pages were in the wrong order. He picked up the book again.

Why were some of the pages numbered in Roman numerals, and others in the Arabic? He flicked through the pages. They followed a logical sequence from one through to four hundred and seventy three, but the numerals were mixed up. Ten pages of

Roman numbered pages, followed by seven or eight pages of Arabic, and so on. The languages of each page did not seem to correspond to the numerals that marked their progress. There were pages of Sanskrit marked with Roman numerals and Arabic alike, and pages of Latin marked with Arabic numbers as well as the Roman type. Martin frowned. Perhaps the translators put them in the logical order but their order was not supposed to be logical. Perhaps Agrippa had not written them that way. Martin smiled, then he would put them back into their original order. If he could separate the book into two parts, one in a sequence of Roman numerals and the other in a sequence with Arabic numbers then perhaps they would make more sense. At least he would be able to read each passage in context with the one before and the next. Martin tore off the spine and began to tear out pages, Roman on the left, Arabic on the right. If someone had gone to all of this trouble to hide what he had written then it must be worth reading.

*   *   *   *   *

Well there's no sense in sniveling, you killed him, and you lit the fire, now you'll have to face up to it.
Anthony tried to stop crying like the voice said, but he couldn't. Instead he placed his hands over his ears and curled tighter, his knees up against his chin now. The earth underneath the bridge was cold and damp, made so by brown water from the river. Anthony had sat here for half the day now, trying to figure out

what to do. His thoughts had been punctuated by fits of despair and tears. Sometimes the tears came so violently that they made him shake, and he had to keep his hand over his mouth to keep from crying out. He didn't burn the place down; all he had done was throw a stone through the window. Maybe there had been a fire anyway and he had not seen it, or maybe the Roberts' stove had exploded while Mr. Roberts was making supper and it wasn't his fault.

Don't be stupid boy, you did it and you meant to do it. You hated that mean old man and you wanted him to burn, you wanted him to die for what he did.

Anthony shook his head, no he did not. Mr. Roberts was mean and old but he did not want him to die, all he wanted to do was to smash his window.

The stone was meant to smash his window that was all.

That did not really matter now. You did burn him and he is dead, and that is what the police will think, so you better do something quick before they throw you in jail forever, and your mother finds out.

At this Anthony burst into a torrent of tears again, his back thudded against the wall behind him as his body shook. He tried to cry out, but his throat had locked into a spasm of remorse. He gasped for breath.

Please don't let them tell his mother, not that, anything but that. Anything?

Anthony fumbled in his pocket for a tissue, now that the tears were subsiding. Perhaps there was a way out of this after all.

102

The tissue was not in his right pocket so he searched his left. Instead of the used ball of tissue paper he found something cold, slim and hard to the touch. He fished it out of his pocket.

There is a way that neither your mother, nor the police will ever find out what you did.

Anthony held the object in his left hand and looked at it closely. A shiny new red Swiss army penknife, the kind that they sold in the fishing tackle shop. He turned it in his hand admiring the colour, and all the gadgets contained within. The voice had gone quiet. Anthony opened out the knife.

*　*　*　*　*

The girl smiled as she span the steel drum to make candy floss for Gregory. Her eyes creased in the corners, to show the beginnings of crow's feet, not there through age, but there because she smiled and laughed a lot, Gregory could tell. He smiled back. She twirled the stick in a slender hand, covered in sticky sugar webs, around the steel drum, gathering pink wool. Twice she brushed straw coloured hair back from her face with her free hand, on which she wore a wedding ring. Finally she was finished, and she held the product up for Gregory to inspect. He handed over the cash and she smiled at the next person in the queue.

Gregory moved on, prize in hand. It was a bit childish, yes, but so what. He took a great mouthful of pink cotton, only to have it melt away almost instantly, leaving the sticky remnants on his teeth and chin. Fairgrounds were great. Over on the other side, past the hoopla stalls and shooting galleries he could see a roller coaster climbing into the sky. He watched as it's climb slowed. It reached the top and paused for a moment, a moment that must have seemed an eternity, and not long enough for the people sat at the front. Then it dipped, hung suspended in the air, between life and death, long enough for the first scream to reach out, and plummeted along the tracks towards the ground out of his sight. He walked on through the mayhem. To the left, on the periphery of his vision the old Merry-go-round was moving. He headed towards it, just to have a look, but it was still. He would have sworn that it had been moving but a moment ago, circling and playing that enchanting music the way they always do. But no. It was as still as the moment he had first seen it; it had not budged an inch. Around the leaping wolf's neck the sign still hung, still unreadable at this distance. Gregory decided to investigate.

As he approached the animals seemed to grow larger, as did the whole machine around which they paraded. It was huge. The wooden rails creaked in the breeze and gave their scent to him. Spices from far away shores. Egypt? China? Russia? Animals of every shape and description from around the globe stood proudly around the central hub, some new, some old, some ancient, and the colours! Gregory had never seen so many colours in one place before. How could the human eye take in so much? He did not know, all he knew was that he was taking it all in; sight, sound and smell. Every sense immersed itself in this wonderful machine and bathed in its glory. The sign around the wolf's neck was clearer now.

Carousel starts at Midnight
(Sorry for the delay)

Gregory sighed. He would love to see this machine in motion. He was sure that it would put all the others in this fairground to shame. Why at Midnight? He stepped forward and ran his hand along the wolf's back. The wood was warm to the touch, unlike cold, dead metal that surrounded more modern rides. Wood breathed and lived, and this was no exception. He wondered why there was only one wolf.

"Because they are so rare in these times"

A man stepped forward from the centre of the ride, his boot heels clattering on the wooden boards. Gregory was startled, "Sorry, I didn't see you there," he backed away slightly, took his hand from the wolf's back. The tall figure watched his hand closely, then looked up at his face, eyes full of smiles.

"That's O.K. young man, I think it's you who was more startled. I was just oiling the machinery."

Gregory nodded. What did not fit in this picture? He was sure that he had not spoken aloud, and yet the man in front of him had answered his question.

"Victor Midnight is the name, pleased to meet you."

Gregory nodded again, backing away a step more,

"Pleased to meet you Mr. Midnight." Then it dawned upon him,

"Then this must be your fairground."

Mr. Midnight smiled, pleasantly and nodded. He sighed and looked around at the land around them,

"Yes, do you like it?"

Gregory felt like a ten year old. He nodded. The man in front was tall, very tall, which was quite intimidating. He stayed back under the shade of the canopy, which hid his features well, although Gregory could just make out a sharp nose and silver hair under his stark black hat.

"Good, then enjoy yourself, tell your friends." Mr. Midnight smiled, revealing perfect white teeth, almost too many of them. He patted the Wolf's head

"And don't forget your free ride at midnight."

Then he turned his back and was gone, back into the centre of his machine

*   *   *   *   *

Midnight is such a strange time. It is not deathly quiet like three o'clock in the morning, when whispers can carry you off to places you would never wish to go, nor is it like the dawn when nothing seems to exist and all is fading or appearing. At midnight, as the clock chimes twelve children shiver and quake in their sleep. Adults lock their doors and dogs stop barking. All goes quiet for that moment, as though the end of the world had just occurred, quietly and without a fuss, only to begin again at one minute past. It is the minute point upon which a penny spins, or a pin can balance before it falls. It is the point where the roller

106

coaster stops and the carousel begins.

Gregory watched the queue shorten as people took their places
for the ride. Five people left to be seated. Why would anyone
want to queue for such a simple ride as this when the fair had
more thrilling and bigger rides to offer? The wind breathed
warm air into his face, carrying the remnants of peanut oil and
salt with it. The queue was down to three.

Other rides were still running, people milled around him, tired
laughs permeating the tinkle of fairground music. The world
turned, but as yet the carousel remained still. Two minutes to
midnight. The wolf still had not been taken, his wolf. Horses,
elephants, ostriches yes, but not his wolf. Gregory itched. The
queue was down to one now, Mr. Midnight ushering people into
their places on the oldest ride in the world. Wooden boards
clattered as people made their way across them, rafters creaked
as they sat astride fantastic animals. Gregory moved closer, there
was no-one else waiting now, and the wolf was still free.

"I've saved a place for you Gregory" Mr. Midnight smiled in his
direction, his teeth catching the moonlight and holding it
prisoner. The spark in his eyes, a white dwarf in each, too bright
to look at directly.

Gregory found himself nodding; he watched a dark gloved hand
caress the back of the leaping wolf. Where was the wolf leaping
to? Where could it carry him? Mr. Midnight nodded, "you will
not be disappointed Gregory, I am certain of that." Gregory got
the feeling that no body else could hear him. People walked
around them both now, ignoring their presence, the man with

midnight skin and moon drenched hair drew closer but did not move.

"This is what you have been waiting for isn't it? There is no ride like this you can imagine, there is no beginning and no end." Gregory was so close now that he could smell the seasoned wood again. He closed his eyes and let the aroma wash over him, through him.

"I know your pain Gregory, I know what it feels like to be one thing and act another, I know what it is like to wish for freedom. Do you remember your dreams?"

Gregory opened his eyes. He was sat astride the wolf, hands gripping onto the soft wooden fur around its neck. Mr. Midnight nodded,

"It's time."

Gregory closed his eyes again to listen to the creak of old wood as the wheels set in motion. The smells and sounds moved together, a groan of wood, a note of music, a laugh, sandalwood and rosewood. He grinned to himself. The ride was picking up speed now; perhaps it would go faster than he thought. Warm air breathed then blew into his face. The music faster now, the smell of old wood stronger, now pine. Fresh pinewood, and grass. Gregory laughed out loud. The music faded, hidden by the rush of wind and the blood in his ears. Fresh pine and salt, perspiration, but like none he had ever smelt. Panting, a growl, grass, the roar of blood. This was like no ride he had ever...Gregory opened his eyes.

The earth was warm under his feet as he pounded his way across the valley, the smell of grass and salt strong in his nostrils. A growl from his right told him to veer right, so he did, following his brothers. The quarry lay ahead, three young deer, cut off from the rest of their family. Gregory grinned as he ran, and his brothers grinned back, fangs glistening in hazy sunlight. He felt the fur ripple around him over sinewy muscle. He was free.

* * * * *

Hannah was beginning to worry. Perhaps she had done something to offend her. She had rushed off in an awful hurry and had offered no real explanation, or tried to call her. It was too late to do anything about it now though, or was it? The clock on her mantelpiece told her it was ten minutes to midnight. She could not go around unannounced now.

Instead she sat back in the armchair and dipped her hand into a bag of crisps. The fair had not seemed such a good idea after all. She had such a miserable day for business that she could not feel justified in blowing money away at a fairground. It was stupid, yes, but that was the way she felt. Perhaps she would call Sylvia in the morning and see if she was all right. No the morning was too late, if anything was worth doing it was worth doing now. She got up and snatched her keys from the coffee table.

* * * * *

Martin shook his head; he could not believe that it could be that simple.

Now that he had placed the pages in their correct order the writing fell into place. It actually made sense. The diagram in the first book, which spanned out like a web was in cabalistic script, used by the ancient Hebrew cabalists to write the secret names of angels and daemons. The Greek and Latin sections of the book dealt with a description of this web and what it meant, the Arabic sections dealt with the history and how the web had been devised and drawn, where the knowledge had come from, and as far as he could tell the Sanskrit sections dealt with how the web could be used. He was not too hot on Sanskrit though so h could not be entirely sure. He rubbed his eyes and yawned, loudly. It was nearly midnight. He could not stop now, this was a breakthrough. How had one man got all this knowledge? It seemed as though the web was a number of things. A map of some sort, to another world, what Agrippa termed as the real place; a diagram of some sort of hierarchy; and a curriculum, or path of knowledge. He would start with the easy part, what the web meant. That was a place to begin.

*   *   *   *   *

By the time Hannah approached Sylvia's driveway there were three minutes to spare until midnight. Her headlights had lit up the iron gates as she passed though, and they had glared back at her. Hannah felt as though she was watched again, as though there should be two great harpies, one sitting on each gate

110

watching all who approached. There probably were and she could not see them. That thought made her flesh prickle up. She hated that gate. The driveway was long and silent, but at the end of it she could see the house. Sylvia had left the lights on in a few rooms, so she must still be awake. As Hannah approached she noticed the lights flickering. Candlelight.

She pulled up to the back gate and switched off the engine. Well, there was no sense in stopping or turning back now. She got out of the car, feeling the warm breath of sea in her face. In the house lights flickered and glowed, warm like the setting sun, basking the place in an orange glow. The house inside was a world apart from it's cold granite exterior, with those worn iron gates and it's guardian harpies. Hannah felt a shiver, what was she doing out here? Cold eyes swept over her back from the base of her spine to the shoulders. It was time to get inside. She ran through the back gate, closing it behind her and around to the kitchen door. She would knock and wait. If there was no answer she would just get back in her car and go home. An owl hooted as though in approval, and on cue. This is ridiculous. She knocked. The door was open, but she knocked anyway. Over on the other side of town she could see the common lit up with all manner of fairground machinery. Occasionally the faintest glimmer of music could be heard, struggling to cross the bay and reach this house.

There was no answer, so she knocked again.

"Sylvia?"

She would have to shout louder than that.

"Sylvia, it's me, Hannah."

She pushed the door open so she could see inside a little better. The bottom edge scraped against broken crockery. Hannah pushed it open and stepped inside.

"Oh my God!"

The floor was littered with broken plates and cups, the work surfaces with shattered glass. What the hell had happened here?

"Sylvia, are you all right."

Stupid question, of course she wasn't. There had been a break in or something. She panicked. Was Sylvia OK? What if there had been a break in while she was here? What if these were all signs of a struggle? A groan escaped from the doorway next to the stairs at the other end of the kitchen. Hannah rushed through the kitchen over broken glass and china. She slipped and cut her left ankle, but ignoring that moved on. There was more to worry about than a grazed ankle. The doorway at the other end of the kitchen led through into a hall passage, the noise had come from here. She gave a brief glance to the bedroom at the top of her stairs on the way past; there was nobody up there. The noise had definitely come from through here. She skipped past a candle on her way through, and then decided to pick it up. She did not know where this hallway led. It seemed to lead down, as in downhill on a slope, and it got darker down there, despite the candles lighting the way, all of then held by sockets in the walls. She let out a clipped, nervous laugh. This house just got weirder and weirder. All the fun of the fair here. She had visited a haunted house at a fairground when she was small, and had

112

hated it. The creaking floorboards and silly plastic cobwebs had scared her stupid. This place was no exception.

"Sylvia, are you there?"

No answer, just that groan again.

She rushed forward and on. The passage seemed to stretch and stretch, and just as she was wondering where in hell it was going she reached the end, and a door. Hannah swallowed hard. The door was shut. The groan came from behind it, louder this time. She put her hand on the handle and squeezed. This was really stupid. What if the burglars were still in here with her, what would she do then? It did not matter, she threw the door open. Inside the room was dark, except for the few candles dotted around. The walls were stacked high with bookshelves, each littered with books, all of which looked older than her. A large round table had its place in the centre of the room and a large red candle on a brass stick in the centre of that. The floor was carpeted, unlike the hall she had just traversed, and two extremely comfortable looking chairs sat around the table Sat at on of these chairs, her head slumped in her hands and sobbing violently was Sylvia. Hannah almost dropped the candle she was carrying.

"Sylvia?"

He voice startled Sylvia, who looked up, immediately wiping her eyes, trying the hide the evidence.

"Hannah, what are you doing here?"

She fumbled for words,

"I thought... the broken plates, are you all right?"

Another stupid question, but Sylvia nodded.

"Yes, that was me."

Hannah sighed, no burglars then.

"No burglars." Sylvia confirmed, "Just me."

There she was at it again, answering questions that had not been asked yet. She wiped mascara from her face and tried to smile. Hannah noticed her hands reaching for a book she had not seen before. It had been resting open on the table in front of her. Before she could get a good look at the page it was open on Sylvia had shut it. She stood up. "Let's go and get a drink."

Hannah nodded, looking to see where Sylvia had put the book she had been reading. It had gone. "What were you reading?"

Sylvia shook her head, "Nothing." She bit her lip as she said this, a red trickle made it's way slowly along the outside of her lip and onto her chin before she licked it up. Hannah shook her head "Oh no, it was enough to reduce you to tears and smash up your kitchen, that is hardly nothing, now what was it?" Perhaps she had overstepped the mark there a little.

Sylvia frowned, "Who are you to come barging into my house and tell me what I must do?" Hannah could feel herself getting hotter and hotter, blood rising to the surface. Were they going to argue now?

"No we are not," replied Sylvia, before she could speak, "and yes I can hear you." Hannah slammed her candlestick down on the table.

"I came over to see you, unannounced, yes, but with good intentions." She could hear her voice rising, "And when I arrived

I found your house in ruins as though you had been burgled."
The corner of Sylvia's mouth twitched, almost into a smile. "I
then hear you moaning and thought God only knows had
happened to you, so came searching through your spooky,
creepy house looking for you." Sylvia sat down, trying not to
laugh.

"Only to find that you are OK after all and the devastation was
caused by yourself in some temper tantrum. I potentially risked
my own life to see if you were OK and you start shouting at
me?" Sylvia stood up and opened her arms, "I am sorry, I didn't
mean to shout at you, but you came in here and...."

"And to top it all you keep answering my questions before I have
even asked them, and you make books disappear into thin air."
She pointed to the table, where there was now not only no book,
but no brass candlestick, only her own. Sylvia sighed. Hannah
had calmed down now, although her chest still rose in short,
rapid breaths.

"So who are you and what is going on?"

They stood facing each other. Hannah did not believe what she
had just said, but she had said it now. Sylvia smiled back at her
warmly, her eyes were pools of light, which Hannah simply
wanted to dive into, but she resisted. The clock above the door
struck midnight with a click as the hands fell into place. The
chimes began.

Sylvia nodded, "There are a few things which perhaps you
should know about me."

Part Two

7. Murder in the dark, and other party games

When Gregory awoke it was with a feeling of some trepidation. His back was sore, his legs stiff, as through far too much exercise, and his head hurt like hell. The sun was also far too bright, and he felt that to look at it would damage his eyes, even through the drawn curtains. He'd had one of those strange dreams again, where a fairground ride had taken him to far away fields and he had been free to run and go as he pleased. That was the entire dream he could remember, just running, then at all went hazy.

His legs felt like he had been running though, or someone had tied all of his muscles in knots. Gregory dragged himself out of bed. He had better have a shower and wash all of this mud and dirt off. It would probably be a good idea to wash his sheets too. In the bathroom he ran the hot and cold taps into the sink first. His face was a mess. He had cut his lip, or bitten it in his sleep by the look of it. There was mud mixed with blood under his fingernails too. Gregory shrugged and went to work with the soap.

*   *   *   *   *

P.C. McRae had never seen anything like this, and he had only caught a glimpse before they were covered up, that is all, just a glimpse. He had seen blood, so much blood that it could not possibly have come from three people. There must have been gallons of it. He had seen them lying in their pool of black blood, covered in white sheets. A pink stain had quickly risen up each of the sheets and he had been sick. He retched until his throat hurt and his stomach muscles gave in. Three bodies, two girls and one boy, all aged between sixteen and eighteen, that is all they could tell. The chief had said they would have to get the forensic lab at Lancaster to have a look at them. The kids would have to be identified by their dental records. He wiped his mouth on the back of his hand and sat squarely on the grass. His helmet lay on its side a few feet away, discarded in the grass. Ambulance staff buzzed around unsure of quite what to do. It was best to move the bodies, that was certain. The police photographer had finished his work, he looked pale, and glanced over at P.C. McRae uneasily. "I have finished here, I'd best get these developed and sent down to Lancaster." McRae nodded, but did not speak. A gypsy boy walking his dog had found the three of them early that morning. It originally looked like more than three bodies. At first he had been told it was difficult to decide which head went with which corpse, but they had pieced together the puzzle. This itself had made him queasy, then he

118

had caught a glimpse of them as they were being covered and up came his breakfast. It was now a quarter past eight. A crowd had gathered wanting to see what was going on and had been asked to keep back. One short glimpse soon discouraged them and the majority of people kept a healthy distance. Close enough so they could tell what was happening, but not so close that they could actually see. He guessed that small towns had to have their maniacs too, eventually.

*   *   *   *   *

Gregory was not the only inhabitant of Seahaven to have strange dreams that night. Henrietta Smith moved around her house in a daze, trying to remember. The horses had been so beautiful. She floated from room to room with their music trailing behind her in soft tinkles, but whenever she looked over her shoulder or turned around they were not there, instead she found the sigh of empty space. It was only after she had opened the front door to pick up fresh milk bottles from the doorstep that she realised she was still naked.

Across the street Thomas Berkley watched her through oily net curtains. He pondered how it would feel to gently push the point of a knife through her smooth stomach. Would it be like puncturing a leather sofa, and make a satisfying pop? Or would it rip, like satin? He smiled to himself as she closed the door. How much, or how little blood would there be?

A small boy passed by his window and he retreated slightly, but

119

the boy could not see him anyway, not behind these net curtains. Howard French hurried along the street so as to get to the end of it and out of sight, just in case his mum came home early, or had forgotten something and turned around. She had gone to the supermarket so he had taken the opportunity to sneak out of the house. She was bound to notice when she got home anyway, but that did not matter, it was the opportunity to get out that mattered. All they would do was send him to his room, which is where he spent most of his time in any event, and he would just go up there and read stories, which is what he liked doing anyway. He had a stash of comics, for reading at nighttime hidden under the floorboards beside his bed, along with some spare batteries for his torch. He would sometimes take these to school as well, although he would have to pretend that he had forgotten something and run upstairs so he could put them in his rucksack after his mum had packed his lunch. She had not found them yet, but was forever telling him that he would forget his head if it was not screwed on tight. He would just smile.

Today he had sneaked out with a purpose. Today he was going to the fair. He had never been to a fair before, not that he could remember anyway, but he had heard other children talk about them, when he could get close enough to hear. Most of the time he spent on his own, in the corner of the schoolyard reading about Spiderman or the Silver Surfer. Sometimes he would even skip P.E. class and read comics. He had a crumpled sick note hidden in his desk at school, which his mum had given him once and forgotten to date, so getting an excuse to sit out P.E. was

120

easy. The other children only ever made fun of him anyway, because he could not see very well without his glasses. He had seen posters for the fair the day before, when he had been out shopping with his mum. She had been trying on dresses again. The fair was on the common at the top of the hill, so it was not very far. He had turned the corner now, so was safe for the time being. If his mum came back early she would be coming from the other direction, so would not see him. He would have to cross Main Street now and head up the hill towards the common. He could see that people were heading that way already, so he followed them. This was easy. He seemed to float in a current of people, flowing towards the top of the hill. He would pass some, and others would race past him, eager currents. All the while he felt watched. Someone, or everyone was watching. Children who were passing him would slow down to look on their way past, then hurry on once they had seen enough. They probably did not recognise him from school, but it was still rude to stare. As he reached the top the current began to slow, as people flowed through the gates. Howard could see the gates now, and on the fence at either side sat five ragged crows. Two on the left and three on the right, oddly asymmetrical. The five crows sat and watched, but they were not crows. As Howard approached he could see that they were children, dressed in ragged jeans and hooded coats, five of them in all, sitting in judgement. A parliament of crows. Howard did not like the way they looked at him, he did not like it at all. Two on the left he recognised. The furthest away looked like Robert Fitzsimmons from his class, and the one nearest he gate looked like James Redfern from the year above, but they did not recognise him. They smiled with wide mouths and wicked eyes. He felt himself freezing in their stare, his feet would not move fast enough to escape. Howard was not sure if he had stopped, but the gate did not seem to be getting any closer. The five crow-boys stared at him from their perch. He felt like he was being scanned. Only instead of Mr. Spock with his tricorder he was being given a mind scan. They were sweeping over him with their eyes to find out who he was, and Howard was suddenly certain that he did not want them to know. A boy brushed past him and through the gates, knocking him off balance for an instant, and his feet were free. Howard took the opportunity and ran through. He did not look back until he was well inside, and when he did the boys were gone.

* * * * *

The morning was not yet over for P.C. McRae. He now wished that he had taken a transfer to one of the Metropolitan forces. Then at least he would expect this type of thing to happen everyday. He would expect not to know what he would be called out to and to have a nasty surprise around every corner. As it was he had never expected the nasty surprise, and this made it all the more unpleasant. Another body had been found floating face down in the river. This time it had been found by three children who had been playing a game of pooh sticks from Seahaven Bridge. They had all dropped their sticks from one side of the

122

bridge into the water and ran over to the other side to see who's came out from under the bridge first. The body had floated out ahead of them all. P.C. McRae tried desperately to hold down the rest of his stomach lining whilst the scene of crime officers did their work and photographed the body. He had left the consoling of the three children, the youngest of whom was six and the oldest nine to W.C. Johnstone as, quite frankly, he was not up to it. He was probably as upset and disturbed by all of this as they were. The boy's skin was pickled slightly, but not bloated, so he had not been in the water for very long, and his throat and left wrist had been cut by what was probably a pen knife, or something similar. Possibly the worst thing was he recognised the boy. It was Anthony Doyle.

* * * * *

Whilst P.C. McRae was on one side of town dealing with the discovery of Anthony Doyle's sodden and bloodless corpse the control room in the town centre had gone crazy. After the three bodies had been found earlier they had taken repeated calls from people with information about the crime, most of them amounted to no more than wild stories of beast men with claws and fangs, but they had some leads to go on. Resources however were beginning to be stretched and the seams were showing. Reports had come in of anything from fights in the town square to burglary and the discovery of Anthony Doyles body as it floated out from under Seahaven Bridge like Eeyore in a

123

macabre version of the Winnie-The-Pooh story. The latest in all of this was the report of a serious gas leak on Shore Street. Thus it was that while P.C. McRae struggled to keep himself intact by Seahaven Bridge, P.C. Dickenson found himself organising the evacuation of Shore Street in the early afternoon. He was attempting to persuade the occupants of number twenty seven that they should vacate the premises temporarily when the fire brigade and Gas company arrived. About time too. Ironically the occupants of number twenty seven seemed to pay more attention to the Gas company than either the police or fire department, especially when the possibility of compensation for any damages to property was mentioned. Within five minutes they had the Street sealed off at each end, and a crowd had gathered at both ends of the small street.

They had so far managed to evacuate every house with the exception of number twenty three, which was, as he had been reliably informed by the neighbours, the home of Henrietta Smith, proprietor of Henrietta's Hats.

Nobody knew whether she was in or not. P.C. Dickenson got on the radio and asked someone to check out her shop, to see if she had opened up. The firemen were becoming agitated. They would just have to break in anyway, in case she was there, there was not time, and if she was in and not answering the likelihood was that something was wrong. The Gas man returned with the news that the leak was in fact coming from number Twenty three. Great. P.C. Dickenson got back on the radio.

"Has anyone found out whether Henrietta's Hats is open yet?"

The line crackled, then the answer came back.

"Negative, she hasn't shown up at all today."

Right, time for action then. P.C. Dickenson gave the go ahead for the fire department to break in. torches at the ready they began swinging their axes. Within five seconds the front window was vacant, shards of glass everywhere. The smell of gas was overpowering. He could hear the team leader shouting for the rest of them to go gently inside, he did not want any sparks. In through the window they went.

They made their way inward only to encounter another locked door. This woman had obviously been very security conscious. "O.k. masks on everybody, let's not take any chances in here." The other three donned their oxygen masks. "Crowbars now, no axes, we can't risk a spark. Torches on." They set to work on the inner door. This was going to take them a bit longer.

*   *   *   *   *

Thomas Berkley watched with interest as the police and fire brigade scurried like ants around number twenty three. Some of them had gone around the back now, presumably to get in that way. He had felt a short moment of panic when the policeman had come to his door, he did not know what he would have done if he had wanted to come inside. Not everyone would understand. The knives were out on the mantelpiece for decoration. He found them to be beautiful works of art, each and every one of them, but not everyone else thought so, so he did not usually let anyone see them. Only that man at the fair had understood, he had said that he had collected things too, and nobody understood him either. He had told Thomas that it was all right for him to collect things, perhaps one day they could swap a few items, or show each other what they had got stored away. Thomas thought that he would like that. Someone else to talk to about his hobby, and about where he wanted his hobby to go next. The man at the fair had asked if Thomas had ever though about using any pieces of his collection. Yes, he had. For the moment though he had not done anything with them, he did not want to spoil them. He watched the parade of uniforms in front with some curiosity and vaguely wondered what would have happened to Miss Smith by now if she was still at home.

*   *   *   *   *

Inside the house the air was becoming hazier the closer they got to the back. Carl guessed that they were heading towards the kitchen, which was the logical place for a domestic gas leak. He somehow doubted that they would find Miss Smith alive. Out back, ahead of them he could hear the other crew working their way forward. They had already come through two doors, and two of them had been dispatched upstairs to see if she was up there, although he doubted that. It was highly likely that she had tried to top herself. The old head in the oven trick. By the size of the gas leak here she had been there all morning. The two of them were faced with one more door to go, the kitchen door. The

126

thumping about upstairs told him that the other two were still looking, so she was not up there, she was behind this door, that meant she was dead. Sometimes he hated this job.

This door looked fairly ordinary so they could prize the gap next to the handle wider and force it open. It was old so it would probably be swollen in the frame, they would have to force it. He set to work around the handle and removed the lock mechanism. That was not so bad, now all they needed to do was push.

It would not budge. The door was swollen fast, more stubborn than his four year old daughter. The two of them put their shoulders to it and heaved.

The spark that Carl saw at head height came as a warning of what they had missed, and was about to happen, but the warning came too late. In that second or less he realised that this door had been so easy because it was a standard kitchen door, but instead of having bolts on the outside, to stop people getting into the house from the kitchen, it bolted from the inside. The spark told him all of this. It told him that she had bolted the kitchen door because she did not wish to be found, that she did not mean to hurt anyone, and that his family, his wife and daughter would miss him. Then everything was gone.

In the rush of searing hot air, part of the stairway pushed it's way out of the front door and the street sidewall above. Glass shattered outwards from the upstairs windows and charred furniture leaped out at the officials standing below. There were no screams or shouts from inside; the loudest sound was that of the glass shattering. Flames licked briefly at the walls and ceilings, but were short lived, leaving them scarred and blackened in the blink of an eye. It was over in minutes, but all who watched knew that there could have been no survivors. No matter how short lived, fire is not that merciful.

*   *   *   *   *

Thus the web works it's way inwards. Not out towards a never ending and ever widening span but inwards towards a single purpose and finite vision. Each arm and spiral weaves its way subtly to the centre, an infinite variety of means with a common cause. This Cornelius Agrippa knew, and Leonardo DaVinci, and Imhotep too, or perhaps they were all one and the same person, who is to know. As eager fingers trace the web and read they feed on the knowledge of a thousand before them, and with each feeding the knowledge grows. With each person the knowing is assimilated for those who will read the web in the future to come, thus each reader becomes the past, and is at once assimilated into the possible future. That is the nature of the web. As each reader reads he becomes part of the intricate web, his life's line is drawn into the pattern and he makes up yet another strand, working it's way into the centre. Thus Martin, reading the will of others was to gain their knowledge and experience, and yet leave a trace of his own there for the next reader to see. With the passing of time the knowledge and experience become stronger and he contributes to the future of this universe. Unknowingly he becomes the book that he reads, and his life becomes a chapter for others to decipher.

*　*　*　*　*

Thomas Berkley was disappointed that he had lost his first experiment to the hand of fate. She was not actually his experiment, not yet, as yet he had merely pondered, but she was to be the first until today. Now he would have to go in search of another. No matter, she was easily replaced. The experiment was to be how each of his collection pieces worked on the same object. He wanted to see if the longer knives necessarily punctured better than the shorter ones, and to see which of the knives would slice better than others. Shape was probably important too, as some were curved to different degrees, whilst others were straight. Some were serrated whilst others were smooth, and so far he believed he had collected every possible combination of several variables. Now he needed an object on which he could test them. They all had to be tested on the same object of course. He had even picked out eight different variations of blade to test, according to degree of curve, size, weight and type of edge, so as to get a good cross section of his collection. So the subjects were all lined up ready, but he had lost the equipment needed with which to test them. He would just have to go and find one of the same build as number twenty three had been. The same approximate age was important too. Because she had been in her early forties she represented the average person, the mid point in a person's development, and therefore was the correct test environment.

Thomas picked up his tool belt with the subjects attached and fastened it around his waist, then slipped into his long, lightweight Macintosh. This hid them well. He could feel them jangling and chattering around his back, and tapping against the back of his legs and his buttocks as he walked. That was good, it meant that they were still there, and still willing to participate in his experiment. Now he would just have to go and pick out some new apparatus.

*   *   *   *   *

Howard had walked around the fairground for some time now and his feet were beginning to get tired. There were all sorts here to see and do. Things that he had only ever been told about in the exaggerated stories of other children. Stalls cried out to him with their brightly coloured banners, Roll up, Roll up, they said, anything you like, you can win if you try. Howard doubted that. The Gypsies had to make a living somehow, and he did not think they would just give prizes away, the way they claimed. The tents were a different story. He kept away from them, skirted right around them if he could. They whispered and dared him to look inside in soft, cold voices, like canvass whispering against the grass beneath. Machinery roared around him, attempting to hide its fierceness by the soft tinkle of music, but the scream of children drowned out any pretense to the contrary. Howard was nevertheless drawn to it all, as other children had been before him and others would after. The fair, a magical place where fear becomes fun and the possibility of death becomes an adventure. Howard could not help but grin. He had no power over the muscles around his mouth, it was someone else who had hold of his puppet strings now, and he loved it. He wished he had some money so he could play the games and go on the rides.

Something made him look down.

There, at his feet, peeping out from underneath the sole of his left training shoe.

A note. Crisp and blue. A five-pound note.

Howard looked up. He did not know where to turn; instead he stood rooted to the spot. Had anyone seen him? He glanced around. Nobody seemed to be paying attention, not to an ordinary boy in an ordinary field at the top of an ordinary hill, surrounded by extraordinary machines. Not a sole was looking. Howard began to perspire. He could feel his leg shaking, threatening to lift up from the five-pound note, and if there were a gust of wind it would be gone. He bent down. He could pretend to tie his laces.

There, it was now within reach. He pulled the laces of his left shoe loose, just in case and began to tie them. People passed to the left and to the right, but nobody noticed him. His hands trembled and he had to try three times to do his laces properly. People were going to stare if he stayed here for too long, or come over to see if he was all right. Now or never. He picked up the five-pound note and stood up. No one had seen. Howard made his way quickly over to the other side of the fair.

*   *   *   *   *

Thomas sat on the grass and shook his head in desperation. It had all gone disastrously wrong. It was not supposed to struggle or shout. This could have been embarrassing, all of that swearing and shouting in public. He was supposed to try out each of his subjects in turn using different methods, but the apparatus was not supposed to try and escape. Next time he would have to do something to stop it from escaping. The problem was that it had to be killed to stop the screaming, and then he was not able to test the other subjects properly. One had been used on live tissue and the other seven had been tested on dead tissue, after it had been killed. The aim of the experiment was not to test out the subject post mortem, but on a live object. He would have to find another one now and do it properly this time. With all the kicking and screaming he had not even had the opportunity to make proper notes. He looked over at the woman's lifeless body and sighed. He would have to hide this one first. It was getting dark now, so that would be easy enough, he could just throw her in the bushes over there, by the river. Thomas got up and grasped the body under the arms.

"Come on dear, let's go for a walk."

He chuckled, this could be fun. The body was difficult to drag though, and her heels were leaving track marks in the grass. Never mind, she would be found soon enough anyway he

132

supposed. By the time he had dragged her far enough to throw her in the bushes he realised that she had lost a shoe somewhere along the way. One scuffed, blue shoe on one foot, the other foot bare. Mud and dirt had stained the bare ankle where he had dragged her along. He rolled her into the bushes and left her there. Now, where was he going to get another one from?

*   *   *   *   *

Gregory was beginning to feel the heat again. It started just as the sun began to set. He must be coming down with something; perhaps he should have finished that course of antibiotics that they gave him to take home at the hospital. He had made his excuses at teatime and gone up to his room to lie down. There was no sense in moping around, he would just have to go to bed and sleep this off, sweat it out like any other cold. Gregory opened his bedroom window, undressed and got into bed. That was the best thing; he would shake this off in a day or so if he was sensible about it.

*   *   *   *   *

Yes, by moonlight it was a lot easier. Just light enough to see up close, and yet dark enough so that people could only see you as a shadow from the distance. This time there had not been as much shouting. Because it was dark she had been scared and had done what he had told her to do, until it had started to hurt, then he had silenced her. He had discovered, by accident more than anything else, that if he cut her throat she could not scream, and took a while to die, so he had time to try out more of his tools on her before she expired. He had only managed to try out five of them before he surmised that she was dead, but it was better than last time when he had only managed two, much better. He could see himself getting very good at this. He was so pleased with his work that he had decided to take a trophy this time, a lock of hair perhaps, or something more personal like a kidney? As Thomas rolled her over onto her front and bent to the task he heard a noise behind, in the bushes. He froze. What would he do now? Replacing the short hooked knife with one hand he drew out a long curved blade with the other, perhaps he could to take two trophies home with him tonight. He crouched and faced the bushes, one hand on the grass to steady himself and one wrapped firmly around the long, curved blade, his personal favourite so far. There it was again, but from behind him now, as though someone was making their way around the clearing. He turned around again.

A low growl issued from his left, what the hell was this? He turned again, knifepoint in front of him. The growling had stopped, as had the rustling.

"Who are you? Who is there?"

Was it someone after his trophy? A thief, or scavenger?

There was no answer, just the rustle of wind in the trees around him. A twig snapped behind, followed by another growl.

Thomas tightened his grip on the knife; there was no way any

134

dirty scavenger was going to take his trophies from him

A growl answered him this time, but not from in front, from the left again.

Thomas turned, shaking now; he had forgotten about the body at his feet and stumbled backwards over her. The dead Jennifer Jones got the last laugh. Out of the bushes, now in front of him leapt something the likes of which he had never seen before, indeed nobody had ever seen and lived to tell. For a moment Thomas thought that he must be dreaming as this could not be happening, then the beast ripped out his lungs.

* * * * *

Howard thought he had best be getting home. It was dark now, had been for about twenty minutes and his mum would be wondering where he had got to. He had spent all but fifty pence of the five-pound note and could not help but feel a little guilty. Whoever had lost it had lost it though, and if he had not picked it up someone else would. He had been relieved that there had been no sign of the five crow-boys in the fair, or they had been watching someone else, but still he could not help but feel a little strange. On his way out there was a rifle-shooting stall, so he thought he would give it a try with his last fifty pence piece (and get rid of the evidence). He turned it in his palm, watching the shining surfaces catch the moonlight. It felt heavy in his hand. The man smiled over the counter as Howard handed the coin over and pointed to one of the rifles in return. "Try that one kid, it looks about the right size." Howard took the first of his three shots and hit a wooden duck square in the middle. The rifle felt right in his hands, like part of his body. He took his second shot and a second wooden duck found itself on the way to wooden duck heaven. If the third shot was his he would have the rabbit's foot on the first shelf. A fitting souvenir from his first day at the fair, and one that he could hide easily as well. A rabbit's foot was supposed to be lucky wasn't it? A third duck went down. Three for three. Howard smiled and pointed to his trophy, which the man duly handed over, "Now that is a well picked prize if ever I saw one, a lucky rabbit's foot for a lucky lad." He seemed to be looking over Howard's shoulder, "Now you run along home lad, before your mum gets to wondering where you've got to." He winked and Howard grinned back at him. "Thanks Mister." He skipped away, trophy in hand. The soft, white fur brushed against his fingers and nestled into his palm as though it had always belonged there. Howard plunged it into his deep pocket, where it would be safe, but kept his hand in there just in case. He was on the way out now and could see the gates up ahead, but something was telling him to turn around. He did not want to. It was like he had been before, running away from the crow-boys, only worse, he had to look, but did not want to, really did not want to. Howard looked. There was nothing there. He sighed. Just the melee of people climbing on and off rides, in and out of tents. In the corner of his eye there was something though. What was that? He turned his head slightly, did not want to look directly at it, but wanted to see. He was not sure, but it

136

was some sort of Merry-go-around. Kid's stuff really, only this one looked different. It was a lot older than he had seen in any books, and the animals looked strange to him. What was stranger still was the silver surfboard right at the front. He was sure.... no it could not be. Was it? Was it the Silver Surfer's board? Howard shook his head, as though having a conversation with himself. No it could not be, not on a ride that old. This ride had to be a hundred years old and the Silver Surfer comics had not been going that long. They did not even have surfboards a hundred years ago. But there it was. At the front of the ride, a big silver surf board. It was closer now and Howard realised he had been walking towards it all this time. He realised that he had let go of the lucky rabbit's foot and grabbed hold of it again. Senses swam back to him and he stopped moving. There was someone on the ride. Not on the merry-go-around part, but inside it, deep inside. That someone was watching him from the shadows, Howard was sure of it. He turned around and walked as quickly as he could towards the gates at the edge of the common. The eyes that he could not see burned into his back and he could almost feel his jacket smouldering. It was going to catch fire in a minute. He hurried onwards faster now and looked up. The gates were dead ahead, and sat on either side were five crows, but they were not crows were they. The five boys watched him as he approached, but Howard carried on walking. He should not stop now, something was happening here that he did not like. He gripped the lucky rabbit's foot as tightly as he could and walked through the gates, past the five crow boys.

Behind him he heard one of them say "Goodnight Howard." but he did not stop to reply, he kept on going.

8. Sylvia Cruz and the Eternal Harlequin

"So how old are you then?" Hannah would not even look at her now, she sat with her arms folded on her knees, bent forward. The room swayed around her, candles flickered. Sylvia shrugged, "I don't know."

That was not strictly true, she had not told her from the beginning, and it had been a long time, but she had a rough idea. "But you were alive during the French revolution, right?" Sylvia nodded, "Yes, I think so." She wished she had not started all of this.

She also wished that Hannah would look at her and give her some sort of reaction. Hannah rocked back and forth gently. She gazed at the books on the shelves in front of her. They were old, so old. "What else do you remember?" Sylvia shrugged again, she felt like a naughty child, "Lots of things." Hannah nodded. "So are you more than five hundred or less?"

Sylvia bit her bottom lip, "More, I think." Hannah closed her eyes and smiled, but it was not her usual smile, it was not the smile that told Sylvia she was enjoying herself. "You think." Sylvia nodded.

"Well are you more than a thousand then?"

Sylvia sighed, "Yes, probably, look does this matter?"

The reaction came at last. Hannah stood up, almost throwing the table over as she did so. "YES it does BLOODY MATTER!" It was a good job the library was sound proof. Hannah's arms were flailing about now; she was beginning to look frightening.

"When I'm told that I'm having an affair with a thousand year old witch I think I have a right to get upset, don't you?" Sylvia winced, "I am not a witch, I am ...."

"A manitor, whatever..."

"Manitou."

"OK, Manitou then, you are still not fucking human are you?" That hurt. Sylvia shook her head, this was not fair.

"Yes I am."

Hannah stared at her with eyes that wanted her to shrivel up.

"Oh, right. So am I going to live to be a thousand then am I?" She did not give Sylvia a chance to answer.

"Well AM I?"

Hannah's face was now as red as the fire within her; Sylvia could see that this could be dangerous. Whatever happened she could not leave knowing what she did. "No, I have been trying to explain, the older I get the more human I become." Hannah sat down again. She did not look as though she was listening, but Sylvia carried on anyway.

"I have chosen to be mortal now, so I will become more human as time goes on." Hannah just stared into space.

"So eventually I will die, like everyone else."

Hannah snorted, "So how long have you got left then?"

Sylvia shrugged; she was doing that a lot lately, "Probably another hundred years or so, no more than that." The laughter that came from Hannah took Sylvia by surprise. The feeling of surprise was not altogether unpleasant. Hannah was shaking her head as she laughed, tears were trickling down each cheek, a conflict of emotions. "Do you know what some people would give to live over a hundred years, let alone what they would give for what time you've already spent?"

Sylvia closed her eyes and fought back tears. Could she tell her of the seven thousand years of sorrow, of the loneliness she had felt in all that time, doomed to be alone in an ever changing world, where every person and every creature would despise her for what she was, an accident of creation? No she could not tell her, only her own kind would understand, and she was among the last of them. She was becoming more human by the day, it was getting so hard to change shape now that merely trying exhausted her. She had not walked as a beast or bird for over four hundred years. She was proud of the crow's feet she had developed over the last ten years or so. At last she was beginning to age. So how could anyone tell her she was not human?

She opened her eyes and looked directly at Hannah, this time forcing her to return the gaze. As much as she hated doing this it was the only way. Hannah looked back at her, their eyes fusing at the contact.

"Do I look human to you?"

"What?" Hannah frowned, her brow began to crease in a distant cousin of anger, and Sylvia repeated herself again.

"I said, do I look Human?"

Hannah nodded, "Yes, you look it..."

"Well what is the difference then? For our purposes I am and will always be." Hannah nodded, why she was just accepting this she did not know, but she felt OK with it. Having a thousand year old lover was not so bad, she could do worse, and they could live out their lives together as normal, as though none of this had ever happened. She felt sleepy now, wanted to go to bed, and she wanted Sylvia with her. Yes, she would sleep on it; it was not such a bad thing at all. Sylvia was kind, thoughtful, intelligent, wise, not to mention very attractive. Hannah smiled and stifled a yawn.

"OK, but just don't pull any of your hocus pocus on me OK?" Sylvia fended off a wince, "No problem, my hocus pocus days are largely over anyway." Hannah nodded, "I don't want you changing into a bird or anything freaky like that on me either." Sylvia nodded. Hannah yawned, everything was becoming blurred and she felt so very very tired. "Can we go to bed now?" Sylvia nodded, "yes."

She blew out the candles one by one as they left the library, but could not help catching a reflection of herself in the mirror as she extinguished the last one. Another faint line had appeared underneath her left eye. It wrinkled the skin, giving her a more pronounced crows foot when she smiled.

*　*　*　*　*

Martin could not read any more, it was now a quarter past four in the morning. His eyes were sore and the letters and symbols on the pages in front of him were blurring into one. Perhaps he needed glasses for when his eyes became tired. He sighed and put the book down. A quarter past four. It was so quiet. He had managed to decipher most of the web now, only a small part, at the centre remained. This was written in yet another code. It seemed that each spiral and each line of the web was written in a slightly different way, almost as though several people, or a hundred or more people had written, or had a hand in it. It was entirely possible of course that Cornelius Agrippa had written this over several decades though, as this was his life's work. The web was, as he had thought, a map, although not in the conventional sense. It was a map of knowledge, if such a thing could exist, and detailed a path that one had to take to gain that knowledge, although it was not specific on what that knowledge was. It went on to say that many had taken the path to become One and that they too were written into the web as part of the path. Many more would take it until the destiny of all was complete. Was Martin going to become one of the many? Was he already one of them? He was still puzzled. He did not know any more what he was supposed to be learning. All he knew was that he now had to finish it and learn the lesson properly. He did not and could not remember anything specific, but knew that he had learned and that he now knew more that he had ever known.

But that could also be said of the average person every day of their life. With every new experience and every new day we assimilate new knowledge and learn something that we did not know before, or at the very least have our beliefs confirmed or denied. But there was more to it than this. Martin was just not sure how much more, or just what the more was. Finally he switched out the light and closed his eyes to sleep.

Patterns moved in the shadows as his mind organised itself, as it had always done. The Librarian glided down corridors placing this thought in that file that idea in this box until it came to a door at the end. The door had not always been there. The door was new. New things in the library were good, usually, that is what this was all about wasn't it? Martin would pick up new ideas and new thoughts and The Librarian would put them into a logical order, as it always would. But not today. The Librarian had run out of ideas and thoughts to file, and there was this door. What was behind this door? There had never been a door at the end of the library corridor before. The Librarian would look up the file marked doors and see if there were any clues there. It did not want to go opening strange doors without any idea what was going to be behind them.

* * * * *

By morning the fog that had been experienced by all earlier that week had materialised again. This time it was not to cover the arrival of a fair, as the fair was already here. James Redfern's

144

mother was worried. She worried about her son. He had been acting so strange lately, staying out until all hours of the night and answering her and his father back. He had never been like this before, he had always been good. He was out again already this morning and she did not know where he had gone. Surely an eight year old boy was not supposed to be this way. Children didn't grow up that quickly these days did they?

Sylvia was already up too, but had not left the house. She stood at the back door, looking out at the fields beyond, or what could be seen of them. The fog was becoming progressively thicker, spreading out from its centre on Seahaven Common. It was strange for it's centre to be the top of a hill, but it did not really surprise her. The fog was heading in her direction.

She had left Hannah asleep upstairs. She had looked so peaceful, now her mind was at rest. She could not help but feel slightly guilty about doing this, but it had to be done, or things would have got out of hand. What if Hannah had told someone? That would have been messy. She would have had to move again. She traced a slender finger along the new lines in her face. She had paid for it after all, and Hannah would suffer no harm.

Hannah stirred in her sleep upstairs, rustling among the sheets. Sylvia smiled. Everything was going to be all right. She was not sure about this fog though. Perhaps the bastard was planning to pay her a visit. It was typical of his style; he could never resist playing with the elements. Well if he was going to come in she may as well leave the door open for him, or he would only come down the chimney and make a mess, or squeeze himself through the letterbox or something. Now where would she wait for him? The library was probably the best place, down the corridor at the far end of the house, in a sound proof room. Yes the library was best; she did not want Hannah dragged into this. Sylvia left the back door open and made her way down the corridor to the library at the bottom. Hannah was safely asleep until she wanted otherwise, so all she had to do now was sit and wait.

*   *   *   *   *

This was not good at all. This was decidedly weird. Gregory had woken up in the early hours of the morning in his parent's garage. He had been asleep between his dad's old Mercedes, with the dust cover over it, and the family Volkswagen. He must have been sleep walking again, and he was naked. Who knows where he could have got to? He would have to see a doctor about this, or perhaps he could get his mum and dad to strap him into his bed at night. He should certainly not sleep with his window open or his door unlocked. What if he had wandered around town naked? Who would have seen him? He was blushing at the thought. This was bad news.

Luckily he had woken up early enough so that the majority of people had still been asleep. He had gone around the back of the house, climbed up a drainpipe onto the roof of the garage, then up the corner of the wall, where the bricks stood out and into his bedroom window. Yet again he had mud all over him, dried on as though he had been rolling around in it before returning to the

146

garage. It was too early as yet to take a shower though; he would have to wait until a bit later. The clock in his bedroom told him it was a quarter to five in the morning, and the sun was on the rise.

*　　*　　*　　*　　*

By the time the clock struck six Sylvia was bored and tired of waiting. If He was going to pay her a visit, then He should get on with it. It was typical of Him to keep her waiting like this, wondering when He was going to show up. It was a power thing, trying to assert His dominance as usual. Or perhaps He was scared. The more she thought about Him the more annoyed she got. How dare He do this to her after all of this time, just when she was getting settled again. She was also on the verge of becoming human and all it would take is something like this to mess it up for her. She looked around her at the books on the shelves. This place was becoming a bit tatty as well; she really should make an effort to tidy it up. Perhaps she should prepare herself for him. There was no telling what nasty trick he would have up his sleeve this time. She called one of the books over and it obeyed, placing itself on the table in front of her obediently. The table lantern winked into life, so she could see more clearly. Now then, where should she begin? It was best to set up some sort of protection. Perhaps she should create a temporal stasis in this room, that way she could do what she wanted and not get any older, just in case he got nasty with her.

He might not even come in here, but she would refuse to see him if he did not. So what else did she need then? Some salt perhaps, and some rosemary? There on the top shelf in the orange box. The box made it's way down to the table for her, as she could not quite reach. A clock. She needed a clock. Her wristwatch would do. Sylvia took it off, and with the necessary ingredients in place she took off one of her shoes and smashed it to pieces with the heel, then scattered the fragments in the air. Before they could land they were taken. Sylvia smiled. She had never really understood where the ingredients actually went to when she did this sort of thing, but did not really wish to know. It was the end result which mattered, not the how or where of it. This done she sat back to prepare herself for the wait again. It only took five minutes before she realised that she was bored again. He was doing this on purpose, keeping her waiting that is. He knew exactly where she was, had to unless he was slipping in his old age. No he must know, if she knew where he was then he knew where she was, that was the way it worked. Whilst they were connected as members of the same race it would always be so. The quicker she got this over with and was able to become fully human the better, then she would be rid of him for good, and he would never be able to find her again.

"Well Celaeno, It's been a long time."

She looked up. He was here in the doorway. As usual he had chosen an unusual appearance. In the dim light she could see him framed against the doorway dressed in black garb. A long and tattered coat made him look like a crow, perhaps that is how

148

he had travelled here. From the silhouette she could not make out any of his features, just the silver hair and silver stars of his eyes.

"My name is Sylvia now, and I would appreciate it if you would knock before you decide to come in."

He smiled and rapped his knuckles on the doorframe. By the time the sound had died he was seated in the chair opposite her with his feet up on the table. There was something different about him this time. Not good, just different. Underneath he was the same old pure evil bastard that he had always been. She watched him carefully as he sniffed the air around him, like a dog trying to catch a scent. She took the pause as an opportunity to shut the door behind him. She asked it to shut and it obliged, the latch snapping quietly into place. He did not flinch, as though he had expected this.

"It's nice to see that you still want to be alone with me Sylvia."

At least he was courteous enough to use her new name.

"Nice temporal stasis you have set up here. A precaution?"

She nodded.

"What do you want?"

He frowned, and leaned forward, taking his feet off the table, "Don't be so rude. We were getting on so nicely then."

Sylvia leaned back in her chair, retreating from his protruding face. The scorn must have shown on her own. "Don't give me that shit Aleph, I don't want any part of whatever it is you're doing, so just piss off and leave me alone."

He looked faintly surprised.

"Now Sylvia, where do you get such language from?"

"Television. It's an invention of the twentieth century; you know the one we currently live in. You should wake up and try living in it and you may learn something."

He shook his head and tutted.

"My name is now Victor by the way. I believe it is a new name from this century." Then his face too turned to scorn. "So don't lecture me you little witch." That was it, that was enough. Sylvia spat directly in his face, hitting him just below the left eye.

"Don't call me witch you little prick. Get out of my house before I put an end to you for good."

Victor Midnight smiled, then grinned, and then laughed out loud. Sylvia was glad she had taken the precaution to sound proof the room. His laughter was getting on her nerves, and it was making the room shake.

"My my you sound just like a Hollywood film star. Did you plan that speech? Is that the best you can come up with?" He stood up and the room ceased to shake. "Don't ever threaten me again." Sylvia shook herself and forced a laugh. "Don't flatter yourself you egotistical novice. I could snap you like a twig right now and you know it. The only thing stopping me is the fact that the Elders may find out and I'm just about on the verge of not caring any more, so don't push me any further." She could feel the nails of her right hand digging into the flesh of her palm, drawing blood. Victor Midnight did not seem to care, he stood and looked around the room without paying the slightest bit of attention to what she had just said, as though it was a small child

150

shouting at him and not someone who was his equal. She stood up to face him. She could see from his face that she was never going to be rid of him. He would follow her wherever she went just for the pure hell of it. It was time to get rid of him for good. Time to use her back up plan.

He finished looking around the room.

"You weren't planning to use that witch iron on me were you Sylvia?" He pointed to a black knife on the shelf over his left shoulder, but it was not there any more. It was in Sylvia's hand. She lunged at him and plunged the blade straight into where his heart should be. The knife passed through him as though it were made of nothing more substantial than mist. Victor Midnight laughed, his breath crawling all over her face.

"Now, what was that you were saying about snapping me like a twig?"

She backed away into the far corner of the room, it seemed so small and cramped now, as though he could just reach out and grab hold of her, which he did. What was going on here? He smiled, showing gleaming white fangs. "Now I am going to drink your blood and show your dry worthless body to the bitch you have hidden upstairs, just before I rip her heart out and tear up her soul." Sylvia shook, she felt the anger build up inside her, until finally it came out in a glass shattering screech.

"NO." The sound was deafening, she lost the senses to her own ears for a moment. Victor reeled backwards away from her, hands over his ears, screaming. "What have you done? I can't hear." She gathered her might and blew. The room went strangely still for but a moment, and a look of realisation grew over Victor Midnight's face. Then a wind started to pick up. No he was not going to allow her to send him back, he would come and visit her again another day. The wind howled but he stood his ground, unmoved by the tempest around him. Sylvia kept it up nevertheless. The net result was that he could not get near her and he could not get out of the door. They were both trapped and she could keep this up forever, that is the nature of temporal stasis. Victor Midnight smiled. "So that is how you want it my sweet? There's no point. I am not acting entirely on free will any more so neither you nor anyone else can control me." He winked at her, putting the starlight out in one eye, and with a flutter of black feathers and a wisp of grey smoke he was gone.

Now just what the hell did that mean? Sylvia collapsed into the chair yet again. Someone had bound him. That is why she could not harm him, because someone had bound him to them. Aleph, or Victor Midnight as he was now known had become a curse. She laughed out loud, but no one outside the small library could hear her. It was time to get out of here. If he was a curse he could only go where this other person went, so she could get away from him then. She would have to take Hannah with her. Sylvia rushed out of the library and up the corridor; she would leave the temporal stasis in place in case she ever needed it again. Once into the kitchen she checked the time on the wall clock above the back door. The whole episode had taken less than a minute in real time.

*　*　*　*　*

Later on that morning Howard sat on the carpet in his room reading storybooks. He had left the Silver Surfer comics under the floorboards, that is where they were best to stay. He did not really want to look at them any more, somehow they had become frightening. He tried not to imagine what would have happened to the person who rode the silver surfboard at the fair, least of all what would have happened if that person was him. He tried to imagine a life doomed to surf from planet to planet in the universe, never finding his way home, and having to fight with space creatures every day of his life. He could not imagine the loneliness even when he tried hard to. He wondered why the Silver Surfer never cried. He had probably got used to it, but he still always looked sad. His mother had not chastised him when he got home, like he thought she would. Luckily she had been so pleased to see that he was okay that she had promised to take him to the fair if he wanted to go again, as long as he went with her. Howard however did not want to go to the fair again. His mother had squeezed him so tight that he felt she might break his bones, but his bones were okay. After all she had been crying and that had made Howard cry too.

*　*　*　*　*

Hannah was having such a lovely dream that she just point blank refused to be woken up like this. It just was not fair. She felt that she had not slept so well in her life as she was doing now, and in her sleep she could feel Sylvia's warm body next to her. That was the dream. Not much, but it was how it felt that mattered. She smiled in her sleep and nestled further into the pillow. Sleep was good, awake was bad; that made her frown. Don't spoil it now. Someone was shouting through her pillow, far away in the distance. She had to wake up. No she did not, she wanted to stay here with Sylvia. She wished that whoever it was would just go away and leave them alone. She turned over and faced the other way in an effort to get away from the noise and placed an arm around Sylvia. Sylvia's soft eyes opened. "You have to listen to me Hannah." Hannah nodded and smiled, leaning forward to kiss her, but Sylvia's face retreated so she could not reach. This made her frown again. "Hannah you have to listen to me." She nodded. "We have to wake up now and leave this house before something terrible happens." Hannah nodded. That was OK as long as Sylvia was coming too. Sylvia smiled, "of course I am coming too, I want to be with you everywhere." Hannah smiled again and opened her eyes.

The room was in semi darkness and Sylvia sat at the edge of the bed stroking her hair, "Come on Hannah, wake up, we have to be going." Sylvia was already dressed. Hannah stretched and yawned, "What's happening?"

"We have to get out of here as soon as we can." Sylvia smiled back, "But everything is going to be all right."

9. Five, ten, fifty fold

Howard held his mother's hand very tightly. She had told him that it was a dangerous road and had made him hold on to her, but he would have done anyway. They were going shopping. The best thing of all was that they were not going shopping for clothes. Oh no, they were going to get an ice cream, then they were going to look for some more story books, so she could read them to him at bed time. The best bookstore was Winterson's on Mill Street, because they had the largest children's section in the world, or at the very least in Seahaven, and that is where they were going.

Howard grinned from ear to ear, the widest grin that he could ever imagine. What had brought all of this on he did not know, because the usual treatment that followed an excursion or other mischief was an early night followed by a ban on television and going out at all. Bans of this type had ranged at anything from a day for not doing his homework to two weeks once for going fishing instead of going to school. The particular day in question had been so lovely that Howard had decided to take a left turn at the end of the street instead of a right turn, and ended up by the river, so he had stayed there until he heard the school bell for final play, then had gone to the last hour of school. The last hour was always the best because Miss Clements usually let the children choose an activity to do, but not for Howard this time. He spent the last hour in the headmistress's office waiting for his mother to come and get him. Every morning since then his mother had dropped him off at school personally.

Anyway, that was all in the past now, he had been relatively good since then, perhaps that is why he was getting the treat. Ginnelli's Ice Cream Parlour stood out in the High Street like a jewel set in granite. Its shop window displayed all the colours of the rainbow in fifty varieties of ice cream. Howard was sure there could not be that many flavours. He had tried to count how many there could be once, but had given up at strawberry. The door was always wide open, letting the aromas drift out into the street, where they seemed to capture and hypnotise passers by. Everyone in Seahaven had said at one point or another that it was difficult to walk past Ginnelli's without going in. Howard gazed into the window of the magical Ginnelli's. Inside there were a dozen or more stools set at a circular table top with a great hole cut in the middle. In the middle is where the waitresses, and sometimes Mr. Ginnelli himself stood, dishing out the ice cream from huge tubs arranged around the middle. "Come on then!" His mother was calling him from the doorway. Howard peeled his eyes from the window and ran over to join her inside. The place was huge. Everywhere he looked giant posters depicting grey people smiled down at him. His mother

156

said they were movie stars, although the people had not been grey in any of the movies he had ever seen. They were all grey because they were so old, so he was told. Everyone got that way when they were old. They sat at the big round table, and one of the waitresses had to come out and make his stool taller so he could see over the top of the counter. Wow. He was not sure if there were fifty flavours but there were certainly lots. He counted past strawberry without even trying.

"So what can I get you young man?"

The waitress smiled at him with a bubble gum smile. Howard sat, mouth open. He had to choose?

"Well Howard, what flavours do you want to try, you can have three scoops." His mother pointed to the various bins full of colours and scents.

Howard closed his mouth and swallowed, he could not sit here all day could he? Three scoops was a lot, but it was still difficult to choose. Now if she had allowed him fifty scoops that would have been easy, but three out of fifty was hard. In the end he opted for what seemed most obvious.

"Can I have chocolate, banana and lemon please?" His mother nodded and the waitress smiled, "Chocolate, banana and lemon coming up."

Soon the waitress brought over their dishes. Chocolate banana and lemon for him, and chocolate with raisins for his mum. They tucked in.

You did not have to sit down and eat your ice cream, of course. Howard had noticed several people walk in and order ice cream cones to take out. The sit down ice creams were bigger though. After Howard had demolished his strange mixture his mother took out a tissue and proceeded to wipe his mouth. He hated this part, but it was an unpleasant necessity. He would rather have her do this here, inside than stop in the middle of the street as she sometimes did, licking or spitting on the tissue first before scrubbing at his face with it. He had seen it being done to other children too, and they looked just as miserable as he felt. Whenever a child spotted this happening to him, or he had spotted another boy undergoing the same treatment they had always given each other that look. The look that said 'I'm glad it's you and not me'. This time it was over relatively swiftly and she seemed to be gentler with him than normal. It was only on the way out that he spotted something that would plague his dreams that night. Robert Fitzsimmons, or rather the boy that was not Robert Fitzsimmons had walked into Ginnelli's with another boy who Howard did not recognise. The older boy ordered their ice creams, in cones to take out, while Robert hovered around one of the grey pictures on the wall. He stood strangely as though he were a coat cut from different cloths. The tailor had run out of material and used some of this and some of that, until the grain was all wrong. Howard watched him as he and his mother prepared to leave. There was no definite change, but something was different, and the boy he was with was odd too. They did not talk like boys, nor did they walk like boys. Robert, who was barely older than Howard, by a month or two, walked like his grandfather would if he had young boy's body. It

158

was as though he had grown so incredibly old overnight, but his body had not caught up yet.

* * * * *

It was terrible they had said, the things that people could do. How inconceivable it was for a human being to do such things to another human being. We are not alone in this though. Lions were known to eat lion cubs just so they could procreate with a lioness that would want to replace her children. Humans though. They seemed to do it just for fun.

Gregory read the article in the Morning Star with an uneasy mixture of fascination and horror.

> Police denied any allegation of misconduct yesterday in the matter of the commons murders the coroner's court heard, although an inquiry is still to be headed into the disappearance or misappropriation of major evidence. Although it is uncertain as to exactly what evidence is alleged to be missing, sources close to the coroner report that the only admissible evidence in this case has been the bodies themselves. In a move unprecedented in Seahaven's

long history it is likely that a curfew will be announced in the next few days. Not since the Second World War have such measures been taken, and never in time of peace.

As Seahaven reaches the national headlines for the wrong reasons many are left wondering what has brought this terror to the tiny and once quiet fishing port.

Gregory put down the paper, his hands trembling slightly. Dried blood and sweat still clung to the underneath of his fingernails. They were fairly long now, half an inch over the end of each finger, and were strong too. He had tried to cut them earlier and had found that he had to resort to his dad's wire cutters in order to cut them at all. He had only managed to cut down the nails of his left hand, the right hand; using his left to cut with had proved nigh on impossible. He would have to ask his mother to do them for him. He would have to scrub them clean first though. The mud too. He had been covered in mud on both mornings when the bodies had been found hadn't he? Mud sweat and blood was not a good mixture with dead people turning up everywhere. Mud, sweat and blood were not good things to have all over you

160

when you woke up, especially if a murder investigation was being carried out in your neighbourhood. The police were going to restart their questioning soon, and that would mean a house to house search, disguised as a friendly visit. They would come and they would probe and they would find the bloody towels and mud stained bedding under his bed. He would have to wait until he was sure his parents were out for the day, and then wash everything, or even better burn it. But it could not have been him could it? He would have remembered something like that wouldn't he? Even if he was sleep walking he would still remember pulling someone's arms out wouldn't he, and the screams, would they not wake him up? Gregory decided that burning the paper was the best thing to do as well. There was no use in worrying his parents. His stomach growled at him, he felt so hungry all the time these days, and yet he had no appetite. Had the reports not said that the victims had bites taken out of them, or were they not partially eaten? Perhaps it did not say that, perhaps this was Gregory's fertile imagination. Gregory got up from the kitchen table. It was time to get busy. Sheets first, then a bath. Then he would have to find some way of locking himself in for the night. It was better to be safe than sorry.

*   *   *   *   *

Dr. Harvey Masterson, chief coroner of the West Coast district summoned all of the strength that he could to stop himself from shaking. He would have to let the official photographers in again to photograph the evidence for a second time now that he had seen it. He would be glad to leave this room and have the orderlies tidy up after him. There had been many victims of serious accidents who had passed before his eyes, many of whom had been infinitely more damaged than this, but somehow they had been easier to take, easier to deal with because they had been accidents. It was not difficult to accept that a machine, or a motorbike could destroy a leg, or render a body so deformed that it became useless and died. But this was far beyond acceptable. A person had done this. A man or woman, possibly who he had seen passing in the street on Sunday afternoon. Whoever had done this may have even smiled at him, or spoken to his children. It could have been anyone, or could not have been. Harvey did not think that anyone could have done this. Whoever had found it necessary to break their legs and then tear out their arms was not anyone. Whoever had then spread open their rib cages in order to eat the soft tissue and organs hidden away inside, and had ripped open their throats, all of this with bare hands, could not be considered as ordinary. They were, however still out there.

*   *   *   *   *

Five crows sat in disorder around a canopied wheel. Each draped over a stranger beast than the first, or squatted on the wooden floor, making the whole sight sit wrong. From a distance the wood of the carousel looked warped, but no, occasionally the five shapes that threw it out of symmetry would move. They were alive and it was not. Five crows and five shapes, all of different sizes, peered from the darkness of the carousel where sky blue swam in blood red and sandy yellow bled into bruised purple. Never had the rainbow been so awful to behold as here, in the twilight of the carousel. The horses stood frozen, nostrils flared, the elephants waited breathlessly with volcanic frowns on their petrified faces, and the tigers plotted with the patience of stone. Five crows with the faces of children stood, sat and squatted. They too waited. The canopy overhead fluttered in evening breeze, pushing the daylight away from the wheel beneath. As clocks moved on so the darkness advanced. At first around the carousel, bathed in shadow, then darkness. Then the darkness would spread outwards, a cancer eating healthy colour, until all was drained into lifeless grey. Even the streetlights bathed their subjects in a jaundiced yellow glow; there was no colour there.

In the darkness still five crows waited in the guise of boys. All with feather ruffled hair and dirt-under-fingernails hands. This was not strictly true. In the daylight they were boys, all of them. With smiling muddy cheek faces and their mother's eyes, but in the darkness they were something else. In the darkness, when colour had bled away they were a mystery. In the greyness of that dark light they had lost their boyishness, but had not become men. Instead they were at home hiding among cold, painted animals of the carousel, falsely cheerful and with fakery in their smiles. What can be more evil than a boy who has had the love bled from his soul and the fire drawn from his heart?

"Come in boys."

At last, what they had been waiting for. Mr. Midnight stepped out from the centre of the carousel, extending his hand to one and all. Five gloved fingers and five invisible strings for five crow-boys. They stood and for a second struggled to find questions. What were the questions they tried so hard to find? Mr. Midnight smiled his gaping smile and they forgot, bathed in the moonlight of his soul. That smile swallowed them whole and spat them out again, washed of any petty feelings or emotions. Finally they followed him to the centre, there were things to discuss, important things which he had to tell them, and plans to be made.

*   *   *   *   *

So darkness falls and silence sweeps over all, but not quite. The fairground holds back the silence, its music and shrieking machinery a safe haven amidst the sea of silent black a place where people can find refuge among the machinery of death, away from the quiet uncertainty of the night sky. The darkness was beginning to fall now, and the fairground would be full by the time it had arrived in its completeness. The older Gypsies gathered together, whilst the younger ones kept the attention of visiting folk. They must keep their attention away from what was happening here. It was time to right a wrong, time to correct that curse with which they had been lumbered. The Elder stood

164

among them, his brow heavy with their worries. There was no sense in worrying about it, they would just have to do something that is all, this had gone on for long enough. He must be stopped. They all agreed, in a murmur of voices as one, although none could look. He could smell the fear in the air, coming from every one of them, and all of them as a whole, so surely It could smell that too. They must ask him to leave them alone, petition him to leave them be, and if he would not go? The Elder felt the crackle of nerves here, but told them that they must be strong. It was only one, despite all of Its disguises, whilst they were many, and as many they could unite and defeat It. If it would not go then they would find a way. They would find another wicked soul to willingly take on this curse, for that is the nature of a curse; it could be taken from them by another, but not given. They had paid enough for what they had done, and the punishment must fit the crime, not outweigh it. This sent a wave of restlessness among them. They did not like to be reminded of their wickedness, but he would remind them anyway, and he would continue to remind them of how wretched they had been and how this had come to pass. Then perhaps they would mend their ways and having mended them keep themselves from straying. No longer then would they stray from the path of their ancestors, no longer would they indulge in exogamy and cavort with the evils of other tribes. Perhaps they had learned their lesson. Then it was time for that lesson to end. He turned and looked towards the carousel. In there somewhere, deep in the heart of all that twisted metal and tainted wood sat the Angel of their deliverance and the Demon of their punishment. The creature waited for him, waited for this moment when they would come to him and ask to be freed and The Elder knew that both sides of it would weigh their promises and their penance against their crime. He hoped that they had paid enough.

*   *   *   *   *

This was not a joke. It was getting dark and his parents were due back soon. Gregory paced around his slowly shrinking bedroom. The walls seemed to grow in height and the floor space decrease as he lurched from one foot to the other, and that terrible heat was on him again. It was too unbearably hot for him to be wearing clothes, but he did not want to take them off, that would just be admitting something. Admitting what? He did not know, but it would definitely be admitting guilt of something. His shoes had come off though; it was comforting to feel the soft fibres of the carpet, gripped between his toes. He also felt tiredness and fatigue washing over him in waves. Something deep inside him was willing him to sleep. Even standing and pacing back and forth as he did he could feel himself drifting, as though floating in warm water, only his skin was hot. His cheeks burned and everything he touched felt so cold, so he paced in the middle of his room avoiding everything. Then it was true, he was going to change, like the American Werewolf in London. That was crazy, but he could feel the burning, and his skin was itching. It itched so terribly that he wanted to peel, no rip it off his body. He must keep the clothes on. Only that way would he know if he had changed in the night? His clothing would rip, or be torn off his body wouldn't it? He must think of a way of locking himself in now before it was too late. He could lock his bedroom door and windows, but that would not stop him unlocking them later, or breaking the door down, or smashing a window. What if his parents heard him thrashing about in the night and came to investigate? They would not be able to get in, but if they were alarmed enough his father might break the door down and who knows what would happen then. No, it had to be somewhere safer than that. He locked the bedroom door and windows anyway, while he thought of another way. Gregory dropped the keys into the bottom drawer of his wardrobe and sat on the bed.

This was ridiculous. He had a fever that is all, from the operation. What about all of those people and the blood and the mud on his skin and in his bed? All of this on the same nights as the people were killed. He had walked in his sleep that was all, there was no such thing as a werewolf, or beast man, or whatever. Things like that just did not exist, they did not happen. Then he had walked in his sleep and somehow killed those people anyway, with his bare hands. No that was not possible, surely the screams would have woken him. He would remember something. It could not have been him or he would have remembered something, anything. Then it had to be someone else, but what about the mud and the blood under his fingernails and in his bed? It was not someone else, it was him and he had changed into some kind of animal, like he had in his dreams. No he was not an animal. Then he was mad, which is it to be? He was so tired. He could not let this happen, not again. He could not let himself loose on this town. There must be an answer, a remedy, a magic medicine that would make it stop. His head ached and he was tired, and now his stomach was joining in, a gnawing pain where his appendix used to be. Hunger, extreme and painful hunger, gnawing at him from the inside. It was not hunger for popcorn or chips or pasta. This was a base hunger which he knew only deep within his heart. This was the hunger that all animals felt before the hunt, the same hunger that drove them to kill. No that was not him. It could not be him. Gregory had to lie down, only then did the aches and pains die away, reducing themselves to a gentle throb, reminding him that they were there. He was cooking slowly from the inside, or not so slowly. Gregory closed his eyes.

Please God don't let this happen.

He clenched his stomach to try and push away the pain, but this made the heat worse still. Why him? He would have cried, but his body was too hot now, his tear ducts dry and barren, tiny deserts.

Please God don't let this happen.

He repeated the litany over and over, begging the something, whatever it was to leave him be, but still the heat grew. He could not keep these clothes on much longer, he felt that they were in danger of burning, but refused to take them off, refused to admit guilt.

Pleasegodontlethisappenpleasegodontlethisappenpleasegodontlet
hisappen.

God was not listening.

*   *   *   *   *

Martin stood in a long narrow corridor, which stretched for mile
upon mile in both directions. Mile upon mile of bare walls,
however at each end he could see a door, miles in the distance,
and upon each door a plaque of silver and gold. He must choose
a direction quickly before The Librarian realised he was here. He
was not supposed to be here, this was a forbidden place. Martin
did not know how he had come to be here, or how he had found
the way, or even how he had got in as there was no door that he
could see; yet he was here and he was not supposed to be. The
Librarian would be displeased. He was here now though and he
had to find a way out, so he would have to choose a direction.
The lights dimmed around him, staying lit where he stood, but
now the two doors were obscured in shadow, then darkness.
Martin set off towards the left. As he walked the light followed
him, directly overhead, throwing the corridor behind him into
darkness and revealing a foot or so of the corridor in front at a
time. His footfalls fell flat on the tile, as though confined to the
space within the light. So no sound could escape, that was good.
The Librarian could not hear him. And since he could not see
past his own light he assumed that anyone else in this corridor
could not either. He was safe then. Martin had never seen the

librarian, or even heard it, however he knew that it existed. He just knew, and had always known, just as he knew that he should not be here. Martin picked up a pace now, and the light followed suit overhead, soundlessly. He stopped and the light stopped. Martin pondered a while, then stepped backwards. The light stayed still. He retreated further and the light refused to follow. Martin now stood on the edge of the light, he could feel darkness behind him. What would happen if he turned around and walked the other way? He did not know. Would the light disappear as he walked out of it? Martin turned around and tried to peer into the darkness, he could not see anything from in here. He leaned forward, pushing his face out of the sphere of decreasing light. Wind soared about him and screamed in his ears, blowing his hair about his face, threatening to pull him off balance and throw him into the gaping chasm below. Darkness pulled at him, dragging him forward, begging him to leave the sphere of light and fall forever downwards. Martin stepped backwards, once again into the light, staggering as he went. So he had chosen the direction and now had to stick with it then.

He pressed on, forward this time, and the light dutifully followed suit.

An hour or so passed and he had to sit down and rest his feet. By his reckoning he had been walking for about an hour, so must have covered at least three or four miles. The stone floor and walls were cold as he pressed against them. Dreams were not supposed to be so monotonous. He thought they were supposed to be entertaining, but then if they were too lively surely they

170

would wake the dreamers up. So they had to be boring or tiring to keep the dreamers asleep. He stood up. There was no sense in sitting around, he may as well press on.

Another hour passed. This was ridiculous. He was getting nowhere here. The whole point of walking was to get somewhere. One decided upon a destination and set off, with the aim of reaching that destination in as short a time as possible. Well, he could not turn back the other way so he was stuck really. Martin pressed on. A moth buzzed overhead, fluttering its dry wings franticly. There was no source to the light that Martin could see, so it looked like the poor creature would be searching forever too. But where had it come from all of a sudden? Martin stopped just short of walking into a large, oak door with a gold and silver plaque in its centre.

The plaque read:

Rules of the Library

1. Silence must be maintained at all times

2. Books must not be removed from the library

3. Note taking is not permitted.

4. No food or drink

5. Strictly no insects.

Martin looked above him at the frantic moth. Sorry pal, but you can't come in. He was about to look for a way of stopping the unfortunate moth from following him through the door when a spider leaped on it from above. Within seconds the poor creature was cocooned and paralysed, ready to be served up as the spider family dinner. Martin shrugged; spiders were not insects were they? No, so it was OK to go in then. He turned a large gold handle and pushed the door open.

Inside the room was well lit, with a warm orange-yellow glow, as from a fire. It was another long corridor, although not quite as long as the one he had just experienced, and wider. The walls were covered in shelves, and on each shelf books in every category he could think of and a few more besides. He could feel the warmth on his face. Martin stepped inside.

Among the shelves at each sides there were still more corridors, and Martin soon realised that the walls were in fact made of books. Books and files instead of bricks. No wonder they were not supposed to be removed. Books everywhere he turned, but no index system. What was the point in having an archive or library without an index with which things could be found? Martin shook his head; there was no point, that was the point. A sign hanging down in the centre of all this read:

Are you a member?

Of course he was a bloody member, it was his dream wasn't it? The sign retreated towards the ceiling sheepishly, until it had disappeared out of sight. The shelves did not seem to be set out in any particular order either. There was only one thing for it. He would have to try and find The Librarian.

"Can I help?"

Martin turned around to see where and who the voice had come from.

"Yes, I..." He stopped.

The figure smiled at him without smiling, his eyes laughed

172

without humour.

"Hello Martin, what are you looking for in here?"

Martin stood still. There was something wrong here. This man was not supposed to be in here, with Martin, in Martin's library, in Martin's dream. The air in here had gone stale, as though too old to breath, or breathed by too many. The man gestured towards a table and chairs, which had appeared to their left. "Why don't we sit down?"

There was something about the voice, it did not compel him, but he felt that it was the obvious thing to do, so reasonable, so he sat down.

The stranger sat opposite.

"Now, what is it that you could possibly want in here? The books are all so dull." The stranger looked around them at the books on the myriad of shelves. They did all look grey and colourless, but didn't everyone dream in shades of grey? Martin was not sure what he had come here for. He had just come here, it was not a choice, it was a dream that is all and that is how dreams work. "There was nowhere else to go." He replied.

The man smiled again, this time showing silver teeth. "Well there you are wrong. You could have gone to the other library down the hall. Now there is a place, full of colour and imagination, a real place of dreams."

Martin shook his head. "No, I couldn't turn back once I had set off, the light would not let me." He had also walked about eight miles so was sure as hell going to spend some time looking around this place now he had got here. "Anyway, who are you?"

The smile disappeared, just like that. It did not fade, or
metamorphose into something else. It just went, in an instant. "I
am The Librarian of course." Martin shook his head. "No you're
not." The man sat back in his chair, pausing for a moment,
thunderclouds gathered on his brow. "And how would you
know? Of course I am, and you are trespassing in my library.
Now get out." Martin stayed where he was. This was his dream,
no one else's. "No chance."

The man froze for an instant. There was a moment when, like a
child who is asked a question he does not know the answer to,
because he was not listening in the first place, he looked straight
at Martin with a glazed expression. Then he gathered wits about
him, "What did you say?" delaying tactics, so he could think of
the answer.

Martin smiled, "I think you heard me. For a start this is my
library, whether you are The Librarian or not you have no right
to throw me out. Secondly you are not The Librarian in here."
Martin was certain of this. He did not know how, but he was
certain that he would recognise The Librarian when he saw it.
Besides, this was his dream and he could say and do what he
wanted to in it. The man gave no reaction to this. Instead the air
in here was becoming thinner. Still the dark figure sat quietly,
waiting. Martin was finding it hard to breath.

"Hot in here?" The voice rasped in his ears, not so reasonable
now, more demanding. He felt that he would have heard this
voice at a whisper from the other side of the world. It buzzed
like an insect back and forth, fighting for a way out of his mind,

impossible to ignore as it flew and crawled into every corner until, finally the buzzing faded. The insect had died. Martin felt that he would pass out soon. The gulps of air he drew in were searing his lungs like steam from a freshly boiled kettle, and they were not enough.

"Who are you?" The words coughed themselves up from his throat, coarse and barbed, scratching him on their way out. The man leaned forward, so that once again Martin could see his teeth, silver in the artificial light, and the blood red tongue behind them. But didn't he dream in shades of grey? "I am the ancient, I am the land. Time is but my shadow and I am darker than the night. No amount of suffering can equal my own, no pain, no sorrow. I am legend eternal."

Martin wheezed what was surely to be his last breath and tasted the flavour of this man's words. They coated his tongue and throat as he breathed them in, bitter and caustic. He coughed and spluttered, but could not shake the poisonous coating. He could feel it trickling down his throat. It was so hot in here.

"Then perhaps I should open this door."

The heat ceased. Martin gasped the first pocket of fresh cool air, and then another, trying to ease the burning in his throat. He coughed vile phlegm up and out of his body, onto the table surface. There it sizzled, and finally evaporated, taking some of the table's varnish with it. Something had grasped the dark man's attention. Martin followed his gaze. There, at the end of the room, stood The Librarian, with it's hand upon the brass handle of a small wooden door. The door was closed, and he looked over at them both, poised to open it.

"I don't think that would be wise, do you?"

The dark man looked worried, if that was possible. Martin stood up and staggered backwards from the table. "You had better leave now, or he'll open it."

He looked in turn at them both, weighing them up. Would they dare? Martin nodded. The dark man stood and cast his night-drenched eyes over Martin. "I will catch up with you later charlatan." Then he was gone.

Martin's legs buckled underneath him and he collapsed, still gasping for air. The Librarian approached. Martin was right, he did recognise it, although could not remember what it looked like even now. It had fingers, a nose, eyes, a mouth and yet had no face. To look at it Martin could not even entertain the possibility of not knowing what it looked like, but even now as he looked to the floor whilst steadying himself to stand upright he could not recall even if the face was male or female. Finally they stood together, nose to nose but not face to face. The Librarian nodded.

Martin attempted to speak again, now that his breathing was beginning to subside. "What is behind that door?"

The Librarian shook its head. "Wake up."

Martin's eyes opened as he coughed himself awake. Tears streamed down his cheeks and his throat rasped, sore with the strain. He kicked his way out of bed and ran quietly downstairs to the kitchen. Once there he ran the cold tap for a few moments and drew himself a cool pint of water. That seemed to ease the rasping slightly. He must be coming down with a cold. He had that foul, bitter taste on his tongue, obviously the side effect of an oncoming chest infection. Nothing some toothpaste and mouthwash would not get rid of.

*   *   *   *   *

Deep in the centre of a web of twisted metal and tainted wood laid the heart of darkness. A man by form. The Midnight man, Mr. Midnight his name. Where night creeps into every corner and cast shadows over what is there he waited. Here in the void where no man can see and no man can escape his hands reach out, his fingers playing in the minds of the guilty. A touch here, a gentle push there, and the occasional removal of an obstacle. Here in the void he floats mindless and incorporeal, untouched and unreachable, for how can one reach that which does not exist? To reach him men must look only to their mercenary hearts and the dangers and guilt contained there. He exists in us all, as a fragment of shadow or darkness, a shard of doubt, a crumb of guilt. As such he hides away, undetected and unwanted. He lurks in that shadowy place where men and women dare not look, and so remains. Who wants to venture into that dark place? No, it is best to leave that place alone. It is best to keep that door shut, lock your windows and bolt your shutters against the night, for nothing can harm you then. In here Mr. midnight waits. He hides in every darkest corner and every shadowy place. He conceals himself in the deception and secrets of men and women, and when their darkness is dark enough he harvests. The Midnight man sews his seed and nourishes his produce, much like any other. Where there is weather to shield against he shields, and where there is a pest to exterminate he exterminates, for we all must eat and nourish ourselves, and so too must the Midnight Man. The more we nourish ourselves the more we are able to grow, and so too the Midnight Man. But here the similarity ends. There can be no similarity between that which creates and that which destroys. The Darkness feeds on the guilt of those it has infected and all the while grows stronger. It spreads its limbs and stretches its fingers, reaching out to those who pass within its reach. It touches their hearts and finds a way, because there is always a way. Everything has a price and everyone wants something. The young boy wants to be a man, to be free to do all of those things which he is not allowed, every girl wants to be a woman, to take life into her own hands. A writer wants to be read, an artist wishes to be loved, a scientist wants to be recognised. A priest wishes to be heard and begs for a sign, whilst his congregation begs for a million different deliverances. All of these the Midnight Man can provide, and the cost? You will not even miss it. A small part of you which you do not even use, and which many do not even know exists. This then the basis of nourishment and guilt the seasoning, for what is a good meal without the salt and pepper, or the basil and fennel?

*   *   *   *   *

Sylvia tried again to start the engine, but it was no use. Hannah's car was the same. They were not going to get out of here any way except on foot. She looked around at Hannah, who was presently sat on their suitcases on the back door steps. She had taken them out already, when they had tried to start the cars the first few times. Hannah had wanted to call out a garage, but Sylvia had insisted that no one must know they were leaving.

"We need to call a taxi then."

Sylvia shook her head,

"No, we can't risk that, anyone could be driving and they could tell anyone where we are headed."

Hannah shrugged, "Then why don't we get a taxi to Portend and hire a car there, or get another taxi from there, or even try to buy a car?"

"Buy a car with what?"

"I don't know. You are the magic lady, can't you conjure up some money from somewhere?" Sylvia rolled her eyes heavenward, making sure though that Hannah did not see. "It doesn't quite work like that Hannah, unless you want me to look like an eighty five year old by the time you hit thirty." Hannah nodded. "Well how did you get here? You didn't have a car then did you?" this had been puzzling her for a while. She did not think that witches needed cars in order to get around.

"They do if they have luggage, and besides, I got a plane, a train and a taxi, like everyone else." She looked again at the two heavy suitcases. "Do we need all of that?"

Hannah supposed not, not in an emergency anyway. Sylvia looked up the coast road, away from Seahaven. They just had to get as far away from here as they could and as soon as possible. She did not wish to be within earshot of Him when she used the Art again. Something like that would alert him as to what they were doing and he would try to stop them, as he had done here. She wished that she had not started her change, then perhaps she would have been better equipped. Hannah's face beamed up at her, life in her eyes and a girlish smile on her lips. Perhaps though she would not have been as happy.

"OK then, can we leave as much of it as we can behind and make our way on foot, at least to outside the town limits?" Hannah nodded, slowly. "OK, but once we are out of town can you do something?" Sylvia smiled and held out a hand to her, "Maybe."

10. Gregory and the Midnight Wolf

So here we are again, thought Gregory, only this time things
would be different. This time he would not change. He ran, this
time away from the wolves that were calling to him from the
woods. He ran along a tarmac road in his bare feet towards a
crossroads ahead. He would not go to the woods and join the
wolves as he had done before, he would stay away from them.
Behind he could hear them howling and pleading for him to stay,
a thousand cries across a thousand nights, of people locked in
the dark. The woe of strangers alone in their rooms at night, with
only the passing of people in the street below to keep them
company, of despair and longing and the dreadful fear of being
alone with himself. Gregory wept as he ran, salted water filling
his eyes and screwing up his face, but run he did. He would face
the loneliness and despair rather than be with them again. So he
ran and he ran until his feet bled with the thunder of his heart
and like a kite with it's strings cut, which lands where it will, he
landed at the crossroad's. There at the centre sat a man. Cross-
legged on the tarmac, His two legs crossed as did the two roads.
It could not be the same man that he had met before. It could not

be the same moon drenched hair and eyes aflame with dreams. Not here in his dream.

Victor Midnight stood upright, moving in one fluid motion surrounded by the flutter of darkness and gazed fondly at him. He smiled his starry smile and held his arms out open, as wide as oceans.

"Hello Gregory, it was nice of you to come."

Gregory shifted from one foot to the other. It would be just as strange to be welcomed to your own house as to your own dream. He said nothing, instead Mr. Midnight continued; "Now I said you could come and see me here whenever you wanted to talk, so what's troubling you?" The tarmac felt sticky with blood under Gregory's feet. He tried to shake his head, to say that nothing was wrong, but the tear tracks on his cheeks betrayed this as a lie. Mr. midnight reached out a hand across an impossible distance and brushed a stray droplet away. His touch was gentle, like silk billowing in a soft breeze, and suddenly he was face to face with Gregory. Eye to eye.

"I don't want to change into that monster again."

Mr. Midnight shook his head, "No, of course you don't." A pause, then "What monster is this Gregory?" Gregory shook his head.

"I don't know. All I know is that there is a monster in me somewhere and it comes out at night." he felt small and young. Mr. Midnight towered above him. Mr. Midnight nodded, his smile as warm as the noonday sun, but all around him black feathers scratched the air. Gregory continued.

182

"Ever since I had my operation, you know, to have my appendix taken out, I have been having these strange dreams", he looked around him at the road and the forest, the meadow. All were fading now like an old painting, only the crossroads and the dark man in front of him remained clear. "Like this one and lately they've been getting worse." This had to be a dream didn't it? He looked at Victor Midnight for some guidance, but the man, or creature he was remained silent.

"Much worse."

Gregory waited for some answer, some sign that the dark man understood. The road waited too. Not a bird in the sky, nor a creature on the ground. Silence threatened to crush his sanity, only his own breathing and the sound of blood in his ears held back the pressure. Then Mr. Midnight Spoke.

"What has been happening in them Gregory?" His voice a whisper, almost like a child. Gregory felt the words tug at him and was compelled to speak.

"I've been dreaming about being a wolf and running along with a pack of wolves in the wild."

Mr. Midnight smiled. When he smiled he seemed to do it with his whole body and soul, the crossroads joined in and the sky lit up with a golden hue. "And what could possibly be wrong with that?"

This made Gregory pause for a moment. He was not sure. No, he was certain that this was a bad thing, the dreams were not normal.

"There is nothing normal about dreams Gregory, they are the

means by which we express our feelings are they not?"

Gregory nodded, "Yes, but these aren't healthy, in them I...." He could not say it. Mr. Midnight raised one eyebrow, which in turn made the corner of his mouth twitch upwards, a half smile. "You enjoy yourself?"

"Yes, but there's more to it than that. I have sex with other wolves, and I kill and eat wild animals." He could feel heat rising in his cheeks. Surely it was not possible to blush in a dream. Mr. Midnight smiled, "But it is only a dream Gregory, we are all permitted a little secret fantasy in our dreams, and as you are a wolf then there is no harm in you enjoying the company of other wolves, is there?" His voice took on a soft growl, which reached outwards and into Gregory, fluttering in his stomach. He felt hunger. Gregory sighed, "I'm not a wolf, I told you before, I merely keep having dreams where I'm a Wolf."

"Then why are you not a wolf now? Or are you not dreaming?"

"Because I didn't go to join them this time, I'm trying to keep away, if you hadn't noticed."

The dark man withdrew from him a pace, without pacing. The tarmac moved him. He stood a while watching the sun rise overhead and set in the distance, a speeded up film but without the artificial haste. It seemed so leisurely.

"So you have a choice then, over whether you are a wolf or not?" The moon had now risen in place of the sun, and it's light seemed twice as brilliant. It was more pure that the orange of the sun. White iridescence.

Gregory pondered this for a while. Then, "That's what I'm trying to find out, I think." He continued. "Since I have been having these dreams I have started walking in my sleep and waking up in strange place. Like the other night when I woke up in my father's garage, and the night before when I woke up in bed, but covered in mud." He looked for a reaction from Mr. Midnight, but did not appear to be getting one. He was too busy watching the moon. "And on each of the nights when I have walked in my sleep people have been murdered." A star fell from the sky, leaving a trail of pale fire behind it and Mr. Midnight sighed and bowed his head. "And you think that it's you who have committed these terrible crimes."

"Yes."

"Why?"

What a question. Did he believe because he thought himself capable? Or because he wanted to do these things? "Because I was covered in mud, and I'd been sleepwalking, and what else am I to think has happened?"

What else could it be?

"Could someone else not have done these things?"

That was the answer. That was the redemption he was searching for, yes they could have and he would be innocent. If that were so then why did he feel this guilt?

"Yes I suppose so, but I think it's a bit too much of a coincidence, and I don't wish to take that risk. It all adds up and points to me, no questions about it. I'm changing into a werewolf or some killer monster every night and I'm killing people in my sleep, and it has to stop." Now he was breathless. He felt the same inward crush he got when he had run a great distance the same exhaustion, the same breathlessness, but from within, like part of him was running.

Mr. Midnight held his arms open again, like harbour gates and Gregory felt himself pulled by the tide towards him "So why have you come to see me?" Gregory shook his head and gasped for the words to say. "I haven't. I was running away from the wolves, that's all. It's as simple as that."

"It sounds to me as though you are just a little confused about all of this, that's all." Midnight's voice, a whisper in the grass again. Gregory caught the aroma of dewy grass in his nostrils. The hour before dawn, when all is quiet, waiting for the first of the day's creatures to stir. No one makes a sound not wanting to be the fist to wake in case... In case the sun did not rise. Gregory shook his head, he was not confused, he knew exactly what was happening.

"In that case where are we standing right now?"

Gregory looked around. They were standing at a crossroad's. There were trees behind him, starting at the sides of the road a bit further down and gradually taking over the road itself, as though it disappeared into the woods. Ahead of them he could not see properly, but it looked like the road wound it's way up to a town of some sort, although he could not tell how large this town was. It had a church, the spire of which could be seen from here, and he guessed that this was at the centre of the town, so it was probably quite small. To their left and right the road

186

stretched on, in a straight line as far as the eye could see. At either side of these roads fields of tall grass and cereal crops swayed in the gentle breeze.

"We're at a cross roads, with four different directions to go in."

"Is that all?"

Could that be all? Was a road ever just a road? Or was it always the beginning of a journey? Sometimes mud was mud and rock was just rock.

Gregory shrugged, "Yes."

"And where are you now."

The trees had not disappeared. The road was still under his feet. Gregory wrinkled his brow against the sunlight peeping over the horizon. It was uncanny but the Dark man always seemed to position himself with the light at his back, whether night or Day, morning or afternoon. How long had they been standing here anyway? "What do you mean?"

Midnight drew closer. "I mean, if this is a dream where is the real Gregory?"

The tarmac felt real enough, the grass smelled real, the sigh of leaves in the trees above sounded real.

"In bed, probably, or sleep walking somewhere."

Mr. Midnight's chuckle also sounded real.

"Then let me explain." Mr. Midnight sat down on the tarmac, so Gregory followed suit.

"You are dreaming. So it doesn't really matter what you do, you can't hurt anyone else in a dream can you?" Gregory shook his head, he supposed not. The problem was though all of this felt so real. What if his dream could actually cause harm? Those people had all been murdered hadn't they?

"If you have never suffered any harm at the hands of someone else's dream I think we can assume that the same goes for you here, that your dreaming will not actually harm anyone." Mr. Midnight sat down again, cross-legged on the tarmac. He did not so much sit down as float down, and bid Gregory to do the same. Gregory did not feel so sure about this. The ground was cold, and it would look odd to any passers by, but this was his dream right? He followed suit and sat down. Midnight continued, "I think your confusion lies in whether you think you are asleep or awake and whether the things you do in your dream can affect real people in the real world." He paused waiting for a reaction. Gregory could feel those silver eyes scanning him for any sign of recognition, a twitch of the nostril, a flicker of an eyelid. Suddenly Midnight spoke again as though he had received the sign he waited for.

"I think that you are also worried about whether what you do in your dreams is right or wrong, good or bad." He shook his silver mane slowly as though in sadness or disappointment. "This is irrelevant here, because it's a dream. It doesn't matter what you do because no one will ever know."

Did that matter?

"There are no consequences nor moral ramifications nor obligations here, this is your world Gregory, so use it as you will."

Gregory nodded, to hell with what anyone else thought. They

188

could not get to him here; they could not judge him or make snide remarks about what he did or how he looked. Here there was no college teacher, no job foreman to tell him what to do and how to do it, only himself. The wolves did not judge him, they accepted him for what he was.

"Instead of making yourself miserable and tearing your hair out over this I think that you should just turn around and go back into the woods to enjoy yourself."

Gregory looked around him and sighed. It was true, he was slightly confused, but he was sure that it was not as simple as that. There could not be any doubt. Confusion or uncertainty was not enough here. If there was any doubt that it was not him who was killing all of these people then he should stop himself from changing, even in his dreams. Mr. Midnight shook his head.

"No, if we went around in our daily lives wanting every thing we did to be done without any doubt or uncertainty we would be so afraid of living that we wouldn't live."

"What do you mean?"

Mr. Midnight smiled, and let out a small chuckle,

"Well, it is like this."

Gregory sat and Mr. Midnight stood, pacing slowly too and fro. Gregory listened and Mr. Midnight spoke, his voice like leaves in autumn wind.

"We represent to ourselves in dreams bizarre and unusual behaviour," He began, "Which would seem extraordinary, or even insane if we were awake." Gregory nodded.

Mr. Midnight looked directly at him, gesturing to his own

clothing, black and ragged, the tattered feathers of an old crow. "How many times have you dreamed that you are dressed in the finest of robes at a ball, or at dinner, when in fact you are naked in bed?" Gregory shrugged. Probably every night. A smirk spread across his face at the sight of the dark man flapping theatrically in front of him, black coat tails fluttering in the wind.

"Now when you say you are dreaming that you're here, in fact, by virtue of the fact that you are dreaming you must be asleep and therefore probably in bed."

Gregory thought about this, and Mr. Midnight seemed to pause in order to let him do so.

"Now this dream, as you say, seems as real as the times when you are awake, so either one is false and the other true, or they are both false, or they are both true representations of what is happening." He stopped and nodded at Gregory, who nodded, even though he was not entirely sure of what Mr. Midnight was getting at.

"Lets assume for the moment that one is a dream and the other is not, because if one causes the other, or dreams the other then it would be reasonable to assume that one is real and the other isn't. The one that is the dream is a thinking thing, a thing created by thought. It can't be measured and does not physically exist."

Gregory interrupted. "What about sleep walking, that is dreams having an effect on the body isn't it?" Triumph, but for a moment. Mr. Midnight smiled and lowered his face to be closer

190

to Gregory, his voice softening.

"You may be sleep walking now, but I don't see two of you here. You physical body can't travel over into your dream world. That would be impossible, wouldn't it?"

Gregory looked up at The Dark Man and every muscle in his body conspired to make him nod his head. He could do nothing but agree.

"So because my dreams aren't real they can't affect the real world?"

Mr. Midnight jumped in the air, his shout startling Gregory. Lightning flashed silently across the sky and then burst into a thousand starlings, which scattered in all directions. "Yes! That is it. Likewise the real world can't have any effect on the dream world. The two are separate and individual. So what you do in your dream world is irrelevant to what happens in the real world and visa versa." Midnight's smile was contagious and Gregory could feel it spreading over his own face, infecting him. So his dream of being a wolf couldn't affect anything in real life. It didn't matter what he did in his dreams. Gregory could understand this part, but what if this wasn't a dream? "What if this is real and the other is a dream? Or if neither is a dream and both are real?"

Mr. Midnight placed a long fingered hand over his own chin. His eyes dimmed a while, the celestial fire retreating whilst he thought and then they burst forth into splendid light again. Gregory could not look directly at them.

"In either case it doesn't really matter what happens here, as it won't affect the other world. There is no physical connection or communication between the two, so one can't affect the other. As long as you are happy doing what you do here then there is no reason for you to stop doing it."

The moon had set now and they sat in pitch darkness. Midnight's hair had lost its glow, only the fire of his eyes fed Gregory's sense of sight. The sum would be moving up soon. How long had they been here?

There was one more thing though.

"But what if that's not the case? What if I'm hurting another dreamer, or another real person here in this world?" Midnight circled around him and the sun rose in the sky again, peering over the horizon and stretching the rays of its arms out with a gigantic celestial yawn.

"How can you be sure that what you see and experience is actually happening and know for certain the effects of what you do?"

This threw Gregory completely. It seemed such an absurd question to ask. Of course he could see and feel what was happening, he was not blind or deaf. Around him the sun was climbing in the sky, clouds dispersing as though blown by a powerful wind. The tarmac was cold against his legs where he sat, but he did not mind the cold, it reminded him that he was still here, and still human.

"Of course I know what I see and hear and feel, that's ridiculous."

Mr. Midnight opened his mouth wide, threatening to swallow

the world and everyone in it, and laughed. The sound of breaking glass scattered on the four winds.

"Can you be sure that I am how you see me? That black and white are to me as black and white are to you?"

Gregory nodded, "Yes, I think so." This conversation was going nowhere. He tried to stand so he could walk away, but found that his legs could not move. The Dark Man had not finished.

"Then describe how I see the world right now. Describe Black to me."

He couldn't. A thousand and one images came to mind. Ink spilling on a white table cloth, the paint in a childhood picture, the shoe polish he used everyday and the stains it left on the kitchen floor, a crow sat on the gates of the common. No matter how he tried though Gregory could not think of words enough to describe the shade of black, without resorting to calling is simply black.

Mr. Midnight nodded, "No, you can't. It isn't possible to look through the eyes of another to check our certainty, so we can never be certain. Try and see the world as it really is and you will find that you can't. So how can you be sure that anything is true?"

Gregory did not have a clear answer to this. "If I went around thinking in that way I would go mad. I have to have something that I can believe exists or there is no point in getting out of bed in the morning." The sun was high overhead now and their shadows had disappeared. Gregory had been watching them move around him in a decreasing circle. It seemed as though there were more than two people casting those shadows. There were too many and now they were hidden out of sight.

Mr. Midnight nodded,

"Yes, you are right, but you still must have a method of checking what is real and what isn't. Even the fact that I am talking to you right now may, or may not be a dream, and it may even be a figment of your or my imagination."

Gregory grinned, here was something the crow man had not thought of,

"So how do I know that what you are telling me is true then, if you don't necessarily exist?"

Mr. Midnight did not even flinch. Instead he twirled around on the spot triumphantly, sending a flurry of tattered black feathers skyward.

"Even if I am a figment of your imagination you are free to discard me as you wish. But if I'm a figment of your imagination telling you all this then I'm part of your thought process and therefore part of your knowledge, the only knowledge of which you can be certain. You thought me up so these thoughts which you are having, unconnected to anything outside must be true."

This was probably true. And the Midnight Man was probably right here, but there was still no sense in taking the risk. Even if it was a far fetched risk that him turning into a wolf in his dream could possibly affect him in the real world then he could not and should not do it. He could not be responsible for any more deaths, no matter how small the risk. And there was no harm in him doing nothing in his dream either, just in case.

Mr. Midnight sat down in front of him again, this time sadness in his eyes. They overflowed with the sadness of a thousand or more lost childhoods.

"Whatever you decide to do Gregory you must follow your heart and take life by the lapels whilst you still can and force it to give you what you want. You are the centre of all of this, no one else, there is nothing else. Don't waste it. Who is the Beast? Is it Gregory or some other who shares Gregory's body? Who has the right to that body?" Mr. Midnight shrugged a huge Gallic shrug, "Perhaps they both do. Do you need it all of the time?"

Gregory shook his head; no he did not need it when he was sleeping.

"If both beings then are figments of the other's imagination then it doesn't matter what they do. Likewise if they both perceive their own world the events don't affect the other, or anyone else. You cannot be sure that everyone else even exists let alone perceives the same as you. We are only players in a cosmic arcade game Gregory, so play how you will, but games are there to be enjoyed not to be suffered."

He reached out and touched Gregory's face again, his hand warm with all the lives he had seen and soft as stars.

"Where you belong is where you are happy Gregory. Are you happy in that other world where people pass you in the street without seeing you and listen without hearing? Does anyone in that other world care what you do or where you're going, or even know you exist at all?"

Gregory could feel himself beginning to cry again. He had done a lot of crying lately, more than he had ever done in his life up to now. He was eighteen years old and he was sat in the dark on a lonely road, crying, with only an imaginary person for company. The wolves howled softly behind him in the distance, begging for him to join them again.

"Here you can be happy and free Gregory. Go and join your friends and run with them for ever."

He nodded. It was time to go.

The road felt cold against his feet now as rain started to slap against the tarmac. Gregory walked towards the trees, the Midnight man standing at the crossroads behind him and the wolves waiting ahead. Mr. Midnight stood and waved his long fingered hand in a farewell, his tattered coat of feathers flapping in the breeze, threatening to take him up into the air, soaring high above. Gregory looked the once, and did not look back again. He did not want to see him disappear, did not want to see where or how he would go. Perhaps he would fly with the wind, transformed into a giant crow, or perhaps he would be blown apart like so many fragile black feathers scattered on the winds. Gregory did not know, he could not be certain. All that was certain was that he was here and he was tired. He was terribly alone and he did not want to be alone, nothing else mattered any more, nothing else existed. Even the road he walked and the wind he felt lashing now at his face were all but an imaginary backdrop on the world he had embraced as his own. The wolves up ahead leaped over each other and laughed their fearsome laugh to see him coming. They at least would be happy to see him and he would run with them tonight, and any other night he chose, or perhaps he would stay here forever. The trees were just ahead now, a stone's throw away, if he could find one. There at the side of the road was one ripe for the throwing. Gregory liked this place. He stooped to pick up the stone, only to find himself on all fours anyway. He grinned and growled to himself, it felt good to be the wolf again, and that is all that mattered. By the time he reached the trees he was running at full pelt

11. Sylvia

They were not going to make it out of here before dark. The moon was already out and the first few stars winking open as though waking from a day long slumber. The suitcases had become heavier and heavier the longer they had dragged them, even though they had decided to leave behind most of their belongings on the pretext that they could always come back for them later, once things had died down a little. Hannah stopped in the middle of the road. Darkness both ways, not a car in sight. She could not tell how far they had come from the house since they had switched off all the lights, and could not tell how far they had to go, since they were not actually headed anywhere in particular.

"This is ridiculous." She gasped, "We need a plan."

Sylvia stopped just ahead of her and dropped her suitcase on the tarmac. It landed with a brittle crunch. Hannah was right. They were not going to get anywhere like this.

"Perhaps we should rest for five minutes, but then we have to get moving."

Hannah snorted and shook her head. "We don't have to do anything. We can stay here, or go home and get a taxi or something." She looked at Sylvia, trying to guess her thoughts, trying to gage exactly what she was so afraid of. "Surely whatever or whoever it is can't be as bad as all of this."

Sylvia nodded, "Yes it can." She could still see his twisted and distorted face, inhuman in its sheer hatred and anger. She could still taste his breath on her, all over her, crawling like insects over her skin. "We have to get as far away from here as possible without drawing attention to ourselves otherwise he'll kill us."

And being killed by Him would not be like dying in a car crash or falling from a high window. It would be infinitely more painful and unpleasant, and far more long lasting.

Hannah nodded, she could see that Sylvia was serious about this and at once believed her. She did not believe her because of what she was saying she believed her because she was scared, like she had never seen her before. "OK, then we should just move on as quickly as we can then. And when we get to Portend we'll have to buy a car, or steal one or something." She stood up and stretched her arms. "So let's go."

Sylvia gave her a big smile and wrapped her arms around her neck. She squeezed her so tight that Hannah feared she would never walk again.

"Hey Sylvia it's OK, we will be OK" She could feel Sylvia's tears trickling down onto the side of her face, but Sylvia gave no answer. Eventually, with the moon at it's brightest and the eyes of stars wide open and attentive they started on their way again.

A little further up the road and another obstacle became apparent. It was difficult to see at first, with the distance, but as they drew closer Sylvia spotted them first. Two police cars blocking the road. Stood around the cars, with torches sweeping the road ahead of them stood four police officers, possibly more. Sylvia stopped Hannah in her tracks and signaled for her to be quiet. The faint crackling of a police radio made itself heard over the still air, but she could not hear what the voices were saying. Sylvia wished she had brought a bag of ingredients with her, but had not been thinking straight. She had just wanted to get out of the house as soon as possible. Hannah could now see them as well.

"Can they see us yet?"

Sylvia shook her head "I doubt it, not yet anyway." She looked into the trees at either side of the road. "Perhaps we can get past them that way."

Hannah did not like the sound or the look of this.

It was now dark, however they were used to the dim light, and the moon, being full did cast sufficient light for them to see. Sylvia, of course, had no problem anyway, but the moonlight did help Hannah. The trees formed a barrier at each side of the road now, beginning as a thin covering and gradually growing denser

200

and denser the further away from the road she looked, until eventually, about twenty yards or so back from the road they threw shadows upon shadows so nothing could be seen in there. Gnarled and twisted wooden arms obscured any pathway and it was so dark in there. It was so dark. Hannah peered into the trees, to try and make out a shape or a line, but there was none. Any shadows cast by the moon's light failed to register in that dark place. The air was not black; it was stronger than that, as though it just absorbed all of the light. Hannah feared that the light was not the only thing it absorbed, perhaps it absorbed life. Perhaps if they ventured in there it would absorb them too. "That's a childish thought Hannah, stop frightening yourself." Sylvia replied in response to Hannah's thoughts, but Hannah could tell she had been thinking something similar, by the emotion betrayed on her face.

They were not going to get past a roadblock. Sylvia thought that she could possibly slip past herself, but she was not going to leave Hannah alone in this place, alone and vulnerable to Him. The trees stood still, waiting. They were the only hope of getting past the police. There was no doubt as to why the police were here. With all the murders going on they were probably sealing off the immediate area in an attempt to apprehend the killer or killers. Sylvia knew that they would not catch the real killer; they could never catch him, as he would not allow it. So the trees beckoned them forward. Branches bowed to let them past and leaves, tickled by a soft breeze brushed against their faces, as before they knew it Sylvia and Hannah were in the woods and the road was out of sight. Hannah looked back only to find warped wood in the way. Branches had closed in and it was as though the road had never existed. There was more light in her than she had expected, however she still had to keep hold of Sylvia's hand, or keep in touch by whispering into the darkness to stop herself from losing her way. Their suitcases were a problem. Sylvia sighed. She should have shrunk them before they left, but again she had not been thinking straight. A branch whipped out at her and slapped her hand. She nearly dropped the suitcase. "Dam!"

Hannah looked up from the forest floor, where she had been paying attention to what she had been stepping on. She tripped, lost her balance and fell forwards, into Sylvia, sending them both crashing to the ground, wood snapping and leaves falling around them. Sylvia giggled softly, trying to get her breathing under control again, "You oaf."

Hannah slapped her on the arm, "Just get up."

"Shhhh" There was something out there. Hannah obeyed and instantly closed her mouth. She tried to hold her breath to listen, but all she could hear was the rush of blood in her ears.

Sylvia crouched, turning her head this way and that. "I thought I heard something."

Hannah stood up, and brushed leaves off her jeans. "It's just the police on the road, we are probably closer to them than we think. Perhaps we should move deeper into the wood. "

"No, it was not that." Sylvia looked behind them, in the direction they had come, "It sounded like someone was following us, not ahead of us. They carried on moving when we had stopped, but stood still once they realised that I heard them."

Hannah peered into the woods, the way they had come but could see nothing. Branches and darkness, that is all that was there. Sometimes that was enough. "Stop it Sylvia, let's just get going again." Sylvia did not like this. She did not like this one bit, not even a fragment of it was what she would have called pleasant. There was someone or something watching them and following them. The something was at home in the woods. It had no difficulty moving around and seeing in here, not like them. She tried to find it, but could only feel it all around them, as though it was circling them at a distance. Only the circling motions were getting smaller. It was closing in.

"No Hannah, stop. There is something following us. It's moving very fast and it's closing on us right now."

Hannah could feel the fear very strongly now. Not from herself but from Sylvia. Fear mixed with excitement or curiosity. Whatever this thing was Sylvia wanted to meet it. Hannah did not.

"Which direction is it coming from?"

Sylvia could not be certain, whatever it was it was fast. It was circling around them at great pace, closing in with each circle. It was some kind of predator, she could feel that by it's own excitement, and the way in which it circled so that they didn't know which direction to run in. It was trying to confuse them, which was working.

"Which direction?" Hannah was panicking now because she

could feel something else as well, this was so strong. Hunger and hatred, that is all this creature felt, and it was coming their way.

Sylvia turned and grabbed her by the arms.

"I don't know, I can't tell, but I want you to lie down." Hannah did not want to but had no choice. Sylvia threw her to the ground and crouched, waiting. "Close your eyes Hannah, you may not wish to see this."

Hannah did as she was told, but not for long. She could feel the creature pressing closer now and the curiosity was too much. She opened her eyes again. Where Sylvia had crouched there now crouched another creature. It was still Sylvia, that is, it was still female, but there the similarity ended. Her fingers had grown in length, it seemed at first, but on inspection Hannah realised that they were no longer fingers. Sylvia's hands had been replaced by talons of a sort, and her feet the same. She had her back to Hannah now, so her face could not be seen, although she could just make out the line of her jaw, with fangs protruding like sharpened tomb stones from either side. Her hair and body were largely the same, although now the back of her dress was tearing as two protrusions forced their way out, one from each shoulder blade. What the fuck was going on here?

"Hannah," The voice lisped and rasped slightly, although retained much of it's softness, "I asked you not to look."

Hannah closed her eyes again, although not before noticing that the protrusions from Sylvia's shoulder blades were unfolding into wings of some sort. What were those bird women from

Greek mythology called now? Was it Harpies?

"Yes, now shut up and keep your eyes closed, I didn't want you to see me like this."

The other creature was getting closer now, Hannah could feel it. She could feel the anger and hatred; she could feel the hunger and something else.

"Wait!"

Too late.

The trees seemed to leap out at Sylvia. They came alive and leaped out, bowling her to the floor. Only when the rush of leaves was over could Hannah see that it was not the trees. Whatever it was it was covered in fur, and it was huge. Sylvia, in a flurry of feathers and shrieks had been thrown against a tree behind her and the creature was advancing with hatred and loathing in its eyes. It paced towards her, not slowly as one would have expected in a horror movie. It didn't growl and taunt her, as she lay helpless, one wing flapping uselessly by her side. Instead it moved with speed which Hannah had seldom seen, except on television wildlife documentaries. It moved with the swiftness and efficiency of a wild animal. There was no wasted energy here, no waiting or pausing, giving it's prey time to escape, it leaped once throwing Sylvia against a tree and tearing great gashes in her abdomen and shoulder, then pounced towards her winded and stunned body with teeth bared.

No this could not happen, not to Sylvia. Hannah threw herself in the way. "STOP!"

*   *   *   *   *

Martin could not figure the exact meaning of his dream, but that was nothing new. He always could eventually, but never straight away. There was something different about this one though. This time it had been about him and not about anyone else. He very rarely dreamed about himself. What kind of library was that anyway? He had never seen one like it. The strangest feeling was that it was almost as though the dream had actually happened. As though he had really gone to a library, inside his own head, and someone had been there waiting for him. Weird. He also could not for the life of him remember what the Librarian character looked like, and the image of the other was fading quickly, which was unusual because he could always remember his dreams in detail, usually. The other character, what did he look like? All that Martin could now remember was that he had been dark, like a crow. That was all. The darkness of this man had stood out like a beacon, absorbing everything around him, trying to suck in all of the light and anything else that was in the immediate area. Whoever he was he had not wanted Martin to be in that library reading those books. Someone or something was trying to stop him from finding the truth. Martin looked over at the closed book on his bedside table. A thin leather strip marked the page where he had left, the page that contained the web. Martin reached over and picked the book up again. It fell open at the correct page and he resumed his reading. There he was, near the centre, just an inch or so to go

206

before he had deciphered the lot. The meaning was not entirely clear yet, but he was sure that he could do this.

*   *   *   *   *

The creature landed directly in front of her. Hannah held out her arms to ward it off, she could hear Sylvia gasping for breath behind her. The creature snarled but slowed.

There was something more to this, what was it?

Sylvia's breathing was slowing as life's rich blood flowed freely from the gaping wounds in her shoulder and abdomen. She could no longer feel her left arm, nor move the left wing behind it. She could not find the words to call out to Hannah. She could not find the strength to tell her to run, and get away. Instead all she could feel was a burning inside as the wounds slowly became infected. Infected with what she did not know, but they were becoming infected nevertheless.

Hannah did not look behind her to see how Sylvia was doing; she kept her eyes on the creature. There was definitely something wrong here. Apart from the creatures obvious abnormality in that it was some sort of hybrid between a bear and a wolf, there was something hidden deep inside. She could feel not only the anger and the hunger that she had felt from it before, but there was pain there as well, and was that fear? Despair? Loneliness? The creature grunted, as though answering, and slavered, sending droplets of stinking saliva to the forest floor. She tried not to look at its paws, with those claws on the end, one of which could rip her into two very separate pieces. Instead she looked into its eyes.

It advanced, making her cower away, then backed off slightly, hopping from leg to leg, unsure of what to do. There was such pain there, such that she had never felt before. Hannah could feel herself beginning to cry. Her eyes filled up with the creature's pain and despair. It was so lonely, so alone in this place. She felt confused. What did all of these people want, why could they not leave it alone? It was hungry, so hungry and yet that hunger never went away. No matter how much it ate the hunger would never leave, there was never enough. Hannah nodded and knelt down, between Sylvia and the creature, still painfully aware that Sylvia's breathing had now slowed dramatically. The creature sat on all fours now, watching her. It let out a low, rumbling whine. Hannah reached out a hand, but it growled menacingly, so she withdrew it. What was wrong with it? The creature looked her up and down, then back over it's own shoulder into the dark woods. When it looked back Hannah saw something that made her peer closer. In it's eyes, there was something, she did not know. Its eyes were no longer wild, they were almost human or ape like in their calmness. They did not match the creature's claws. She could feel Sylvia ebbing away behind her. She could feel sticky moisture against her back where she leaned against her, protecting her. Was that blood? She dared not look. The creature grunted again, and advanced on all fours, now more like a wolf than a bear, but still huge. On all fours it must have stood as high as Hannah's chest. She reached out to try and stop it but

208

it gently nudged her out of the way, toppling her over to Sylvia's side. Hannah watched as the creature approached gingerly. It sniffed and looked Sylvia up and down as though trying to measure her, stopping at each of the wounds it had made in turn, inspecting them. Then it did something extraordinary. Hannah could do nothing. She sat and watched as it licked at the gaping wounds it had made, and with each lick they seemed to close a little more, until the blood had stopped flowing and only open scars remained. Four close together across her left shoulder, and four of the same down the centre of her abdomen from midway between her breasts down to her stomach. Her dress hung in tatters around the two wounds, dark with blood, but the blood had now stopped flowing. The creature looked her up and down once more and tilted its head slightly to one side, confused over her appearance. Perhaps it was curious to see another hybrid like itself, Hannah was not certain, however this was a mixture of two or more creatures that was for sure. She reached out again, and this time it allowed her to touch it's coarse fur, which tickled the palms of her hands. She drew closer and placed her arms around its neck. The creature grunted and stirred, although allowed her to continue. Hannah bent forward and whispered in its ear, making the creatures ear twitch against her breath.
"Thank you."
The creature growled, this time not as throaty or as threatening as before, but she released her arms anyway. The pain had receded to a dull throb, the hunger to a distant memory. As she withdrew her hand it caught on something, pulling it up and

away from the creature's fur where it had been hidden. A gold chain, absurdly thin against the creature's neck glinted in the moonlight, and below, underneath tight against its throat hung a crucifix of all things. Hannah reached out to take hold of this, but the creature growled and batted her away with the back of a huge paw. The weight almost crushed her chest and sent her flying into the undergrowth yet again.

When she opened her eyes and looked up the creature was gone. She rubbed her now bruised chest with one hand and thanked the Lord, or whoever was listening that it had not used its claws.

*   *   *   *   *

Whilst Martin slept with an open book on his lap, the pages folded and ruffled where it had come to rest the Librarian within him worked. It had been necessary to send him to sleep again so that it could file all of the information and, of course, figure out what to do about this door. It had tried finding a definition of door, but this had not shed any light upon the situation.

Door: a hinged, sliding or revolving barrier for closing and opening an entrance. An entrance or exit. Open the door: create an opportunity.

This was interesting enough in outlining the nature, but served absolutely no purpose in finding out what was behind the door. What opportunities lay in wait behind it? The Librarian stood in front of the door now, deciding whether to open it or not. If it were unhelpful or even out of date or false information then he

210

would simply shut the door and seal it. There was no such thing as good or bad in a library, no good or evil, only information. There was therefore absolutely no harm in opening this door to see what was behind it. That other fellow, the Dark Man had been agitated about this. He had not wanted the door to be opened. Perhaps then it contained some information, which could be used against him and his like. That in itself had to be good. The librarian tried the door. It was locked. This was absurd. It could not be locked. Martin could not possibly lock a door against him or bar him from seeing any information. Unless the information behind the door did not belong to Martin, so he did not have a choice. But then what was it doing in here? The Librarian was puzzled and examined the door closer. There were markings which had appeared on the surface, scratched into the wood as though by fingernails, although with greater precision. Some of the strands and lines were deeper than others although it was obvious that this was a web of some sort, with symbols along the length of each strand, only the centre was missing. So Martin was trying to break the code and unlock the door then. Good. Then The Librarian would be able to open it and see what was inside, but it was best to take a look first before letting Martin loose in there unsupervised. There was no telling at the moment what may be behind it. The Librarian tried to peer through the keyhole, but could only see darkness. Perhaps it was best to let Martin wake up and decipher the rest of the web then. The sooner he could do that the sooner this door could be opened and the library could get back to normal, with a bit of extra storage space. Now where was that information he was looking for? The references that Martin had asked him to find. They were over in the Mythology section, under Immortality.

*   *   *   *   *

When Sylvia finally opened her eyes she found herself in her own bed again. It was a quarter past three in the morning. Her head throbbed and she did not have the strength to sit up. Her shoulder and stomach ached terribly, as though someone had tied knots in them with piano wire. Every time she moved her muscles threatened to tear themselves away. Hannah was sat by the bedside, and smiled down at her, eyes red and sore from too much crying.

"What happened then?" Sylvia rasped, her throat sore. With the word came a dull pain in her chest and she did not look down because this would hurt her shoulder, but guessed that she was badly bruised at the very least. Hannah took hold of her left hand and placed another on her forehead, brushing her hair back.

"You had a little scuffle with our resident bigfoot, but survived." Sylvia coughed, and could almost feel her chest caving in. "I feel like I was run over by a train."

Hannah nodded, "I think you have a few cracked or broken ribs, but your arm and stomach are going to be OK, there's no infection." Sylvia smiled,

"Since when did you start playing nurse?"

"Since you started getting above your station and picking fights with people twice your size."

Sylvia nodded, "OK point taken, now I've got to get up and we have got to get out of here."

Hannah pushed her back down, sending a wave of piano wire pain through her left shoulder, "No you don't we're not going anywhere. If you remember the roads are blocked, and we are in no fit state to go rambling through the woods or swimming across the bay."

Sylvia's head was swimming at the moment, but was gradually clearing the mud, getting a sharper picture. She felt a stab in her right shoulder blade and shifted over to her side, away from it. Hannah blushed and turned away, "I didn't know what to do with that." The skin was bulging out, protruding about a foot out of her back, like a poorly erected tent. Sylvia twisted her shoulder and shrunk the protrusion back out of sight again. "It happens."

Hannah nodded.

"I must have passed out before I could change back." Hannah wanted to ask what that was, but thought better of it. Sylvia nodded, "No you don't really want to know, it's not very pretty, but sometimes comes in useful." She watched for a reaction on Hannah's face before adding "And I haven't had to do that for about a three hundred and sixty years." Hannah merely nodded, "So don't do it again."

Sylvia stroked her hand. There was no sense in arguing, not in her present condition anyway. What would they do now? She would heal a little faster than perhaps another person would, but

213

she still would not be able to move from here for a few days. She looked at Hannah. Hadn't Hannah saved her life somehow? There was something about a beast and Hannah stepped in the way. The memories were still swimming in and out of reach. "So what did you say to it then?" Hannah leaned forward, "What do you mean?"

"Well you must have said or done something to stop it from tearing us both limb from limb, and I am assuming that you didn't sleep with it, so what did you say." Hannah resisted the temptation to slap her.

"I didn't say anything, it just didn't seem to want to hurt us once it saw who we were. It seemed so confused and so lonely, and the pain inside was terrible Sylvia. We have to find him, whoever he is and make sure he's OK, or try to help him or something."

Sylvia was confused, "What do you mean him."

Hannah sighed. "I mean him. It was a person, a man inside a bear or a wolf or whatever it was, as though they had swapped places." That was it, of course, "It was as though the beast had always been inside and someone had made them swap places so the beast was on the outside and the man was trapped on the inside. The beast was so frightened and confused by being suddenly let out that it didn't know what to do, and the man was so frightened and powerless on the inside that he couldn't do anything."

Sylvia nodded, "You are talking about a lycanthrope."

"A what?"

"A werewolf, only it doesn't have to be a wolf, it can be a bear, a cat, a fish, whatever."

"A bird?"

Sylvia almost nodded, but caught the thought behind this. At least her senses were coming back properly, "Yes, but not the way you think. When I changed I was conscious, very aware of what I was doing so it was only my appearance that altered. This creature though, if it is what you think, doesn't have any control over the change and each aspect of it may not be aware of the other. So when it changes into wolf, or whatever, the human part has no control at all, and visa versa. Also the two or more parts are constantly fighting for control, so that the human can only keep the creature away while he's awake, sometimes not even then." she looked directly into Hannah's eyes, "It's very important that you understand this, because I'm not like that creature we met in the woods. The thing which tracked us down in the woods is infinitely more savage than we could ever be."

Hannah nodded, although she did not altogether agree with the savage part. It had just seemed confused to her, and frightened inside.

Sylvia shrank back into the bed. "OK, now can you do me a favour and get me some things from the study at the end of the hall."

Hannah stood in the doorway to the study now, but was still hesitant about stepping inside. It seemed to be still and quiet in there, more so than in the rest of the house. In a house at night you could expect the odd creak and groan of wood, or the rattle of a heating system, especially in one this old, but not in there. She listened very carefully. From inside the study there was nothing, not even the gentle ticking of a clock. She would just have to do this a quickly as possible. They were all on the middle shelf in a box Sylvia had said, so she would just grab the whole box. She also needed a silver pestle and mortar from the side table. Hannah peered around the corner, careful not to step through the doorway. They were there also, and the knife she had described was there on the second shelf.

Right, here goes. She stepped through the doorway with her eyes closed and stood for a while before opening them. Nothing. No noise, just peace and quiet. The room was so still she was afraid to breath, but found that doing so did not disturb anything. OK so time to get the things on the list. It was actually quite nice in here, very peaceful. Hannah imagined that the leather armchair in the centre of the room was very comfortable indeed, and that coffee table was just the right height to put her feet up on. No, she should just get the rest of the things Sylvia had asked for and get out of here, there was something about time being slowed down in here, or the like. Hannah grabbed the box off the middle shelf, which was heavier than she thought, and the knife and the pestle and mortar, then for good measure she grabbed the widest book she could find to use as a tray. Before she could be tempted to fall asleep in that very comfortable chair she was on her way up the corridor again towards the kitchen.

*　　*　　*　　*　　*

Half past five in the morning and Martin stirred in his sleep. Something was happening here. It was a something that would not go away and would change him and the world forever, which was a very long time. Darkness had descended over Seahaven and was not moving. It had staked a claim here and it would take force to move it on, only who had the might to shift the night sky? The birds should be waking up and starting their dawn chorus now, waking up the sun and telling it to get moving, there was a new day to be enjoyed by all, only they were not singing. The time was half past five in the morning and the sky was as black as it had been at half past two. Martin opened his eyes. That was it. Eureka was the word on his mind, but he did not shout it out, it had been done before. At half past five in the morning in the middle of August he had solved the riddle that had plagued him all summer and a little longer. The book he had been studying was open on the floor and Martin was sure that he did not need that now, but he would take a look just in case. He leaped out of bed in a naked frenzy and grasped the book in both hands as though snatching it away from another reader. It was open on the wrong page, where they had been ruffled as it fell. He flicked through to find the correct one. When he at last came face to face with the web he could not understand how he could possibly have missed this in the first place. It glared out from the page, obvious in it's simplicity, like one of those three dimensional pictures made of dots which are supposed to spring

217

out at you if you stare long and hard enough, only he did not have to concentrate here. The pattern was as plain as the light of day. The answer was there for all to see; he had just been asking the wrong question.

* * * * *

Hannah had mixed up the various ingredients in the mortar, grinding them into a fine powder with the pestle under Sylvia's instruction. She had got some matches from the kitchen, although did not know what for, and had even pushed the thin silver needles into the areas around the wounds as Sylvia had indicated, but she drew the line at cutting her with the black knife. This was ridiculous she should just get her to the hospital. "And a hospital won't be able to help me." Sylvia shouted back. "They won't be able to stop the infection which may be in these wounds and God only knows what they will make of me if they take an x-ray." Hannah understood this, but she could still not bring herself to hurt her.

"OK, give the knife to me then." Sylvia took the knife from her, being careful not to touch the blade.

"What metal is that knife made from?" asked Hannah. It looked like old iron, at least in the way it had blackened, but did not feel heavy enough.

Sylvia shrugged with her one good shoulder, "I don't know, probably fairy dust or something. Now we'll work on one wound at a time. When I cut I want you to pour half of the

218

mixture you have made into the blood, and stir it in well with the wooden rod there." She pointed to a thin wooden stick about eight inches in length and half an inch in diameter in the box beside her. Hannah took hold of it. "As the mixture changes colour, it will turn a yellow-brown shade, I want you to strike a match and light it."

Hannah nodded. "A match?"

Sylvia looked at her and nodded, one eyebrow raised slightly, "Yes, a match, OK?"

Hannah nodded again.

"OK, let's do it."

With her right hand Sylvia traced the edge of the knife over the wound in her left shoulder, opening it up again. Blood rose to the surface as though a well had been struck and she gasped, "OK, pour, get on with it."

Hannah did as she was told, the mixture went in and she stirred, trying nor to poke the newly opened wound too much until Sylvia told her to get it in there and almost grabbed the stick off her to do it herself. Once the mixture had changed colour, in a matter of seconds Hannah struck a match.

Sylvia looked straight at her again, "OK, don't wait until it burns out, do it."

She dropped the match onto the mixture of blood and who knows what. Fire spread over the surface of the wound and in a split second was gone, working its way inwards instead of out. It lit Sylvia's arm from within, making her shoulder and her left side glow like a flesh covered lantern. Sylvia screamed, then the fire was gone, and so was the wound, save for a few thin scars, one for each claw.

Moisture dripped from Sylvia's brow and she gasped a tired smile, "OK, now for the next one, but can I have a glass of water first?"

By the time they had finished it was six o'clock in the morning. Hannah put the remaining ingredients back in the box and closed the lid. Sylvia was feeling a little weak, although thought that she could get up now, so she did. She got changed out of the torn dress and into some more practical jeans and a shirt. If they could both walk then there was no sense in either of them sitting around. They may as well go into town and see if there was any other way out. Hannah did not mention it although she was becoming concerned about Sylvia's appearance. Overnight she had developed a grey streak in her hair, and a few extra laugh lines. This was OK in itself, but she did not want her getting so old that she would pass away. As it was at the moment she was fine, more than fine, in fact she was beautiful. Sylvia caught her staring. "Stop it we have work to do, and I'm in too weak a condition for that." Hannah blushed again and turned away to pick up her jacket, "Come on then, let's go"

On the way out Sylvia caught sight of herself in the mirror. She decided that today was a good day to wear a hat.

* * * * *

Milkmen started their rounds and postmen reported for duty as usual, however all were more than a little confused. This was the height of summer, or almost, and it was not supposed to be dark at half past six in the morning. No birds sang, the only music this morning were distant carnival tunes. If one listened very carefully one could trace their origin. They weaved in and out of the streets of Seahaven, up and over buildings, down and through the sewers. For every direction they floated another tune would cross that, forming a web of music over the coast and inland, the centre of which was Seahaven Common, the centre of which was the carousel. And in the darkness of morning it continued turning, weaving its tunes, a different one for every person, notes to suit all and more fabulous wooden creatures to match.

*   *   *   *   *

By the time Martin had got himself up, had breakfast and walked into town it was still dark. He looked at his watch and could not quite believe that it was really nine o'clock, but that is what it said, and that is what the church tower clock said as well, as far as he could make out. Shops were opening as usual. Perhaps the darkness was due to an unexpected or unannounced solar eclipse, although this had not been mentioned on the television this morning either. In fact, the weather girl on Breakfast T.V. had predicted more record-breaking temperatures and sixteen hours of daylight. It was going to be difficult to cram in that many hours of daylight into the rest of today, unless the sun suddenly woke up and stayed awake until one o'clock in the morning. As far as he could see the people of Seahaven were roughly divided into two groups here. One group who did not seem to notice or care that it was still dark at nine o'clock in the morning, and the other who by and large were either panicking or were trying to get on with their daily business the best way they could, always looking over a shoulder to see just who was watching. Martin did not really know which of these two categories he fitted into. He was obviously concerned by the fact that the sun seemed to have forgotten them this morning, but felt that it did not particularly affect him that much. He was more interested in what he had just discovered. Cornelius Agrippa you see, or Leonardo DaVinci, or Aristotle, whatever he wished to call himself was all one person. If he had survived for that long then the chances were he was still alive somewhere. As ridiculous as it perhaps sounded Martin believed that there were some people who could live, if not forever, then at the very least for centuries. He wanted to know if he could find any, to talk to them and find out what they knew, but most of all he wanted to know how. How did someone live forever? He had taken to the street in order to get some fresh air, and partially because he wanted to check out the cost of a flight to Egypt in the travel agent. That was the place to begin, in the cradle of civilisation; he would look for answers there. In the distance, weaving in and out of the darkness he could hear the faint tinkle of fairground music, unaccompanied this time by any shouts of joy or alarm. It

222

seemed out of place today, as though a visitor from another time, or a ghost of the past.

*　*　*　*　*

Sylvia urged Hannah to hurry up. They could not take forever over this. She did not like the fact that it was still dark at nine o'clock in the morning. The darkness meant that He could travel about at his own pleasure. She did not like that one bit. It also meant that he was much stronger than when they had last met in her study. The plan was to check out whether there was any postal service still operating in and out of Seahaven. If there was then they could hijack a post van and get through one of the roadblocks. It had been Hannah's idea as she had expressed concern over the invasion of grey now infiltrating Sylvia's otherwise glossy black hair. It had been a subtle way of telling her that she did not want her getting old too quickly. Sylvia too had been giving this some thought. Perhaps being human was not all it was cracked up to be. There were virtues in extreme longevity, like not having to look old, and not dying just to name two. She did not actually know if they could die of old age as none had yet reached such an age, but by the very fact that she was not this tall four thousand years ago they must actually age, although very slowly. This was all very well now that she was mature, but the first hundred years or so had been hell. Sylvia did not, of course voice any of this out loud. It was not too late for her to change her mind about this. She was not as far along in the change as she had thought, the events in Paris and the recent escapade with Aleph had probably slowed it down a touch, but taking her original shape in the woods last night had certainly put a stop on it. She could probably just as easily reverse the change now as not. Her spirit balanced on a pinhead. She peered through the window of the post office, looking for Hannah, willing her to speed the clerk up a bit. She was posting a bogus parcel to an aunt in Newcastle-Under-Lyne and asking when it would get there, when the next pick up was and so on. This would give them an idea when the post van would be coming and going. They then had to figure out how to hijack it without hurting anyone, or being caught. She was currently at the counter having the parcel weighed.

"Come on Hannah."

The window turned white with moisture, where Sylvia breathed against it, so that she could not see through. She turned around and leaned with her back to the window.

*　*　*　*　*

Martin could not be sure what or who it was he was seeing, but although he recognised her from the town he was looking at her for the first time in this moment. She stood over the road, outside the post office, bathed in yellow light from a weak street lamp overhead. She had turned around now and was facing him, looking right at him. He watched her carefully, and she seemed to regard him with equal suspicion, the both of them measuring

224

the other. He did not know what she thought or where she had come from, but was certain of one thing for the first time in his life and could not speak. She was not human. He could see. She was not human, but walked as one, in disguise. There was nothing sinister about her, nothing that he found threatening, he just knew that is all, the same way that a dog knows the difference between a dog and a cat, or a signet knows a swan from a snake. Sylvia Cruz; at least he thought that was her name, as everyone in town talked about her at one time or another; was not human. As she turned around he thought he could see the shadow of a wing thrown on the pavement in front, but the image vanished. Could she be an angel? He did not know, but he had to talk to her.

Martin stepped off the pavement and crossed the road.

* * * * *

As Sylvia turned around her heart jumped into her throat and the chorus of a thousand wings fluttered in her ears, blood rushing to her consciousness. Someone was watching her. She peered into the darkness until her eyes were directed by default to a part of the pavement on the other side of the road that was more crooked than the rest. No it was not a badly laid wall, it was a person, who now stepped forward. Sylvia shrank back, but there was nowhere to go. She recognised him, but could not recall his name, a sign of impending old age she guessed, and chuckled inside. She pleaded for Hannah to hurry up; this was going to get sticky. She watched his face, his eyes, and deeper. He knew. He did not just think, like the young children who told stories about her being a witch and dared each other to walk up the hill and touch her gate on Halloween. He actually knew. She could not tell how much, but was certain. It was as obvious to him as it was to her that he was on the threshold of becoming.

Hannah was still inside. Sylvia breathed deeply to calm herself down. This was no problem. She could get out of this in the wink of an eye, and it was dark so no one would see.

He stepped off the pavement and began walking across the road towards her.

Part Three.

12. The Healing Touch.

There they stood, face to face. Sylvia watching the minutest movement of his eyes, looking for some intention there, and Martin merely watching. Neither of them spoke a word, but both heard everything. Martin watched her shadow moving around her just below the level of darkness. He watched it's shape, the wings and talons, and he noted it's age. She was not human that much he knew, but what was she? The files in his mind worked overtime looking for a match. Was she an angel or demon? Sylvia heard all of this, perhaps before he had thought it, and a smile grew uncontrollably on her face. This was dangerous, yes, but how refreshing. Someone who knew her, or thought that he knew her for what she really was. Someone with whom there was no pretense and no mask. She pondered briefly whether to let him see her as she really was, but decided against it. He could see her other shadow anyway, the one which was always there just beyond people's vision. She watched the gateway of his eyes carefully, noting the questions that they held, then decided to enter.

*   *   *   *   *

Hannah emerged from the Post office with triumph. The postal service was running as normal, although delays were to be expected because of the roadblocks on all roads out of town. People were being allowed through the roadblocks if they had normal business going to and from town, so post vans were allowed. She looked up the pavement searching in the darkness for Sylvia, who was stood underneath a dim yellow street lamp. Hannah stopped in her tracks. Opposite Sylvia, only a breath away stood someone else. A younger man, perhaps in his late teens. Neither of them were talking, they were just staring. What could she do? There was no way she was going to let him stop them from leaving. If he had been sent by that Aleph, then she would send him on his way before he did any harm. But they could not allow him to leave and tell Aleph what they were up to though could they? No. Then she would have to make sure that he could not talk. Hannah fumbled around in her bag for something that she could use. He was young, but was probably stronger than her so she had to give herself an advantage. Why was Sylvia not doing anything?

Finally her hand gripped hold of something sharp in the bottom of the bag, she caught her thumb on the edge of it and pulled her hand away sharply. That hurt, she had probably cut herself. She felt around again, this time a little more carefully. Eventually she took hold of it by the handle. All the while she kept her eyes on the two figures under the street lamp. She was not going to let anything happen to Sylvia. Hannah pulled a pair of steel scissors out of her bag and began to advance cautiously up the street.

*   *   *   *   *

Sylvia stepped nimbly through the gateway, which Martin had so conveniently left open for her. She walked right in and sat down in one of the leather chairs in front of a large table. All around them books stacked high on shelves stretched as far as she could see.

Martin stood dumbfounded, how the hell did she get in here? She could not just walk into his library. Sylvia smiled to him, "Hello Martin, we meet at last. Why don't you sit down?"

She had to take control of the situation. Martin sat down in a chair opposite, so it seemed to be working.

"Nice library you have here, very sizeable for someone your age." She gestured around her at the books on the shelves. Martin shrugged, "I read a lot."

He watched her closely, could see her clearer now that she had come inside. There were no shadows in here to confuse and hide. She was a very beautiful woman, but he could not let her face and those slender fingers deceive him. He was looking at someone who was not like him here. She was much older, much stronger and much more powerful.

"Very good Martin, ten out of ten for effort there. You are right of course, but what do you intend to do about it." Martin tried to hide his surprise. She could hear him even when he did not speak.

"Of course I can Martin, I'm inside your mind, in your library."
She looked around her, it was a fair size, but she had seen better.
"Perhaps you should come and see mine some time."

He nodded. That would be useful. To think of all the things that
this woman must know made his blood run faster. She nodded in
appreciation.

"I think we can help each other here Martin, don't you?"
Martin nodded, although he could not see how. He wanted to
know what she knew, yes, and he had a thousand questions for
her if not more, but what could she want from him?

Sylvia sat in the leather chair and watched him closely. The boy
was young and yet seemed older to her, and it was true that this
library was very large for someone of his age. She reached into
him further to see what she could find and saw only a door.

"What's behind the door Martin?"

He did not know.

"Do you want to know?"

Martin paused. Did he want to know? He had spent his whole
life in pursuit of knowledge so far, so it would be strange if he
did not. He was not sure. Somehow he felt that what was behind
this door would change the course of his life forever. He had
brushed with something he did not quite understand and there
was living proof of what he thought may exist sat in front of him
now, but he was still uncertain of whether he should proceed.

If he did would he become like her?

Sylvia shook her head, "No Martin, that's not possible I'm afraid
because I was born this way, if born is the correct term. Let us

just say I was made this way and have always been so." She pointed down the corridor to the locked door at the end. "I don't know exactly what is behind that door, in the same way that you don't, but I do know that it will change your life forever, and we both know that it's part of what you have been looking for." He nodded. "I also know that you have a key in your pocket with which to unlock it if you want to."

Martin's hand reached down to his right pocket.

"No, the other one."

He reached into his left pocket and sure enough pulled out a brass key.

What else did she know about him?

"Everything now, except for whatever is behind that door."

"Oh, may I?" She gestured towards one of the shelves.

Martin nodded. Sylvia smiled back.

A book floated out towards her and placed itself on the table in front of her; open at the page she wanted, ready. She took hold of a pencil, which winked into existence and crossed out a word, replacing it with another. "There, that's better." The book closed itself and floated back into position.

How did she do that? Sylvia looked at him again, "I did it because you let me, so you must be able to do it as well." Martin shook his head, no he could not.

"Have you ever tried?" No he had not, "Well go on then."

Martin thought about what to ask for. Did he want to look up Harpies in Greek mythology, or angels? Because he was certain she was one of the two.

232

When he opened his eyes six books floated in front of him, waiting for him to chose. There was not enough room on the table for all of them.

Which one was she?

Sylvia smiled and pointed to the second book from the left. Greek mythology. Martin sent the rest of them back to the shelves where they belonged. The book placed itself on the table, closed. Martin looked up at Sylvia for some help, but she had stood up now and was walking towards the locked door, reading the symbols scratched into the wooden surface.

"This is very good you know, although your translation of the Sanskrit is a little basic." He nodded; he was not very good at Sanskrit. Sylvia had now reached the door; she scratched over one of the symbols. "There, that's better." Martin looked over at her, twisting in his chair so he could see what she was doing.

Which one was she? Aello, Ocypete or Celaeno?

Sylvia sighed, poor Ocypete, what a waste. And as for Aello she had not seen her for centuries. "Don't believe everything you read Martin, we were given such a bad press don't you think? Besides is it important which of the three I am when the other two are my sisters and we are all the same, more or less?" Martin did not suppose so. The book closed and floated back to the shelf from whence it came. Sylvia looked around at him, "Remind me to give you an accurate history some time, instead of relying on those kind of books." He nodded.

"Now do you want to get this door open or not?"

Martin stood up, gathering his courage and walked towards her.

*   *   *   *   *

Hannah approached as carefully as she could, but could not stop the crunch of gravel underfoot. This did not, however, seem to matter. Despite the noise she was making and the uncanny sixth sense, which Sylvia seemed to have at other times, they did not seem to notice her approaching. They did not seem to notice anything at all. She was now stood to the side of them, less than arms reach away and they were not moving. They were breathing but there was no animation. The lights were on, but there was nobody home. It was as though the scene had been frozen and everyone caught in the yellow glow of the street lamp had been switched off or paused as on a video screen. Hannah wanted to reach out and shake Sylvia awake, but dared not. Perhaps this other person had trapped her somehow. Hannah gripped the scissors as tightly as she could and stepped forward to position herself between Sylvia and the boy, holding the points upwards against his neck and under his chin.

*   *   *   *   *

Yes he did want to open the door. The urge to see what was beyond it was overwhelming.
"Do we have a bargain then?"
Martin nodded. Yes, if she helped him to open the door he would use whatever was behind it to help her and her friend

234

escape. Then he could find them later and she would give him the real history of the world, not the rubbish that was printed in the books.

She placed a hand on his shoulder. It was warm, and although alien felt good to have there. "Right then, let's open it."

Martin handed her the key, but she would not take it. "No Martin It's your door, only you can open it. If I was supposed to open it then I would have had the key in my pocket." He supposed this was correct. She did not have any pockets large enough for the key, but this whole thing was a metaphor for something anyway, so what the hell. He lifted the brass key, which felt heavy in his hand and placed the end of it in the lock. It fit like a glove, as the expression went. Sylvia stood back slightly, uncertain of what the door would be hiding. She wanted to be in a position to help or make a quick getaway if there were any surprises in there.

The key turned in the lock as though it had turned there a thousand times before. The action was smooth and solid. The levers of the lock mechanism yielded against the pressure and one by one slid into place. Finally the door was unlocked.

Martin and Sylvia stood in front of it, the one on the edge of realisation and the other on the precipice of nostalgia.

"Open it Martin, let's have a look inside."

He turned the handle and pushed the door open.

Inside it was dark, but he stepped through the door anyway.

A light flickered into life above and around him, throwing its gaze around the chamber. More books. Not many of them, but more nevertheless, and not only that. They were more than that.

The books in here seemed to be alive. They rustled and sighed as the light touched them, almost breathing the fresh air that he had let in by opening the door. Sylvia stood in the doorway but did not enter. It was as she had suspected.

Martin looked around at her. Were they alive?

She did not react. Perhaps she could not hear his thoughts in here.

"Are they alive?"

She nodded, "Yes, they are. They are part of you now, and like you they write their own history."

Martin nodded, grinning. Yes, now he understood.

Sylvia turned around. It was time for them to go.

*   *   *   *   *

"Hannah!"

Hannah froze as Sylvia called to her. She felt Sylvia's kind hand on her shoulder and let the arm holding the scissors drop a little. The boy in front of her shrank away, then upon turning around and seeing her ran for cover behind Sylvia. "What the hell do you think you are doing?" He shouted. Hannah ignored him, "Sylvia are you all right?" Sylvia nodded and took hold of her hand, relieving her of the scissors.

"Yes I am fine. Hannah, meet Martin. He's going to help us." Martin smiled at her meekly, casting uneasy glances at the scissors: now safely in Sylvia's hand, then with a flick of the wrist not. She winked at him. Hannah placed an arm around

236

Sylvia's waist and took comfort in the safety there. "Nice to meet you Martin."

They did not shake hands.

*   *   *   *   *

By noon that day it was still dark. There had been a chaotic period for almost an hour between ten and eleven o'clock when the street lights had automatically switched off, and the council had to take emergency measures to get them switched back on again. This was going to cost them some money on their next electricity bill. A few shops remained open, but most had closed for the day. There was no point in staying open with so few people around. Was it twelve noon or midnight? For those with analogue clocks there was no way of telling. The sky remained more than overcast. The sun had not shown up for work today, called in sick. Only the fairground at the top of the hill carried on as usual. Darkness was no hindrance there, it allowed the brightly coloured lights to play freely and dance on the wind. Martin sat alone in his room watching the fairy lights through his open bedroom window. Mid day and it was still dark. Those two were certainly on the run from something all right. They were on the run from something which denied the sun it's right. He sat on the edge of his bed and counted the minutes. It was strange how a simple thing like darkness could change the course of someone's day so dramatically. Here in Seahaven shops had closed, people had stayed in and locked their doors,

and Martin had just had the single most bizarre experience of his life so far. He had met a Harpy outside the Post Office and she had proceeded to enter his mind somehow. She had shown him things in there which he did not know existed, and then asked for his help to escape from the dark town of Seahaven. If he did not know better, with it being so dark outside, Martin would have thought this to be a dream. But he knew that it was not. He had not been dreaming then, and most certainly was not dreaming now. He wondered if they were on their way yet, the Harpy and it's companion. He wondered how he would find them again. The Harpy had told him that he would find them when the time came, but Martin did not know what that meant. All he knew is that somehow, with her guidance he had put up some sort of smoke screen so whoever it was who was looking for them could not see them and would not find them. This would enable them to use some sort of trickery of their own to make a fast exit. He looked out of his window into the darkness and could not help himself wondering how far they had gone. How had they gone there? Had they flown? Had they just gone? Smoke billowed up to his window from the street below, as though something was on fire down there. Martin stood up and leaned out of the window to look. Nothing, and the smoke had gone. It must have been a thin patch of fog. He turned around.
"Hello Martin."
It was him, the dark man from his dream.
The man nodded, silver hair tussling as he did so, like silver wind chimes playing in the breeze without a sound.

"I thought it about time we met in the flesh."

Martin eyed the doorway, his only real exit. He stood with his back to the open window, one floor, and fifteen feet up. Could he jump out of it and have a safe landing. He was not sure, but he certainly could not get past the man who now stood between himself and the bedroom's only door.

"You could jump I suppose," the man said, now already by Martin's side looking down at the pavement below from the open window. Martin did not see him move. "But I don't think you could guarantee a safe landing do you?" Martin sat down on the bed, away from the window now.

"And please don't even think about trying to make it to the door, because I can guarantee that I will get there before you, and you don't really want to put me to all that trouble and make me angry do you?"

Martin sat still, "What do you want?"

The man laughed out loud, "At last, you speak. I was beginning to think we would never get around to it. Where is Celaeno and that bitch girl friend of hers?"

Martin shook his head, "I don't know."

The man knelt one knee on the bed and leaned in closer. His eyes burned with the fire of stars, blinding Martin in their fury. He was afraid now. The world did not seem such a grand place full of adventure and knowledge any more. It was a place full of dark secrets that were best left unexplored.

"I do not wish to ask you a second time. I assume you know what I am?" Martin could not find the words to answer, his

239

mouth was too dry so he simply nodded.

"Good, so you know that if you don't tell me I will tear the information from you on your way to Hell." These words gripped at martin's throat like a hangman's noose, tightening with every passing second.

"I don't know where they've gone, I only know that they went this morning."

The man sighed, the star fire in his eyes dimmed.

"Why must it always be this way? Why can't people just do as they are told?"

Martin was not sure what he meant. He watched the man form these words with his animate mouth, and the celestial furnace in his eyes spark up once more. Martin's world was consumed in white fire.

*   *   *   *   *

She had been beautiful, that is all he knew, and she had shown him love. She had shown him love even when the beast had taken over. She had looked through the beast at him inside and had loved him. Gregory wrestled with the creature which he now new invaded his body. They did not share as he had thought may be the case and as Victor Midnight had told him. The body was his and the Beast was an invader. It had no right there; it had no right in the real world or the dream one. When her hand had been upon him it had woken him up and made the Beast tired and sleepy. The Beast had wanted to sleep and Gregory had been able to take control, partially. Now he was struggling with all of his might and was winning. He was stronger than the Beast because now he had a fuel for his fire; he had a reason to live. The Beast growled and howled, but there was nothing it could do. In the birth of his new life Gregory was infinitely stronger. The Beast raged within, but remained within. If Gregory could not entirely rid himself of this thing forever at least he could contain it, and if it took over in his sleep he would awake and beat it down again. Gregory smiled and laughed, no growl now, just a human throaty explosion of laughter, all voice and skin, no fur and no teeth. The Beast withdrew, frightened by the laughter, a human sound so alien to it's ears. All it had ever heard were screaming and pain and the fire of it's own blood. Somehow this new sound was deeper. It felt instantly calm, soothed by the warm sounds the human Gregory made. It remembered back to the woods and how the other creature had stood her ground. It could remember her smell, and the warm sweetness of her breath, the softness of her touch, so delicate.

Gregory breathed deeply, and slowly, the expulsion of air driving the Beast deeper inside him, further away, until, like the whistle of a train receding into the night, hurtling into the distant darkness with the cry of a thousand sleepless infants it was gone. The hair on his arms stood up on ends, raised there by goose bumps, but it was his hair. His skin felt rough to the touch, forcing a shiver at every pass of his hand, but it was his skin. He sat for a while on the grass by the river.

It was still dark and there was no telling what the time actually was, because it had been dark forever. His clothes were gone, as were his running shoes. Only the crucifix remained around his neck. There was going to be a problem in getting home without being seen in this state.

There did not seem to be anyone around, so he thought that he might make it part of the way home along the river. Then he would just have to run the rest of the way up his street and hope that the garage, or the back door had been left open. And once he was home? Once he was home he would get dressed and go out again, to look for her. The town was a good place to start, depending on what the time was, and if not there then he would have to look around the fair ground. Gregory watched the silver wolf glide past him on it's way around the carousel again. Perhaps the fair ground was not the best place to go, but if he had to he would. He would leave it until last though.

What would he say to her once he had found her? Gregory could not find the words. They were buried deep beneath him, but they were there, and he was sure they would rise to the surface once she was stood in front of him. Perhaps she would recognise him. He would never forget her, so perhaps she too would always remember him. These were things that he would tackle when he came to them. The most pressing item on the agenda at the moment was how to get home without being seen by the neighbours, or being arrested for indecency.

*　*　*　*　*

Police and emergency departments had been on double duty for most of the day. If the weather itself was not strange enough, then the behaviour of the people of Seahaven tipped the scales in favour of weirdness. The strangest thing, or not so unbelievable, was that P.C. McRae did not really care. It could be said, in his own words, that he did not give a toss what was happening out there on the streets. The people of Seahaven could loot and pillage all they wanted as long as he was left in peace. The short end of it all was that he thought they were all wankers anyway and they quite frankly deserved everything they got. If the Wallpoles had their shop burgled it was only because their prices were too high, and if Mr. Johnson was beaten in the Town Square and hoisted up on the Town Hall flagpole he had probably deserved it, and although murdering the Montgomery brothers was possibly a little harsh nobody was going to miss the pair of bastards anyway. P.C. McRae was sure that the other officers felt the same. No one else was responding to any of the 999 calls, so why should he. The fire department had let two warehouses on the edge of town burn down already. There was no point in trying to save them because someone would only set fire to them again anyway. There had been talk on the radio that a state of emergency may be called and the armed forces may be brought in to police the area and seal off access to the town of Seahaven, but so what? P.C. McRae sipped his coffee and watched the portable television he had brought into the station earlier. He could only get one channel on the thing, but that was better than going out there.

*   *   *   *   *

Gregory soon discovered that he need not have been worried about whether people would see him running up the street naked or not. He did not think, by the look of things, that they would either care or notice. He had already passed two couples becoming intimately acquainted with each other in the main street, four sets of hands, legs and lips gliding over each other, and no one seemed to be paying the blindest bit of attention. The few people who were actually out on the street were otherwise engaged. He had slowed his run to a walk now, as it did not seem to matter anyway, and there was no sense in making himself tired. He had borrowed some clothes from a nearby shop window, which someone else had been thoughtful enough to smash.

Where the hell were the police? He looked up at the Town Hall clock and at the lonely figure of a man struggling to free himself from the top of the flagpole there. The time was only four o'clock in the afternoon, or at least he assumed it must be afternoon because of the people walking about, and some of the shops still being open. The inescapable noise of burglar alarms permeated every street he turned down, shouting out for help to deaf ears. Nobody seemed to want to help. Nobody seemed that bothered actually, and just below the screaming of sirens and alarms the air tingled with the faint, but distinctive jangle of fairground music.

244

Gregory stopped in the middle of the street and looked around him at abandoned cars and broken windows. A naked, panting couple in a shop doorway across the street were shouting and beckoning him to join them, but he declined. What the hell was going on here? No body answered him, nobody particularly cared. Behind him an elderly gentleman took a sledgehammer to the window of a Hoover shop. Gregory decided to move on. He would not go home, instead he would try to find her, and if she was mixed up in all of this he would save her just as she had saved him. The jeans he had borrowed were a size too big, so he would have to find a belt from somewhere, and he needed some shoes. The shop next door was wide open with nobody inside, so what could he do? Gregory stepped through the door and peered into the darkness. "Hello?"

There was no answer. "Is there anybody in?"

Again there was no answer. He closed the door and bolted it behind him. Perhaps there was a telephone in here as well, so he could call the police. He had seen at least three robberies being committed on his walk up the street, and surely it was not right for the people he had seen to be having sex openly in the main street at four o'clock in the afternoon. Children could be walking past or anything. Gregory fumbled around for a light switch. There was a strange smell in here that he could not quite place. His sense of smell was usually good but he could not place this one. It was familiar, like a distant voice, but indistinct. No luck. The light switch could be anywhere. It was probably, in fact at the back of the shop, where customers did not go. Gregory made his way gingerly to the rear of the shop, behind the counter, trying carefully not to tread on anything or knock anything over. The wolf inside him growled, it recognised the smell. Gregory listened, but would not let it to the surface. The smell was very familiar now, as the wolf tried to furnish him with memories. Gregory strained to remember, to recognise the smell, to translate the wolf speak inside. His hand fumbled on the wall at the back of the room, edging it's way along and down and back again until his fingers found the switch he had been looking for. The wolf urged him not to switch on the light; it had seen enough death for a lifetime. Death, was that the smell? Gregory's fingers hovered over the light switch. The smell cleared in his nostrils, salty and sweet. The lights flickered on, at the involuntary action of his fingertips. Blinded for just a moment he stood behind the counter trying to get his bearings. White fluorescent light surrounded him casting a stellar brightness over his world and for those few seconds everything looked sterilised and clean. The counter, the rows of blurred clothing, the shelving stacked with jeans and jumpers, and the pale, clean body on the carpet in front of the counter. He blinked and as his vision adjusted the light became dimmer and not so sterilising. The body was not so clean. A gentleman in his mid thirties rested against the counter with he feet splayed out on the carpet in front. His head was bowed, but Gregory could still make out his features from here, stood at the side of him.

The man had been shot in the chest, probably with a shotgun, by size of the wound. There did not seem to be a lot of blood, his

246

clothing and the carpet had soaked most up, leaving only a minor mess on the counter behind and above him. Gregory reflected on this. It was probably a minor mess compared to what he had seen, but he was sure that if it had happened at home his mother would have more to say about it than that. Most of the man's chest had caved in, leaving a gaping hole where his lungs and heart should have been. Gregory spotted a few fragments spayed over the counter and on the wall behind. He looked at his own hands, plastered in red and grey where he had been groping the walls in search of a light switch. This made him heave. He ran through into the back room, now also lit up, and rinsed his hands under the taps there. He was not sick, he had seen worse, much worse. The wolf would not let him be sick, he had to be strong.

There would be a telephone in the shop somewhere and he could phone the police. He could also change his jeans for a better fit and take a pair of the cowboy boots displayed in the broken window if there were any his size. Gregory rinsed his hands and splashed water on his face. He looked up into the mirror, trying to find the wolf hidden deep behind his eyes. It had retreated, leaving behind a ghost, a vacuum.

The telephone was behind the main counter, so he picked up the receiver, dialed 999 and waited. There was no answer. This was ridiculous. He let it ring some more. There was still no answer. After a couple of minutes he replaced the receiver in its cradle and pondered what to do. There was nothing he could do. He had tried his best. They did have jeans in his size, so he changed as quickly as he could. A brown pair of boots in the window were close enough so he put those on as well. Now at least he was fully dressed. There was nothing he could do about the poor owner of the shop, so he would just have to leave him here. He was dead so there was no point in taking him to the hospital, and if the police were not responding then there was no way he could report it to them. Gregory squatted down in front of the body, careful not to put his knees on the blood soaked carpet. The smell was even stronger now that he recognised it. Stewing blood. He reached into the man's pockets, looking for keys to the shop. At least he could make sure that nobody else came in here and did anything vile to his body or anything. The lifeless body jerked around him, arms flailing as he fumbled around in its pockets. Finally he found the keys. On his way out Gregory grabbed a jacket from one of the racks by the door and closed the door behind him. Once outside he locked the door and pulled down and locked the shutters. He would post the keys to the police station with a note. He guessed that what he had done really amounted to stealing, but there was no point in borrowing from a dead person was there, he would not exactly care whether Gregory gave back the clothes or not. Gregory placed the shop keys in his jacket pocket and set off running. He had to find her and they had to get out of this place before it was too late for them. He ran toward the bottom of the hill, the start of the road up to Seahaven Common. At the top he could hear the music of the carousel, and within that, hidden inside he could hear Victor Midnight laughing.

248

*   *   *   *   *

There was nothing. No sound, no feeling, just a void, floating in the nothingness of notime and suspended in the emptiness of nospace. There was no reason to be here, no reason not to be, it was just simply so. Here there was no beginning and no end. Here there was nothing.

Only himself remained, filling this void. There was no physical body that he could be sure of, no being or thing of which he could be certain. There was nothing beyond him, only emptiness. The only thing that remained were these thoughts, which took up no space and used no time, the products of nothing. I think therefore I am, these thoughts expressed, and in the beginning there was nothing.

*   *   *   *   *

Martin lay still in the hospital bed where he had been placed. He was breathing voluntarily now so the life support had been switched off. It looked as though he was stable, but that did not mean recovering. Nurse Green watched him from the foot of the bed. He seemed so peaceful, but they always did. So young for this to happen. He had slipped into a coma and had not woken up for two days now, just like that. The parents had found him asleep in his room and had brought him into hospital themselves when they could not wake him up the next day. The ambulance service had apparently not been responding, and they had only been allowed to leave Seahaven under armed guard to ensure their return. The poor lad was not going to have any visitors, but she did not suppose it mattered since, in all likelihood he could not see or hear anyone anyway. At least he was stable, which meant he was not dying. His mind was not switched on to the world, that was all. It may just be a matter of time before he woke up. Until then they would continue feeding him and turning him over periodically, like a slowly grilling lamb chop. She wondered if he could dream while he was like this, and then turned away and left the room.

* * * * *

Yes, in the beginning there was nothing, and darkness was upon the face of the deep.

The Librarian stirred from its place of hiding, in the other room, which no one may enter. The lights were out, the shelves were bare. No that was not quite right. The shelves were not quite bare; they were empty or may just as well have been. The books were all the same. He glided up and down the corridor, searching for a clue of where to begin. There was none. The shelves were stacked high, as usual with books, although now all of them were the same. They were all nameless, as though their titles had been erased, and they were all blank. What had he done? The Master was nowhere to be found. He was not asleep; he was just not here, nor anywhere. He must be somewhere. The Librarian searched among the blank books for some kind of sign to show his whereabouts. There was none. Then perhaps could find something in the other room. The new room. That was the place to begin, where it had been hidden in the first place. Something must have happened whilst it had been hidden in there, reading. The Librarian made it's way back to the rear of the library corridor and through the door at the end again. The room was alive, not empty and dead like the place out there. In here the books breathed and pulsed like living beings, and some had already begun to write themselves, but had been stopped, dramatically. That is why it had left the room and gone back to the main library to find out what was going on. That is when it discovered that The Master was missing. The Librarian flicked from book to book in here looking for an answer, until it came across the first one. Was this the first book ever written? All but the first few lines were erased, and a new line was writing itself. Let there be light.

*   *   *   *   *

He opened his eyes to find himself in a strange room filled with books. He was sat at a chair, in front of a desk with a pen in his hand. Opposite him stood what he could only guess to be a librarian.
"Where am I?"
The Librarian smiled as though greeting a long lost friend, "you are in your library, with all of your books."

He nodded, still unsure of what that actually meant. Books, thousands of them lined shelves all around him, stretching in all directions as far as he could see. They all looked the same to him, all of them dressed in uniform grey, with no writing and no symbols.

"If this is my library and these are my books then where is the writing?"

To this the Librarian shrugged, "I don't know the answer to that question, only you do, and you must find it."

He nodded, that made sense, sort of. But what was the use of having a librarian if it did not know where anything was? The Librarian bowed it's head, as though in shame. He nodded his head, it was OK, he was sure that a librarian had some use in here for something. There was a question that needed to be answered first of all though, before he could tackle anything else. "Who am I?"

The Librarian shook it's head and looked up at his face with the sadness of a hundred lives in its eyes.

"That I don't know."

He sighed, "In that case how can you help me?"

The Librarian gestured towards an open door at the other end of the library, "I can show you where to begin, and we can look for answers together there."

He smiled; at least this was a start.

*   *   *   *   *

The fairground was as dark as the rest of Seahaven despite the pretense of brightly coloured lights and music. Gregory did not go through the main gates to the common, which were presided over by the five Crow Boys, but instead circled around it and in through the woods on the other side. There was no sense in announcing himself, and the least contact he had with Victor Midnight the better as far as he was concerned. All he could think about was Her face and Her gentle touch. He would find her and they would escape this place together. He was not going to let the Midnight Man get his claws into her.

The fairground was as full as ever, the people here did not seem to be dismayed by the darkness that had descended over Seahaven and had been present for days. They did not seem to care about much at all, like the people he had come across in the town centre. Nobody seemed to notice him. They were all too busy indulging themselves in whatever crossed their minds at any given moment. It was as though the music blanked out any moral memory, and the closer they got to it and the louder it became the more of this memory it seemed to wipe out. He could feel its pull himself, but resisted. What was the point in resisting? Who cared who did what to whom? Or why? Or when? Or how? Why shouldn't he just join in? The wolf would growl inside and he would snap to attention again. There were two of them fighting this in one body, so he was stronger than most. The wolf, it seemed, was trying to help him here. Like him, it too did not like being manipulated or controlled. Wild animals should not be tamed. Gregory could not agree more.

She, however, was nowhere to be seen, at least not yet. The wolf was stronger up here, it wanted to take over and sniff her out. Gregory struggled to keep it back. He could feel the other things that it wanted to do as well; he could feel its hunger. He could not let it loose, never again. It did not matter what the people around him did or how they behaved, none of them deserved that. The wolf could never be free again. It growled its displeasure inside, so Gregory told it to keep quiet. It retreated into the background. Where was she? Gregory stopped in his tracks and looked around him. Why had he decided to come straight up here to look for her? It was too late to answer that. He circled around and watched the crowds carefully. The five Crow Boys stared back at him, surrounding him in the crowd, watching him. He growled and they smiled back. Perhaps it was time to let loose the wolf. The wolf silently agreed.

"Now now boys, don't get too close or he will rip you apart, like he did all those other innocents."

The voice was unmistakable, like warm summer rain, behind him. Gregory turned around slowly, keeping the wolf in step, straining at the leash.

"Welcome back Gregory, nice to see you again."

Victor midnight stood in front of him now, towering over, and Gregory felt suddenly small again. The Midnight Man placed a hand upon his shoulder in a cold and heartless gesture of friendship.

"We'd better have a chat."

Gregory wept inside; he could feel himself crumbling under the

254

pressure of this hand. He could feel the Wolf getting stronger inside. The wolf would resist though wouldn't it? It loved her too didn't it? Victor Midnight's smile threatened to swallow him whole, he had no choice.

*   *   *   *   *

This is the way it was. He was alive and that is all that mattered. Large sections of the library had been destroyed, or erased and he did not know how, neither did the librarian. The section referring to his past was completely gone. There was no name, no address, nothing that he had actually done. The other information, which he had gathered in a life that he could not recall, was all in here, in this library somewhere. The problem was that all of the books which contained the information were now untitled. Someone or something had been in here and erased all of the titles, the filing system and anything else that could be erased. The only area that remained untouched was the anti room at the back of the library. In here the books were alive, and it was in here that The Librarian had been hidden whilst all of this had happened. It was thanks to this that he could know any of this at all. If the Librarian had been in the main library when all of this had happened who knows what the outcome would have been? At least now he could wake up and try to piece things together.

He opened his eyes and sat up in bed. This must be a hospital, at least that much he could remember, so things could not be that bad. Perhaps then it was just things about himself which had been erased, and not necessarily everything he knew. He counted to five in his head. That was possible, so he had not forgotten everything. He stood up and stretched his arms and legs, feet cold on the hospital tiles. The chart at the end of his bed was in the name Martin Phillips. That must be him.

Martin peeped around the door to his room into the corridor beyond. It was time to find some clothes and get out of here, wherever here was.

Martin ordered The Librarian to search out some information from the Anti room at the back of the library while he decided what to do. He did not know where to begin, but had to get out of here in order to begin. Unfortunately the chart did not have an address on it, just his name and a date of birth, along with some other medical records. The date of birth had another meaning. He vaguely recalled something to do with age. The Librarian returned promptly with what he wanted. Martin blinked and was gone, leaving the hospital room empty.

*   *   *   *   *

This could not be true. He was sure that she loved him. The way she had looked at him, her soothing voice, the touch of her hand. Gregory cried and the wolf within growled. She had left Seahaven. Sneaked away in the night after deceiving him. No that could not be true.

"Yes, she has made a fool of you Gregory, just like all of the others."

No she had not. There must be a reason why she left. He would go after her and find her, see if this was true.

The Midnight Man smiled and looked into his eyes, letting the fire of his own lick clean the wounds in Gregory's heart. "Let her go Gregory, it's just you and the wolf now."

Gregory could feel the wolf within, pacing back and forth. It was upset, it was enraged by what she had done. It too had loved her and had let her live, but she had made a fool of them both and she would pay, along with everyone else who was laughing at him. It was also very hungry.

"No." Gregory said, the wolf had to remain inside.

"I don't have to listen to you. The wolf stays with me, in here,", he patted his chest, "and I choose when or whether to let it out, nobody else."

He looked Victor Midnight straight back in the eyes, the power of the wolf and himself in one gaze. Victor Midnight scowled back, anger rising in his voice now,

"How dare you speak to me, the one who set you free like this." Gregory felt his own gaze wither under the onslaught of Victor Midnight's stare. His eyes seemed filled with the stuff of galaxies, swimming and brimming over into the material world, and where this cosmic stuff touched the world it burned, leaving it scarred with stellar fire.

"You do what you are told you ungrateful little bastard. Now let the wolf loose and hunt her down. And when you find her I want you to kill her and the bitch she is running with. Kill them both!

"

Gregory felt the world receding. He heard his own cry in the distance and felt his own tears warm on his cheek. The wolf rushed past him, and then the world was swallowed in a howl of wild rage.

XIII. The Legacy of Agrippa

Enough is enough. They had eaten their pie as they had been forced to all those years ago. They had taken this curse and had lived with it, but surely this was enough? Surely everyone else was not to pay for their stupidity and impropriety. There was wrong and there was wrong, and this was really wrong, of that they were all agreed. But how to get rid of the demon, that was the problem. They could not just go and leave it; it had to be taken from them, willingly. There was no way they could just simply pass it on to someone else, and who in their right mind would take it freely as they had done all those generations ago. For generation after generation they had been stuck with this curse and never questioned the reason, but now after their forefathers sins had been all but forgotten in the mist of time why should they continue to pay so dearly? The only way, they were all agreed was to trick these people into taking him away from them. Then so be it, they would make it so.

* * * * *

It was dark outside the hospital. Martin did not have a watch so there was no telling what the time was, but it must be late because it was so dark. He ruffled his knotted hair with one hand and looked up and down the driveway. Which way now? The Librarian did not know, it had never really given much thought to such things. The mundane things like name and address and directions to the supermarket had always been left up to Martin. It could not do everything. Martin sighed. Any way was better than none, so he set off to the right and out of the rear exit. This way fewer people would see him, which was probably a good thing. He was still trying to figure out how he had got here. That had been wiped out along with all of the other personal memories. The strangest thing was that he could remember other complex things, like physics equations, mathematical solutions, and the ingredients needed for a temporal distortion, but he could not actually remember his own name. For all he knew Martin Phillips could be someone else. He could have been in the wrong bed, or the nurses could have forgotten to remove an earlier patients chart from his bed. For now this was all he had to go on. His name was Martin Phillips and he was eighteen years old. He felt older than eighteen. The clothes he had found were not an exact fit either, some blue overalls and a pair of tennis shoes that had been folded up in a cupboard along with some cleaning products. He would have to get changed somehow, or people would begin to ask questions. He did not know how, but he knew nevertheless that these were not the sort of clothing he should be wearing walking about in the street. He also knew that he needed some money. That was going to be a problem. The Librarian did not seem to think so. Martin had to try to calm it down on occasions, but he got the gist. The Librarian was enthusiastic about something. It was enthusiasm about all of the new things that Martin now had access to and now knew. Getting money would not be a problem he was informed, they would just take it. Martin was not too sure about this. They would just borrow it then. That was better. He still, however, could not see the point of all of this when he did not even know his own name.

*   *   *   *   *

Many towns and many places, all of them lost. Menes had stood on the edge of nothing and dared the world to be born, and so too Martin now stood. Only this place was no longer nowhere. A path had been trodden by those who went before him. King Menes, Imhotep, Great Rameses, Leonardo DaVinci, to name but a few. All of this he knew, and the path had been charted by the greatest adventurer Cornelius Agrippa He had charted the seas of human existence and the expanses of the mind, and by his writings Martin had come here to this place. Were they all one person? Of this he was uncertain, but was certain in the knowledge that at least they had become one, just as he now joined them in the Web of Cornelius. The web of symbols that made up the path, and showed them all the way forward. This was the path, which Martin had taken, and in deciphering the web he had written in his own strand, for others to follow. Follow to where? This he did not know either. He doubted if any of them had. Which among them was still alive? He was uncertain, although it was possible that it be all or none. The one thing of which he was sure was that it was his path now, and he had to walk it. He was the new torchbearer, and he was the way. There were no others, or he would know of them. There were others though were there not? Yes. The woman who was not human. He had met her. Where? He did not know. When? What difference did it make, time was irrelevant to her, but not to him. He had the knowledge, but not the form. He knew what he had to know, and who to search for, what to look for, when to look, but he did not have what they had, his predecessors. If Agrippa was still alive after all of these centuries then he had to find him. Of all of the many who had walked this earth only a handful were no longer. They had met their prize on dark street corners or at the hand of raging wars. Rameses, Menes, gone. But the others? They were out there somewhere. This brought him back to the woman. Sylvia, but that was not her real name. Greek. She had saved him somehow, written something, made a correction. There was no way of telling exactly what she had done, but the whole library had been cross referenced because of her. She had re routed all of the references into the anteroom, where books lived and wrote themselves. So he would regain most of his memory in time. Only the trivial matters would remain lost, like his name and address, his date of birth. He would just choose a new name if he had to, and what was the use of an address if he was to travel the world? Why did he need a date of birth if he was searching for immortality? Sylvia Cruz. It was not a real name, but it was a start. He would have to find her again. She was the only one he had actually seen, although she was not written into the web. How many more of them were there then? Martin walked until he reached a junction in the road and his feet hurt. A sign ahead of him gave him two choices. Brook was seven miles to the left, Seahaven was three miles to the right. He turned right, following the road, and continued his thoughts.

*   *   *   *   *

Fire and blood is all he knew. The rage within was out. Gregory, dragged along by the force that was his own anger could only watch. He fought for control, but never gained more than a whimper. The beast was rampant and it wanted blood. Gregory withdrew from the world, not wanting any part of what was happening now. These poor people. They pleaded and ran, but the hunger had raged to the surface and it would never be satisfied. In all the lakes of blood and mountains of flesh there could never be enough to quell the raw anger that he now felt. Somewhere deep inside of him the anger and the revenge felt good. It was there in the shadows, and as he watched the carnage fall before him he could not help but feel a fraction of the beast's thrill. In the blackest part of his heart he wanted to burn the world to the ground for what she had done. But he would never harm her. So the others would pay. The Wolf tore and ripped at all within its reach. It growled, punctured and snarled, rending flesh from flesh in the momentum of it's hunger, only the scream of animal fear and the roar of blood to drive it on and on into a night without end.

*   *   *   *   *

This took the biscuit. Now they had to respond and do something. Who would be the one to go up there? P.C. McRae sat with his head in his hands. Shoplifting, burglary and indecent behaviour were one thing, but this was another. There was some kind of wild animal loose on the common, in the fairground and it was tearing people up left right and centre. Someone would have to go up there and look into it. He looked around him at the others in the station house. Nobody wanted to go, but someone had to. P.C. Markson had turned a pale shade of green. He was a family man, had two small children. There was no way he was going up there to deal with some wild animal escaped from a zoo somewhere. P.C. McRae picked up his helmet and car keys, hands quaking. He would have to go himself.

*   *   *   *   *

Martin rounded one of many corners in the road he had been following and came face to face with a problem. Ahead of him, about a hundred yards or so up the road towards Seahaven, two police cars and a makeshift barrier blocked the road. He was not sure what they were there for, but was somehow certain that they were not going to just let him walk past them. Whatever the reason they were there to stop people from passing.

He stopped in the road to consider this for a moment. They may not have seen him yet as it was dark and the overalls he was wearing were of dark blue. He could get around them through the trees, if he was quiet.

He would have to be very quiet. A. He could hear them. He understood what they were saying. Yes, someone had been in there, they had told the trees to watch. The trees quick survey of the trees in the woods at the side of the road told him that this would be very difficult. Someone had been in there. Someone had set traps. The trees bent over and whispered to each other, looking for another victim, but Martin could hear them watching now and waiting. Not for Martin, no, but they would see him and they would inform this someone that there was a trespasser among them nevertheless. So that was out of the question. He would have to walk straight past the police and hope they did not stop him and question him. If they asked him anything other than his name he would be stuck.

Martin walked on.

Fifty yards from the cars now and two of the three police officers stepped out of their cars to meet him. They stood their ground in front of the cars, whilst a third remained on the radio. Martin breathed deeply, here we go.

Twenty yards from the cars now and one of the officers had stepped forward slightly, in a moment they would be face to face.

"Can I help you s........" Martin waved him away, blowing into his face. The officer stopped in mid sentence and dropped to the floor, sleeping like a baby. The other three became immediately agitated, so Martin dismissed the first one in the same manner. The two remaining had now got out of their cars, one of them shouting at his radio handset for backup. They both drew truncheons, but it was too late. Martin had already gone. By the time Officer Peterson realised that he had just broken his colleagues collarbone, both of them being temporarily blind, Martin was already past them and fifty yards down the road towards Seahaven. Behind him he could hear the screaming and shouting of two panic stricken officers of the law. He smiled casually to himself and wondered how silly they would both feel when the blindness wore off in an hour or so.

* * * * *

Ezekiel turned around for the seventy eighth time and sat down again in an effort to get comfortable. This box he had been squashed into was far too small for a cat his size, and there were not enough air holes. It was getting very stuffy in here. He would have some plain words with Sylvia when he got out of here. The whole affair was most undignified. Underneath him he could feel a rumbling so knew that they were on the move. This was one aspect of the journey so far which had actually got better. The noise had been so great and the rattling so furious at

266

the beginning that he thought his eardrums would burst and they would all be shaken into small pieces. Then suddenly the rattling and rumbling had ceased, as though they had been lifted off the floor and were sailing on air. The droning noise, however, continued. He had been in a car before, of course, and a train, but this was neither. He had also, come to think of it, not appreciated the popping sensation in his ears. Most nasty. Ezekiel could not sleep so decided to give himself a bath, which was perhaps a little overdue. Maybe that was the reason he had to travel in this box. From what he could tell he had also been put in a room with other animals. This was most degrading for a cat of his standing. There was even, judging by the dreadful aroma, a dog of all things in here somewhere. Ezekiel tried to remain calm. There was little or no point in getting annoyed at this juncture. Soon enough he would find out what this was all about and where they were going.

* * * * *

"What do you mean he isn't there any more?" Martin's mother shouted down the telephone. He just was not there any more. He had got up, out of bed in a critical condition, and left the hospital. He was supposed to be in a coma.
"I thought you were supposed to tell us as soon as there was any sign of him waking up." Yes, they were, but one moment he had been in a comatose state, and the next he was gone.
"What kind of hospital security do you run there?" It was a

rhetorical question. Mrs. Phillips slammed the telephone down, hands trembling. Her son had awoken from a coma and as far as she knew he could be walking the streets. She stormed out of the lounge into the hallway and snatched her coat from the coat stand in the corner. Roadblock or no roadblock she was going to make sure her son was all right.

*　*　*　*　*

Rage pressed forwards through the trees, snapping wooden limbs as it went. It hurtled onwards away from the town common, and away from the panicked crowds, into and through the trees beyond. It ran, to get away from the smell of death and the rush of blood. It ran because Victor Midnight told it to run. Inside Gregory only heard distant cries and a blur of guilt. This was another world and he was only dreaming. Trees swayed to the side and branches snapped to let it past. Smaller animals hid in primeval fear, and tried to hide this fear, lest the beast would smell them and seek them out. The beast however was not on a mission of hunger. It did not care for the taste of smaller prey, and so passed them in their shelters without a second thought. The beast was on a mission of destruction. It was humans who were the prey, one in particular. This was a mission of hatred and revenge. If she was here it would find her and it would eat her. It would not just simply kill this time, it would eat her so that nobody else could have her or look at her when it had finished with her. Ahead the trees were giving way to tarmac. A road. The beast sped forward towards the road and the cover of trees on the other side, undergrowth and dead wood cracking under foot, spraying into the air behind it as it ran. Two men, both shouting. They clung to each other as though they had not noticed the beast coming upon them, as though they could not hear the approach of death. Past them now quickly, snapping both of them like the branches of a tree, the beast was over the road and into the trees on the other side, with silence behind and darkness in front.

* * * * *

When P.C. Doolitle awoke the first thing he did was to reach for his truncheon. The road was silent, too late. He kicked P.C. Rogerson, who had been lying next to him on the tarmac, snoring. P.C. Rogerson woke with a start, almost choking on his own saliva. He coughed and spluttered, sitting up and rubbing the back of his head. What the hell had happened then? Doolitle was looking at him with a puzzled expression on his own face.

"Are you OK?" He nodded,

"I think so, you?"

Rogerson nodded. They both stood up. One of the cars was in a bad state. The windscreen and headlights had been smashed, and the bonnet dented as though someone had been jumping up and down on it. Peterson was sat, leaning up against the wheel, asleep. Doolitle walked over and shook him by the shoulders to

269

wake him up but did not have much luck. Behind him he could hear the spatter of liquid on tarmac as Rogerson started vomiting.

"What now?"

Rogerson could not speak as his jaw was involuntarily locked open and his last meal was making its way back up, but Doolitle soon discovered the cause. Peterson's head lolled to one side unnaturally, like an old rag doll in drastic need of re sewing. The weight of his head was threatening to pull itself away from his shoulders. P.C. Doolitle also realised that the head was on the wrong way around, it had been turned one hundred and eighty degrees. He let go of the shoulders and the body sagged to the tarmac, it's head landing with a sickening crack. He felt a little queasy himself now and turned around to see if P.C. Rogerson was OK He was not OK, and Doolitle could see why.

The person who had been Police Constable Blackstone was laid out spread eagle on the tarmac in front of both cars. His eyes were open, as was his mouth, which was spread wide across his face. He had been cut wide open from his lower abdomen up to his chin by what looked like several attempts with a butcher's knife, and his rib cage had been separated and partially lifted out of his chest in the process. Blood had started to coagulate in the hollow that the wound had left, forming a pool of deep red, almost black, some of which had overflown onto the tarmac in a star shaped puddle. He looked awful. P.C. Doolitle reached in through the broken window of the nearest car and grabbed the radio mike. He drew breath first, trying to calm himself down

270

and then called for some assistance. It looked like they had both just had a very narrow escape with the Seahaven Slasher, and Doolitle knew what he looked like.

*　*　*　*　*

As Martin marched on the buildings of Seahaven loomed closer and closer. The road wound off to the left, and along the cliff tops towards a lonely house, or straight on in a more direct path towards the glittering town below. Martin paused for a moment and looked in both directions. The house looked foreboding out there on it's own, set above the rest, and a cemetery along the path towards it made it even more so. He could just make out a pair of huge iron gates, each with a gargoyle or other figure perched on the top, barring the way into a private drive, and could see the spire of a large house behind. There was something decidedly strange about this house. He was sure that it had no shadow, as though it should not be there, but it was dark so wasn't that a silly notion? Nothing threw a shadow in the dark. That is true, but he could tell that this place would have no shadow even in bright sunlight. Martin shook his head and carried on straight down the road towards Seahaven. The night air was getting to him and making his imagination run wild. It was just a house that is all. It was a very old and creepy house, but it was just a house nevertheless.

The town could only be a mile or so from here, so it would not take him very long to get there. And then? Martin did not know

271

quite what, but he was sure that it would come to him when he got there. He had to get a car or something so he could get out of here and go somewhere. Where? This he did not know either. He did not even know if he could drive yet, but there was one sure way of finding out. He would have to change his clothes as well, as he was sure that the dark blue overalls he was wearing were not the normal attire for wearing around town. Martin fished a leaflet out of his pocket. It was a curious thing to have. Package holidays to Egypt. Perhaps then that is where he would go next, after he had found a change of clothes. The first set of houses were not far away now so he picked up his pace slightly. There was a garage on the other side of the town, in a street to the left. He could just make out because of the height advantage up here that they sold cars, or it certainly looked like that. They had a forecourt with about twenty or so cars on it anyway, all of different types. That would be his next port of call after getting some clothes sorted out. He would see if he could borrow or buy a car there and make his way out of town again. He would need a map, that was a good idea. Martin started to formulate a shopping list in his head as he walked. A change of clothes, and possibly some spares, a map, a car, some food for the journey. He would also stop off at a hardware store somewhere to see if there was anything else which would be useful. He did not have any money, but the Librarian kept insisting that this was not a problem.

* * * * *

Within ten minutes an ambulance had arrived and picked up the two dismembered policemen off the tarmac, and the Seahaven police had been told that an armed response unit was on it's way from Manchester which would be with them in less than two hours. This was an emergency; the killer was to be considered armed and very dangerous. They should not approach him, and if he was seen he should be followed only. They were to wait for the armed response as back up. P.C. Doolitle nodded and switched off the radio. Another car had joined them since he had asked for assistance, but the two officers were reluctant to get involved any more than necessary. P.C. Doolitle himself had organised most of the cleaning up, whilst they stood by turning green. He was glad that he had served three years with the traffic division before this. He had seen worse, but not much worse. Once the bodies had been taken away there was not much more for him to do there, so he left the other two officers to man the road block and volunteered to take P.C. Rogerson back into town. There was no way he wanted to be here in the way if that mad kid decided to turn around and leave town again by the same way he had gone in. At least they had him contained now, and with the armed response unit on it's way they were likely to be able to corner him somewhere and put a stop to this. If he had his way they would corner him and kill him, never mind arresting him. With P.C. Rogerson in the car Doolitle was all set to climb into the drivers side when he spotted another car heading towards them at speed, away from Seahaven. The two officers behind stepped out of their car, one of them calling out over a loud speaker they had set up.

"Stop your vehicle."

The driver did not want to stop.

"Stop at once, this is a police check point."

Doolitle watched, unsure of whether to just get out of the way or not. The vehicle began to slow, and finally stopped about five feet short of the three police cars. Doolitle walked over carefully, but there was no need. The driver was Mrs. Phillips. This was an interesting turn out. She looked in fear of her life. Her eyes swiveled in their sockets, darting about wildly.

"I just want to see my son." She said feverishly.

Doolitle nodded, "So do we Mrs. Phillips. Would you mind stepping out of the car?" He reached in and pulled the keys away from the ignition and stepped back.

Mrs. Phillips opened the car door and stepped out.

"What is all of this, I'm not the person you are looking for. I just want to see my son in hospital."

Doolittle shot P.C. Robinson a glance. Robinson was staring at her; the mixture of emotions inside had combined to turn his visage a murky brown.

"We would like very much to talk to your son too Mrs. Phillips. Would you mind accompanying us to the station to help us with our enquiries?"

* * * * *

The Librarian had said that money would not be a problem and it had been correct. Martin had walked into the first clothes shop he had come across to find it deserted. Shirts and jackets hung in racks in the middle of the shop, men's on one side and women's on the other. Jeans and trousers had been neatly stacked in their sizes on shelves at the side of the shop, again with men's on one side and women's on the other. There was, however nobody in the place. Martin waited for five minutes to see if anyone would come out, but nobody appeared so he started to try things on. Eventually, within about fifteen minutes he had found a couple of pairs of jeans that fit, four shirts, two jumpers and a suede jacket. He waited at the till, and still nobody came to collect any money from him, so he helped himself. As a last thought he checked the till as well. It had not been emptied, so he took what was there. He felt that after all he needed it more than the owner of the shop ever would. There was also a small selection of sports bags, so he took one of those and put the spare clothes in it, then stepped through the broken glass of the shop's door and out into the street. He was certain now that this was not normal behaviour. It could not be, it did not make sense. He looked around him. Everyone else seemed to be doing it though, so why not. It must in that case be normal for this place. It still seemed inherently wrong, but who was he to question local customs. Martin walked up the street. At least now he had some clothes and some money. All he needed was transport. How would he get to Egypt? By airplane of course. And how would he get on one of those?

He peered up and down the street at the fighting crowds of people. They did not seem to care who saw them or what they did. Martin felt that something was terribly wrong here. He could feel eyes all around, but none of the people here were watching him, they were all too wrapped up in what they were doing. Who was watching then?

*   *   *   *   *

Gregory could hear Victor Midnight's shouts but was paying no attention, or rather the wolf was paying no attention. Victor Midnight had been calling him for the last fifteen minutes, demanding that he come back to the common. He was heading the wrong way, he must turn around. Gregory was beyond caring. The wolf had taken over now and was on the run somewhere, Gregory did not care where, as long as it was away from this place. Victor Midnight continued to call in his head, angry now. It was not that the wolf was not listening, that was not the case. The wolf was just as alert to this voice as Gregory was, but unfortunately the wolf did not understand. It did not speak English. Gregory was the only person it could understand and Gregory did not feel like talking at the moment. He did not feel much at all. The world was becoming increasingly dim and murky, disappearing into the mist. Gregory was glad. He was glad to be rid of a world that had given him nothing but pain and false hope. What could Victor Midnight or this world have to offer now anyway? Why should he turn around?

276

Because I know where she is.

Gregory asked the wolf to slow down and explained why. The wolf slowed to a stop, and grunted. This had better be true. The Midnight Man better not be lying, or he would wish that he was in hell rather than face what the wolf would do to him.

If she was not here by the time they got back then the boy called Martin would be able to lead them to her.

Gregory relayed the message and retreated as the wolf growled its approval. They were going to find her at last, then the pain would end.

The wolf turned around and headed, at speed, back to the town of Seahaven.

*   *   *   *   *

P.C. McRae did not have much choice. The town's people on the common had formed a lynch mob and were calling for Victor Midnight's blood. A rumour had circulated, which he knew to be untrue that the Seahaven Slasher was Victor Midnight. P.C. McRae knew this to be untrue because a description of the Slasher had been released which matched that of the Phillips boy. Martin Phillips had already been identified by a survivor of one of his attacks. There was no choice here though. He had to arrest Victor Midnight, or take him to the station for his own protection. These people were going to kill him. Several of the Gypsies had stood forward and told him that they would act as witnesses in court, and were willing to give statements, which in itself was unusual as these people usually looked after their own affairs. If this was true, then he would have expected to find Victor Midnight dead in a ditch somewhere at the side of the road, and the other Gypsies claiming that he had gone missing or been killed in a motor accident. Why did they all of a sudden want to get the police involved in their affairs? There was also the dog thing. People were claiming that Victor Midnight had set a killer dog on them, which had since run off in the woods. True there were at least seven people dead here, and eighteen or more had serious injuries. They were claiming that anything from a wild wolf to a bear had attacked them. Mr. Midnight, despite all of the injuries that surrounded them here, did not have a spot of blood on him. He could not have done this. The dead had been covered and removed from the scene, and the injured and shocked were being taken away by ambulance staff. P.C. McRae was entirely at a loss in all of this. He had no option but to place Victor Midnight in protective custody, which was something he had never had to do before. The crowd was becoming increasingly menacing, and the remaining Gypsies seemed to be taunting them and stirring them up. If he was going to do it he would have to do it quickly. Victor Midnight had remained silent throughout. He had cast a few knowing glances at the Gypsies who he had travelled with, but only smiled at them as though to say farewell. When P.C. McRae questioned him at all he had been very courteous, but always with that glint in his eye. The glint of fire in his eyes said that he was not telling the truth, and that P.C. McRae would have to arrest him to get any sense

278

out of him. The glint in his eye told P.C. McRae that he knew he had to be taken to the station and protected, whether the rumours and stories of what he had done were true or not.

Finally he made his choice.

"Mr. Midnight, I would advise you that it is in your own interest to come into police custody for your own protection." He gestured around him at the swelling crowd with their swelling capacity for violent retribution.

"Will you come with us to the station please sir?"

Mr. Midnight smiled as warm a smile as anyone on this earth has ever managed. This was just what he had wanted to hear. The policeman, an agent of the town of Seahaven, was inviting him, voluntarily, to go with them. He cast a farewell glance at the chief elder of the Gypsies he had been with for so long, but the elder looked away, as did all of the others.

Then he replied, his voice soft as silk, warm as blood,

"Yes officer, I would love to join you, if you would take me freely of your own free will."

P.C. McRae thought this an odd answer but nodded nevertheless, and opened the car door for Victor Midnight to get in.

*　　*　　*　　*　　*

By the time the armed response unit arrived in Seahaven the crowds of angry people had already begun to disperse, with no one left at which to direct their anger they had gone silently home, or walked the streets in smaller bands, seeking out victims upon which to vent their frustrations. Victor Midnight had been taken into protective custody and Mrs. Phillips was being held in the next cell for questioning. Despite repeated attempts to ask for a lawyer she was told that she was not under arrest so did not need one and the police station did not have to provide one. They would not allow her to telephone for one, or for her husband because the telephone lines were down. They wanted to know if she knew the whereabouts of her son, who they wanted to question about the recent murders on Seahaven Common and the surrounding woods.

On their arrival the armed police set up new armed roadblocks and dispersed their own officers throughout the town centre. With the appearance of the first armed officer looting subsided and the angry bands of vigilantes dispersed into angry and frustrated individuals. Within an hour of their arrival Seahaven was quiet once again.

The Gypsies had already packed up and left. They had seen enough, it seemed, of Seahaven, turned away and not looked back. The summer had gone for them now and it was best to leave behind everything that it had brought with it. The Common now stood empty and silent except for the lonely Carousel in its centre. The wood crackled and spat under flames that the Gypsies had set before their departure, not wishing to take this ancient machinery with them and not wishing to leave it behind.

If a person were to listen carefully, and very quietly they could hear the screaming of animals. They pierced the sky with a razor

280

tone, driving nails at the heart of anyone who would listen. The screaming of a hundred thousand children trampled under foot, or graveyards full of people not wanting to be dead, and they would not stop even through the rain and the howling wind until your blood had curdled in your veins and a tear had leaped to your eye. As the wood burned and paint melted the wooden animals around the carousel's centre seemed to buck and writhe. This was more than the warping of wood. Five crow-boys watched from the edge of the common as their plaything collapsed in on itself and was consumed by the pillar of black smoke at its centre. The time was midnight and once again all stood still, just for that moment, except for the carousel. Heat from the fire, coupled with the cold wind was causing it to turn slowly on its axis; it's macabre zoo parading before them one more time. The animals squealed and spat, reared and bucked against the flames but could not escape their iron bolts. Finally the screaming of burning wood ceased and the carousel slowed once again to a stop. The flames tired now, died down to rest and the black smoke took the spirits of those painted animals away to wherever they would go. Smoke coiled high into the clouds above, dispersing into the heavens and spreading across the sky until all that remained below was a broken and charred wheel.

14. Midnight revisited.

The next morning it was still dark.

The officers of the Manchester Armed Response Unit were beginning to feel uneasy. Things had not been so bad last night; it had been the usual riot gear with armed back up. They had seen and done it a hundred times before. But this morning was different. The sky was not supposed to be pitch black at half past eight in the morning. The crowds were starting to gather again, this time looking for anyone who would get in their way. This was senseless. There was no reason for their behaviour here. They had forgotten about Victor Midnight and the escaped wild beast and the Seahaven Slasher. They had forgotten any reasons why they should be here at all. They were here to loot, and intimidate, they had now gathered for the sake of gathering. Deprived of television and radio, which were now somehow jammed they had turned in on themselves for entertainment. Sergeant Lip trot of the Manchester Metropolitan police had never experienced anything like this in his life. The sky was black; all communications had been cut off with the world outside of Seahaven, including radio, telephone and now the postal service. Seahaven had been effectively divorced from the rest of the British Isles. Nobody was to be allowed in or out of the town limits, and anyone attempting to enter or leave should be stopped with reasonable and necessary force. That reasonable and necessary force consisted of two armed police marksmen manning road blocks on each of the three roads out of the town, and several marksmen placed strategically around the town centre itself. Sergeant Liptrot was under the impression that this was army business and not for the police to handle. With a nine o'clock curfew to come into effect from today the place was in all but name under martial law. From his vantage point in the town square he could see several buildings on fire at the edge of town. Brown and grey smoke clawed it's way skywards, and flames licked above the roof tops every now and then, to taste the air above and try for a hold on buildings across the street. This was madness.

At the far end of high street a larger crowd was gathering by the minute. They had loitered at first, unsure of themselves, but now were beginning to advance. He did not know how many of them were in the crowd, but he did not think that many people actually lived in Seahaven. The crowd continued its advance, cricket bats, chair legs, iron posts, bottles, anything they could grab to hand. Young and old, male and female, most had joined the advancing crowd now. Sergeant Liptrot gave the signal to his men, who formed two lines, one behind the other. This they were trained for at least. He ordered the tear gas at the ready.

*   *   *   *   *

"Sylvia, what are you doing?"

"Nothing."

Hannah frowned and tried to grab the hand mirror off her to take a look.

Sylvia struggled with her for a moment, almost upsetting the food tray in front of her. She let go and Hannah took the looking glass away from her. She was right.

"I would not call this nothing."

Sylvia shrugged,

"I was just curious that's all, I wanted to see what was happening."

Hannah grinned, "You'll never learn will you."

Sylvia shook her head, letting a strand of black mixed with grey hair fall over her left eye. "No." She grinned back, then chuckled, "And you wouldn't have me any other way."

Hannah peered into the hand mirror at the scene contained within. She could see crowds of people fighting and a police station in the background.

"How do you do that?"

Sylvia took the mirror back gently, "I'll show you one day."

The plane lurched slightly and she grabbed hold of her gin and tonic, to stop it sliding off the tray. "How much longer have we got to go?"

Hannah looked at her watch, "About three hours I think."

Sylvia sighed and looked out of the window. All she could see were clouds. It was much nicer to travel by boat. Hannah peered over her shoulder, then down at the hand mirror again. The scene had gone; all she could see was Sylvia's shoulder and the side of her face. It looked strange from this angle.

"So what were you looking for when I interrupted you then?"

Sylvia turned back to her, away from the window. "I was just looking that's all."

"What for?"

"I hope that Ezekiel is all right down in the hold. Do you think he'll be all right?"

Hannah frowned, and wondered how someone could be so down right stubborn.

"OK, when?"

Sylvia's brow creased slightly, her mouth twitched up at one side, bringing out laughter lines. "When what?"

Hannah smiled at her, looking into her eyes for as long as possible. She could almost forget they were on an airplane surrounded by people, almost.

"When are you going to teach me?"

Sylvia blushed and took hold of her hand, "Soon."

Hannah was not sure, but for the briefest moment she felt that she had caught one of Sylvia's thoughts, the one which had made her blush. No, it must be her imagination, wishful thinking.

*　　*　　*　　*　　*

Clouds of warm vapour rose from within the crowd as tear gas pellets hit their target. The vapour, warm at first spread outwards, like a cloud of dust billowing in the wind, and sought it's way into the mouths and noses of those present. To the unlucky that warm vapour soon became searing hot, burning at them from the inside, threatening to melt their lungs and eyes until the very organs themselves ran in sticky trails down their cheeks and out of their noses and mouths. As the cloud dispersed so did the crowd, blindly seeking shelter from the source of their terror. Panic ensued.

In the midst of that panic Martin stood with one hand over his mouth, watching carefully. Now was his opportunity. Whilst the gas cloud had obscured their vision, coupled with the darkness, it also meant that the police could not see into the crowd either. This was it then. He could see the travel agents three doors down, so ran for it. Martin ran, weaving his way in and out of the melee of wild-eyed people. Twice he ran into someone and pushed past them so as not to be drawn into the throb of adrenaline that permeated the air. He stopped only once, to help a little girl to stand, shielding her from the onrush of trampling feet. She tried to smile, but the gas had gripped her and was forcing tears where light and life had once been. Martin wiped the tears from her eyes and whispered that she would be OK The girl had stared at him for a while with her new eyes, and then had gone, bolting with the rest of the herd, but with the advantage of sight. She looked back over her shoulder once and smiled, then disappeared into the mist. Martin did not see the others watching him. All the while only five others in the crowd

286

had remained calm. Five crows in the shape of boys, spread out among the crowd, feeding them with their malice. They watched him silently. Up ahead Martin could see the travel agent's sign, the neon glowed through the mist and turned the air around it yellow, like a spreading nicotine stain.

The door was shut and locked and the window intact, so he had to smash it to get in. Glass flew inwards and fell dead on the floor, the noise did not escape to the ears of the panicked outside. Martin stepped through the hole he had made into the shop. Inside the air was calm and peaceful. None of the adrenaline that swam in the mist outside had made its way in here. Martin strolled over to the nearest desk and sat behind it, facing a blank computer screen. This was it. He switched on the computer below and waited for the screen to wake up. It did. Images flashed across the screen. Lines of numbers, and a greeting. The box beneath groaned softly in an electronic yawn, until finally a menu appeared on the screen. Martin chose the ticked booking option.

The menu disappeared and was replaced by something that he did not want to see. The computer screen stared back at him blankly, demanding a password. There was to be no negotiation here. It wanted a password and that was that. No say, no play. Martin rapped his fingers on the table and thought furiously. What the hell would the password be? Most people could not even remember telephone numbers, let alone passwords. It had to be written down here somewhere. He closed his eyes and tried to slip into the place of the last person to sit in this chair.

She was going to be glad to be out of here, it had been a hell of a week and this place was becoming weirder by the hour. They had not sold a single holiday for the past two weeks, not even a genuine enquiry. Lipstick in the car, a ford fiesta, and park around the back. Shit, she had forgotten nail polish this morning. Extra lipstick. Brown hair, thinking about going blonde, or auburn, probably easier to go auburn, not as noticeable, subtlety was the key. Getting out of the car, change shoes. Out of slippers and into heels. God they hurt, pinched at the toes and strained the ankles, but all for show. The more leg the more customers. Smile and in we go.

The place is open already, but front doors not unlocked. In the back door, hello to Jasmine, god she looks awful, blonde does not suit her, it would look better on me, and those legs! She should wear longer skirts, or better still trousers. Coffee, wake up girl, into the hall and off with the coat. Hello Jane, be nice the boss is watching, going to win that incentive. Holiday in Brazil, mine, no one else is close, here we go, the desk. Who left their coffee here? Not mine, someone been at my desk, stealing my clients. Switch on, what is that password. Can never remember, in handbag, there in diary, under December 25th, Christmas day, what is it now, oh yes....

Martin punched the six letter word into the keyboard. B-R-A-Z-I-L. For a moment the computer stalled as though it could not quite believe that he had guessed correctly, then, reluctantly it buzzed into action. The demand for a password disappeared and was replaced by another menu. Where did he want to go today?

Martin chose his option and then typed in the word he had been waiting for. Egypt.

* * * * *

The no smoking sign flickered on, followed by the fasten your seat-belt sign and Hannah swallowed the remaining saliva in her mouth. It instantly dried up, leaving her with no comfort what so ever. She hated flying. Why did they have to fly? Couldn't they have got on a boat or gone by train through the channel tunnel or something? And there was another thing.

Hannah leaned over and whispered to Sylvia. "Where did you get your passport from?"

Sylvia looked at her with a mischievous grin all over her face. It was a grin that would have caused any customs official in the world to ask her to empty her bags and strip. "From the passport office, where else?"

Hannah shook her head, "What, with a seven thousand year old birth certificate?"

Sylvia shrugged and waved the question away with one hand nonchalantly, "Well, not quite. I used someone else's."

"What!"

Sylvia looked straight ahead, trying to make this sound like nothing out of the ordinary. "Well the real Sylvia Cruz died when she was two years old, so she is not going to miss it is she? And besides, what am I supposed to do apply for one through the normal channels? Nationality: Manitau, Place of birth:

Ancient Messapotamia, Occupation: Harpy?"

Hannah tried to hide a smirk. This was not funny, they could get in serious trouble here. "What if someone spots it, or finds out?"

Sylvia laughed out loud, "Do you really think that anyone would believe them?"

Hannah supposed not. The plane began its descent so she shut up. Hannah thought about asking Sylvia the best way to stop her ears popping, but thought better of it. Sylvia was sat next to her with one of the largest grins she had ever seen all over her face. Hannah hoped that she would wipe it off when they went through customs at the other end. She did not fancy being strip-searched by an Egyptian official, or anyone else for that matter.

* * * * *

Outside the riot was beginning to subside. The people of Seahaven were not used to the battle strategies of the Metropolitan Police, and it sounded as though they had got everything under control, and were managing to contain the violence to a small area. Sergeant Barnes sat back in his chair and cast his eye over the cells beyond the steel door. He had left the door open, so that he could hear anything untoward. That Midnight character had proved to be very slippery. They had originally taken him into custody for his own safety, but when they had questioned him he had confessed to everything, with a smile on his face. The bastard had actually smiled as though he was admitting to a practical joke. Yes, it was his animal which he had let loose on everyone at the fair, and yes all of the people who had been murdered had either been killed by himself or he had asked people to do it for him. Sergeant Platt scratched his head and rubbed his eyes. The bastard had even told him that he did not regret any of this, and that he would do it all again, and would continue to do it if they did not lock him up. The worst thing of all had been the shock that he had experienced upon entering the room to interview Victor Midnight. Up until then he had not seen the man. He had never been up to the fair, although his children had, which made him shudder at the thought of what could have happened to them. He could smell it before he entered the interview room. This was a smell he had experienced before, a long time ago when he was with the Merseyside CID. He had experienced the same feeling that once when he had stumbled across the humble abode of Michael West, and the bodies he had stored in his numerous chest freezers, and again when he had interviewed Janet Pascalle in a supermarket car park. Sweet Janet had murdered sixteen children and distributed their bodies throughout the whole of the North West, from Carlisle, across to Manchester and down to Chester, via her chain of pet food stores. Sweet seventy two year old Janet. She had been labelled insane, but he knew different. He hoped she would never get out. He hoped she would rot in that hospital until she died, and afterwards as well. But this Victor Midnight, he was all of these together in one bundle of joy, and more. He had been sitting in the centre of the room on a small wooden chair, behind the interview table as Sergeant Platt and P.C.

291

McRae had entered the room. He had looked up at them as they entered and smiled, a scar across his face. He had wished them a good evening. These words, welcoming and polite from any other's lips had twisted as they left his mouth. They had writhed like a snake, full of venom and hatred. The fingers of his left hand had rapped on the table in rhythm, unpolished nails clicking on it's wooden surface, the sound of a dog giving chase. Throughout the whole interview Victor midnight had smiled and had looked at whoever asked him a question without flinching. The man was not sane. He was not human and Sergeant Platt had wanted to smash his face in. After two hours of his detailed accounts of how and when each body was found he was charged with sixteen counts of murder with the possibility of more pending further investigations. He had smiled and told them there would certainly be more.

Now he was safely locked up in the far cell, at the end of the corridor. The light around this cell seemed to be dimmer than the rest, as though he cast one great big dark shadow over everything, everywhere he went. P.C. Forsythe emerged from around the corner with a steaming mug of coffee in hand. The mug had Sergeant Platt's name on it.

"For you sarge. How is he doing in there?"

Sergeant Platt nodded, and reached out to take possession of the coffee. "He seems to be as quiet as ever. He's stopped talking now anyway."

He looked up at Forsythe, "What was he talking to you about?"

Forsythe shook his head. "Nothing much. He was just going on about how it had been right for him to kill all of those people. Sick bastard." Sergeant Platt nodded and lifted the mug to his lips. P.C. Forsythe watched eagerly.

Sergeant Platt twisted his mouth up, upon tasting the contents. "Is this coffee all right? It tastes bitter."

Forsythe watched him closely, a bead of sweat appeared on his brow, which Sergeant Platt thought odd.

"I think it may have gone past it's sell by date sir, I'll get some more tomorrow."

Sergeant Platt nodded, "Yes. Make sure you do." It was warm and wet though, so he took another mouthful. The taste faded after a while, so he took another on. "It's OK when you get used to it."

Forsythe smiled back at him, but was not really smiling.

Sergeant Platt felt strange. His stomach was beginning to ache, and the ache was growing.

What the hell was going on here? The ache had turned into a burn and he fell to the floor, clutching his stomach with both hands, sweat washing over his face as though someone had placed his head under running hot water. "Call an am..." he could not get the words out.

"Amb......bula......" Why was Forsythe just staring at him?

As the room went dark Sergeant Platt still had not managed to say what he had needed, so Forsythe said it for him.

"Ambulance?"

There was no reply.

He reached down and took the keys from the chain around

Sergeant Platt's waist. He was sorry, but the Midnight Man had offered him more than the police or Sergeant Platt could ever offer. In return for a little rat poison in the coffee he had been offered riches beyond his wildest imagination, and the chance to get Sylvia Cruz into bed. All because Mr. Midnight had recognised him from the fairground, when he had taken his boy to the fair. It was the first time Derek Forsythe had ever been recognised by someone as important as Victor Midnight, and Victor Midnight could see the potential within him. Forsythe ran down the corridor towards the cell at the end and placed the correct key in the lock.

"Well done Derek, now the reward shall be yours."

Derek smiled, the reward was going to be his, and it had been so easy.

"All you have to do is to remove Sergeant Platt's head. You will find a saw in the basement, and make me a standard we can be proud of."

Forsythe tilted his head to one side, like a dog listening to it's master, but was puzzled, "A standard?"

"Yes, " Mr. Midnight continued, "Like a flag. You will find a pole in the basement along with the saw."

Forsythe nodded, now he understood, he started off down the corridor, towards the basement door.

"I'll be waiting for you outside."

Forsythe ran down the basement steps. He would not disappoint the Midnight Man, and the reward would be his.

294

That had been relatively easy, now for the difficult part. Martin logged out of the computer system and switched it off. The ticket would be waiting for him at the airport. He had a connecting flight from Manchester to Paris de Gaul and then on to Cairo via Air France. His flight from Manchester was at half past seven tomorrow evening. The difficulty arose in getting a passport and a visa for entry into Egypt. He did not know where to start. Perhaps he would have to fool his way past customs. In the back of his mind the Librarian was trying to tell him something. There was something about a dead man's eyes. Yes, he could use that one. The liquid inside a dead man's eyes. He could use the liquid to make an ink, which would alter the appearance of a document. He could make his own passport. But first he would have to find the essential ingredients.

Martin looked carefully out of the front window of the shop, to make sure that the coast was clear. It was not. There were police advancing up the street, driving away the remaining people who had tried to reform. He would have to go out of the back door. Martin walked to the back of the shop and down the corridor marked 'Private, Authorised personnel only'.

He passed a kitchen, and finally reached what must be the back door. There would be a small car park beyond this, and freedom. He unbolted the door and kicked it open.

Outside the air was dark and cold, and Martin walked calmly out into the car park. There was nobody else here. Where now was the obvious place to find the ingredients he needed? The local cemetery was no good. Eyes were quick to rot away, and it would take too long to dig up a body, especially if he had to dig up several in order to find a fresh enough corpse. A morgue was better, if there was one. But there was no way of finding out if there was without arousing suspicion.

He could look in yellow pages and let his fingers do the walking. Martin smiled, what an excellent idea. He headed for the nearest telephone box, which he had seen in the Town Square.

Down the side alley and out again into the main street he emerged behind most of the police, who seemed to have driven the remaining rioters back quite a way. The Town Square was to the right, away from them, so he should not have much trouble. He waited for the last of the police to pass the alley, then cautiously crept out and made his way down the street, keeping as far to the side, against shop windows as he could, so as not to be seen. The police and rioters were way behind him now, so he picked up his pace. One then two, then four figures emerged from the darkness ahead of him, then more behind them. Four crows in the shape of boys, leading a hundred or more people. Martin ducked into one of the shops, to let them pass. They had circled around, behind the police and had now cut the main bulk of this riot squad off from their headquarters in the Town Square. The small group seemed to be growing larger as they advanced up the street towards the police at the top. Martin watched as they headed on a collision course. He saw one of the crow boys light a wick of cloth, draping from a bottle and saw

296

the bottle launched high into the air above them. It hurtled in an arc down into the middle of the police in their riot gear. Martin turned his back on the scene and ran towards the Town Square, not caring now. He saw the explosion in shop windows, which lit up the sky briefly, and he felt the heat on his back.

As he ran he passed one, then another police officer sprawled in the road. They had been over powered by the second regrouping. This looked as though it was getting serious. It was no ordinary riot. This was not just a gathering of disgruntled citizens or the protests of the dispossessed, this had the stuff of revolution in it. The Revolution of Seahaven, something for the history books.

As he ran Martin had a thought and stopped. He looked down at the broken and bruised body at his feet. This man no longer needed his eyes did he? Martin looked around him, looking for a reason not to do this. If someone were watching he would just walk on and not do this. Nobody was watching. Up ahead he could see armed police surrounding the police station. They were not looking at him; they were calling for someone inside to surrender themselves. Mutiny by the Seahaven Police force? It would be difficult to get to the telephone boxes now, and as they were not watching Martin thought he had no option. He opened up the silver penknife he had been carrying in his jacket pocket and knelt down in front of the limp body.

*   *   *   *   *

Robert Fitzsimmons knelt on one knee and twisted the wire

connectors the way that Mr. Midnight had told him to do. He did not quite know what plastique was, but had been told that a pound in weight was a lot, and Mr. Midnight knew what he was talking about. It seemed more like cold play dough to him though, only it smelt funny. He kept one eye on the police surrounding the police station next door. They would not see him here, they were far too busy trying to get that mad man out of there. He smiled, as the final connection slid into place. There that was it. Bonfire night. He leaped to his feet and switched on the mobile telephone that hung at his side. The number had been pre set and all he had to do was press the send button. His phone would then call the pager connected to this plastique, and it was bonfire night all over again. He wanted to do it now, only Mr. Midnight had told him to make sure he and his new brothers were far away, on the other side of town when he did. They could go up to the common and watch from there. Robert laughed and ran across the street, back into the shadows.

*   *   *   *   *

Mr. Midnight would be so proud, thought Derek Forsythe. He had done a grand job. His hard work would pay off too, because now he was sure to get his reward. The Midnight Man was going to be so pleased with his work that he would definitely give him the reward he deserved, which was only just after all. The saw and the wooden pole had been in the basement, just as he had said. The pole had been a little too long, but Derek had sawn off one end and made it shorter. He had also found a sharp knife down in the basement, which he had used to whittle one end of the pole to a point. This made the last part of the job easier. Then he had gone back up the stairs to finish the job. Mr. Midnight had already gone, but he had said that he would meet Derek outside hadn't he? Yes he had, so there was nothing to worry about then. Derek would finish the job and would carry the standard outside for Mr. Midnight to see, and they would march triumphantly forward. To what? He did not know. Somehow the plan in his own head had not gone that far, but he was sure that Mr. Midnight would enlighten him as he got outside. Derek had not found the second part of this task very pleasant, but had thought happy thoughts while he sawed. He thought about the money he would have and about what Ms. Cruz would look like naked in his bed, and somewhere in the middle of these thoughts he heard a thud and there was no more to saw. Yes the spike he had made on top of the pole did come in handy; it made the construction of the standard a lot simpler. Derek patted himself on the back for this, what a good idea that had been. Finally with the standard ready he stepped over the headless corpse of Sergeant Platt and walked towards the front desk. Around the front desk and towards the door he could hear Mr. Midnight calling him to come out and show his hand. What did that mean. He must mean show everyone what he had made. The Midnight Man would be so proud now when he saw what a good job Derek had done of making the standard. He would be the standard bearer and they would march up the street, like the

Roman army, towards his prize. The mayor would shake his hand and an envelope would be passed to him. Their pictures in the paper, bright summers day, on the Town Hall steps, and she would be smiling at him from the crowd, just waiting for him to take her now he was so rich and powerful.

Derek smiled so hard, he could barely conceal his excitement. It was a good job he had been to the toilet before he began, or this may get embarrassing. He opened the door wide and picked up the standard. Outside he heard the click and shutter of cameras. They were taking photographs already. Police with rifles had lined up outside. They were going to give him a twenty one gun salute. Derek smiled, but kept his cool. It would not do for a man in his position to betray emotion now. Such a powerful man must behave as though this was normal, and perhaps now it would be. Perhaps now everywhere he went people would give twenty one gun salutes. Derek hoisted the standard high and stepped out onto the front step of the police station. There was a pause as people admired his work, and he told them to take a good look, then the officers sounded their twenty one gun salute.

* * * * *

Martin watched as the reason why the police had surrounded the police station became evident. He could not see who the man was, but could see quite clearly what he was carrying. This had all got way out of hand. Someone's head on a pole, complete with police hat for identification purposes. He stared in disbelief

300

for what seemed like minutes, while the air around grew dense and heavy with silence. Seahaven was a small town, a fishing port. It was not the kind of place where people rioted and cut policemen's heads off and jammed them on the end of poles. That stuff belonged in the dark ages. It was the stuff of tales about Vlad the Impaler or Genghis Khan. The armed police brought the man down, shattering the silence with gunfire. Martin recoiled, covering his ears, then looked down at the sad body at his feet. What had he done? The body did not stare back at him, it could not stare at all. Instead the two caverns of black threatened to draw him in, to drag him down into their blackness. What the hell had he been thinking of? Martin dropped the knife in his hand as though it had offended him and stepped backwards. Surely he was not as bad as the rest of these people. There was a world of difference between himself and the man who had carried that severed head on top of a pole wasn't there? Before he knew it Martin was running. He ran and he ran, until he could no longer hear the shouting in the streets behind him. He ran until the paving stones were replaced by grass under his feet.

*　*　*　*　*

Flames spread over the pavement and then died down, and more were thrown to replace them. They were well and truly trapped. Nobody had expected the people of a small town to be as sophisticated as this when it came to tactics. Whoever was leading them was obviously very experienced in some sort of urban warfare. Sergeant Liptrot felt that he had no option but to call for the rest of the armed unit. They may even have to ask for assistance from the local armed forces. He had never had to do this in all of his fifteen years of service. As another cocktail of fire rained overhead, clattering down on upraised riot shield he radioed for back up and told them to hurry.

*   *   *   *   *

Whilst police reinforcements headed towards the town centre, and the armed squad prepared themselves for the possibility that they may have to open fire on civilians en masse, many people discovered the urge to leave Seahaven. One by one and two by two cars crept as quietly as possible along the only roads out of town. The roadblocks could not possibly stop them if there were enough, and they could at least show that they were not connected with the riot in the town centre in any way. They were in fact decent citizens, trying to escape from the urban horror within. To the delight of many the police on roadblock duty had largely given up the effort. They were after one man, and as long as he was not allowed to leave then all was well. As long as people did not mind having their cars searched thoroughly then they could leave and go wherever the hell they wanted. The queue of traffic now tailed back a quarter of a mile on all roads out of the town. Suddenly it was a good idea for everyone and his dog to go and visit that Aunt he had not seen for years, or an

302

old friend who lived a long way away, the further the better. They could read about Seahaven in the morning papers. In the distance behind them windows were smashed and people raged in the streets. The sound of gunshots cracked through the air, making many of the people in exile shudder. What if they had not managed to get out? Who was doing all of the shooting? The gunfire continued, and in the middle of it the entire town centre erupted in a ball of flame, shaking the ground under their feet.

*   *   *   *   *

The explosion reduced the town square to a crater, along with two thirds of the armed police. The remaining third had escaped when they had rushed to form back up for the riot squad further up the street. Fire raged like a wounded animal around the crater, pacing back and forth. They had been lucky. If it was not for the ferocity of the riot then they would not have been called away and all of them would be dead. The explosion halted the violent crowd, almost shocking them into looking at themselves. As glass shattered all around them, all over town, not a window left intact by the blast, they stopped. It was not sudden, like switching off a light. It was more gradual, like a steam train running out of steam, or a lighter that runs out of gas. It slows down, but tries to continue until it just cannot any more. There was no stop, it just stopped somehow. Before anyone realised it they were sneaking back home, and leaving the police to pick up the pieces and wonder what had gone wrong. Later this whole episode would be used as a training scenario for budding young officers. The Seahaven scenario, where there was a no win situation. Within half an hour, with nobody to guide them the crowd had completely dispersed. The police made no arrests, there was no point. There was nowhere to hold anyone in custody now that there was no police station. With no police station there was also no Victor Midnight. All they needed now was Martin Phillips and they could wrap up the enquiry and get out of here, the sooner the better.

*   *   *   *   *

Five Crow Boys stood uneasily in a semi circle and watched Victor Midnight. He looked at the broken and burned wheel in the centre of the common and groaned. It was a groan the likes of which they had never heard and never expected from one such as him. Earlier they had been jumping up and down and whooping with joy at the sight of their bonfire in the streets below. Robert had sent the phone signal at just the right moment. The pager had answered and a split second later BOOM! The town hall had disappeared in a ball of burning hatred. The animal fire consumed the building, swallowing it whole, and not contented with this feast, had started to eat other buildings, until the whole town square was on fire. Then Mr. Midnight had turned up. The first thing he had seen was his carousel, burned to the ground by the Gypsies as they departed.

He wailed and they had covered their ears. The wail, like the scream of a thousand long dead and gone steam trains faded and was replaced by the groaning of the dead, and their tortured souls. Mr. Midnight turned to them all in turn, so that they could see his pain. His animals, all of them a thousand years old and more were dead, wasted in a senseless act of revenge by the Gypsies. He showed them in his glare how they had bucked and writhed to escape the flames, but had been unable because they were fixed and bolted in place. The five of them watched and said nothing, lest he release his anger at them. Instead with a great howl of rage he released it into the world. Robert looked at his four companions and watched their hair turn white as so did his. They watched together as white fire consumed the Midnight Man, starting in drips from his eyes and mouth, then bursting from every pore, flashing and searing into the air around him. He roared and the wind roared with him. He dripped fire from his eyes and mouth and the rain lashed forth in unison. Mr. Midnight raised his arms and demanded that the earth shake, and it obliged. A storm raged in the sky above, spreading out over the town. Wind picked up speed, and the five crow boys were forced into the centre, next to the Midnight Man as he dripped with stellar fire.

15. The Last Waltz.

Angry clouds stamped their way across the sky like vengeful gods and unleashed their vengeance on the town below. Winds howled like dogs in the streets. For each street a different wind, all converging upon the Common above, and in their madness the winds fought mighty battles raging across the town. The winds fought with all at their disposal, launching cars as missiles, using roofs as shields and lampposts as battle lances. Lightning cleaved the sky in two and then again in four, and thunder roared out in anger at the people of Seahaven, shaking them from their pretended slumber. The battle raged on, each wind throwing bricks and paving stones, trying to injure the immortal and incorporeal enemy.

Somewhere on the edge of town fire had been roused from its rest. It had joined the battle as a car was hurled into a petrol station. Sparks flew and in anger fire had spoken, waking his brothers all over town.

Fire raged and winds wrestled in the streets.

Within half an hour the fire had spread to the main high street, being uncontainable in the force of this tempest. Houses were coming apart brick by brick and being swallowed by the ravenous winds. Police began the evacuation. There had been no weather warning on the evening news, or on their radios, as all communications outside Seahaven had been cut off. Now as the winds tore down houses brick by brick and uprooted telegraph poles, wrapping telephone wires around buildings in a giant game of cat's cradle there was no other choice. The centre of the storm and the calmest place seemed to be the common, on the hill above Seahaven. If this were some sort of hurricane, which it certainly looked like then that was the calm centre. Nobody, however, had ever heard of a hurricane standing still before. About a quarter of the townsfolk had already been sent up there, and the police were doing their best to keep everyone calm. It was difficult to stay calm when your house was disappearing before your eyes and being thrown up into the black sky. Where would it land?

Were they simply swallowed up into a black nothing, or were they carried to a distant place. Somewhere on the shores of a tropical island did native Indians watch as houses built themselves on the beach, or did it rain bricks in Mongolia? Where does thunder go when it dies?

*   *   *   *   *

Martin made his way out of the town centre and up the hill towards the common. Since he had started his journey the wind

307

had picked up speed and force, and a look over his shoulder confirmed that the town was disintegrating behind him. In the last ten minutes people had joined him, in a rush to get out of the storm and up onto the common, which appeared to be the centre. The gates ahead had been torn wide open and people were flooding onto the common, falling over each other in their effort to escape the wrath of the storm. Each had a guilt, which they ran from. The guilt chased them with great gnashing teeth in the guise of a storm, seeking retribution for all they had done and thought in their sinful lives. The people of Seahaven ran up the hill and through the gates of the common, dragging Martin with them, whilst behind them their town burned and their lives were torn down and dragged up into the black sky. Martin felt a familiar sensation of being pulled towards the gates at the top. This had happened to him once before. Only then the tide of people had been gentle and had urged him to relax and flow with them. Now a torrent raced towards the gates, threatening to drown anyone who fought against the current. It threatened to drag them down and drown them in gravel and bruises and crush them under the weight of their own guilt. Martin could taste the guilt all around him, and the fear that their guilt had come alive and wanted to take them. Take them to where? He looked up, peering into the black sky, and the darkness within it. In there, where your screams would be silent against the howling of winds below, suffocated in violent clouds.

The gates approached with alarming speed as he bobbed along in the current of human lives. Sat atop each gatepost was a crow in

308

the shape of a boy. Two of them, one at each side. The leered at the frightened crowds as they entered, watching closely. For what? Martin did not know, but all who passed through the gates looked up at these boys with fear in their hearts, afraid of being cast back out into the world below by these two frail children. However, Martin could see that they were not so frail. Inside them was the strength that darkness brings to your nightmares, which seem trivial by day but terrifying by night. The innocent creak of an old house as it cools at night, and the hoot of an owl, or the eerie call of an unknown animal in the darkness amidst the secret whisper of trees, all of this was contained in that look, as they watched you enter their ground, through the gates and onto the common. Martin ducked his head down as he approached. He glided through the gates, only once feel the cold sweep of eyes across the back of his neck as they scanned him in the darkness, then he was through.

The air up here was somehow calmer, as though he had stepped into a large, spacious room. The wind was but an echo of the past up here, something that raged outside, out of the protection and comfort of this place. It battered against the open gates trying to force it's way in, but the gates were just to strong. Their old rotting wood was to secure to allow the storm through. The calmness of the air up here did nothing, however to calm the people who made it this far. They gathered in groups, some huddling against each other to fight off the cold, others at the edge of the common, as far as they could go, watching the destruction below. All thought of their lives vanishing like dust thrown into the wind. Their houses and belongings strewn all over the town, the country, or the world.

He watched the skies, but there was nothing to see, so he watched the people instead. Among them there were but a few who did not share this dread. Five boys who had become like crows, feeding on the carrion of others. These five watched with pleasure as the fear grew among the townsfolk, feeding on this emotion as though it were a delicacy. These five watched in turn by a lone man, if that is what he was, at the centre of this all. Martin saw him before his eyes stumbled across his confused form. He saw him as a whole, encompassing this place, feeding on it like a rat feeds on suffering and remains. He saw him causing this destruction so that he could feed on what remained behind, and take what he could from the souls of men and women. He saw his shadow over the earth, blocking out the sun, then his eyes stumbled across his form. A lone man sat on the edge of a broken and burned carousel in the centre of the common. His eyes bled with unseen fire and his tongue glowed with the burning heat of stars, as though the words he uttered would scorch the earth and burn the ears of any who heard them. Martin shuddered, for the first time that he could remember he was actually afraid, and he tried to stop himself. This man could smell it. He watched the man carefully from within the crowds, circling so as not to be found out. The shadow crouched around him like a cloak, hiding him from the eyes of men. Martin remembered a shadow like this once before, in a woman named Sylvia who was not Sylvia, but this was a darker shadow than that, a thousand times darker than the sin in any heart, or the imaginary fear in any mind. The shadow crouched about the man, a Midnight Man, ruffling in the breeze like the feathers of a giant crow, darker than any raven could ever be. It absorbed all light so there was no telling how tall he was or how wide, nor what shape. He was just there. His hair and teeth and eyes that brimmed with white fire blazed forth from the shadowy cape, but remained unseen by all, except for Martin. The winds whispered to him and waited, but he did not whisper back, he let them wait. Martin knew that the winds would wait for days if necessary. They would wait for him to command them and they would do whatever he said. He stood up, and as he stood, Martin could have sworn that the air parted, to let him pass.

*   *   *   *   *

P.C. McRae watched the skies with fear for what would have happened to his own house. He lived fairly near the common, so perhaps his house would not have been as badly affected as some of those near the Town centre. He tried to calm people as the entered the common, getting them to sit in their groups. A cart had been brought up here with coffee and tea making facilities, but he knew that a cup of tea was not going to make all of this go away. It was possibly the worst storm this century and he was telling people to sit down and have a polystyrene cup of tea. They would have to wait until the storm subsided enough to venture back into the Town centre and assess the damage. Only

311

then could they open whatever buildings remained standing as makeshift shelters. The storm did not look as though it would ever subside. Like the darkness it looked as though it was here forever. Earlier he had quietly arrested one maniac who had been preaching an end of the world sermon. He had been handcuffed and placed in the back seat of a police car, which was now parked at the rear of the common, away from prying eyes. The last thing they wanted was a maniac trying to panic people more than they already were. P.C. McRae was beginning to take this end of the world stuff more seriously. He was pondering this when he saw Martin. The Phillips boy was up here, as bold and brazen as anything. He was up here and walking about among these people as though the blood on his hands and the lives of those policemen he had spilt all over the road meant nothing. P.C. McRae tried his radio, but it was still not working. The interference had become worse since the storm started. He cursed silently and made his way slowly towards the boy. As he walked he passed P.C. Trevitt, who was trying to explain to a group of people that it was against the law to light a fire on the common, he tapped him on the shoulder and signaled for assistance. Trevitt nodded and followed. His radio did not work either. The two crept through the crowd and split up, so as to approach him on each side.

*   *   *   *   *

Somewhere in the whirlpool of people around him someone had

uttered a curse and Mr. Midnight pricked up his ears. Someone in the crowd still felt malice even among all of this devastation. He smiled his arctic smile and peered among them. A policeman. Who were they following? He swept his gaze across the crowds of people, up and down among them, in and out of their heaving bodies until his eyes met another pair who did not move to let him past. The boy was here. The boy who he had left a human vegetable.

*   *   *   *   *

Martin froze. The Midnight Man had spotted him and was smiling. He knew that he was here. He watched the cold fire of those eyes sweep over him and into him like harpoons, barbed and inescapable. He was flooded with images of darkness and pain, a lifetime of fear which was to last for ever. This is what the Midnight Man was promising him, as he had promised those before him. Only he had the cure, the cure of Midnight and darkness. Take the cure and you will be saved, like the crow boys. The crow boys. What were they now? Were they still human? Could a puppet of flesh and bone without fear and without remorse remain human?

Martin fought, and at once, when it was too late realized that the Midnight Man had held him there for a reason. The heavens turned and as above so below the world turned with them. Martin, too late realised that danger was at hand. Before he could react the Midnight Man smiled and released him from his gaze. Martin found himself face down in the dirt with both hands behind his back and a knee in his chest. He had the right to remain silent. His pockets were turned out, while he remained face down in the dirt, the pressure of a knee in his back, and his legs were kicked apart. There were no weapons. All of this was a blur now, and echo around him as though it was happening to someone else. He did not have to say anything, but if he did not he was in deep shit if it came out in a trial. What trial? He was being arrested for the double murder of Police

Constables Peterson and Blackstone. Martin shook his head violently.

"I didn't do it, " He screamed, "It wasn't me, it was him." He tried to point towards the smiling darkness ahead, but could not move his hands.

He was yanked to his feet by the handcuffs that now secured him. P.C. McRae stared back at him calmly and coldly. "You either come with us calmly and without fuss or I'll beat the living shit out of you right here."

Martin shook his head violently, shouting back, so everyone around him could hear. "You don't understand, " The words spat from his mouth, throwing saliva in all directions, "He's not human, he's a demon. He wants us ...." he did not finish the last sentence before P.C. McRae yanked hard on the cuffs again, spinning him around and placed a cold truncheon against his neck from behind. Martin found the words cut off, along with his breath.

"Shut the fuck up and move." McRae pushed him forward. They

314

were going to throw him in the back of a police car along with
another nutter they had nicked earlier and lock the door. Then
they were going to leave him there until things had calmed down
and they could get to the police station. Martin could hear all of
this going on inside McRae's head, like it was a radio
transmitter, only all radio transmissions were down weren't
they? He could see the Midnight Man watching them and knew
that it would be his turn next. While he was locked helpless in
the car the Midnight Man would come to him and dispose of him
quietly, or worse.

Martin was marched through a leering crowd towards a police
car. Murmurs were spreading. Murderer? Thief? Rapist? The
crowd pressed to see the new exhibit. This is what a serial killer
looks like folks, just like you and me, only rotten inside. But
Martin was not a killer was he? Surely not, he would have
remembered something like that. Martin struggled against the
hold but it was no use, then a miracle happened. Someone in the
crowd shouted and a rifle was poised, then another. P.C. McRae
stopped. He was confused here. Martin turned around. Armed
police had surrounded the burned carousel and were training
their weapons on a man dressed in the finest black clothes at its
centre. The were calling for him to give himself up. Martin
shook his head. It was no use, what could they do against him?
Then P.C McRae shoved Martin against the car, it was best to
arrest him anyway, just in case. A face leered up at him from the
car window, another lunatic, happy to have the company.

"NO!" Martin shouted, "Don't put me in there. Don't you see?

I'm not mad and I'm not a killer. " He felt his head being squashed down into his neck as McRae tried to force him into the back seat of the car. "You don't understand. He will kill you all!"

*   *   *   *   *

Blinding pain and the sting of tears was the only thing left. The world had vanished, washed away in blood, but this had not washed away the pain. Nothing could ever wash away the fear of loneliness and the agony of love. Gregory fought against the beast as it carried him inside itself through the woods, ripping bark from trees and flesh from bodies as though there was no difference. The wolf was tired now, exhausting itself as the rage they both felt swallowed it up. Gregory could feel his senses swimming to the surface again, clouded still in the blood and thumping of his own veins. He fought for more, swam towards the surface away from the beating drum of his own heart. Grass under foot. He could feel the grass, he could feel. But what of the sun, it was gone, like her into the distance. Revenge was not the answer. Gregory rushed on towards the shouting and artificial lights ahead. What was this place? The wolf growled along side him now, lazily, it's energy spent, and the body was his again. He ran onwards towards the common and the fairground. He ran back to the Midnight man, but did not go to make peace or to bargain. This time he would not listen to the lies that dripped like honey from his tongue. This time he would

316

control the wolf and he would let it loose to do his bidding. He would eat the bastard.

Gregory ran and ran, as he had always run, but now at last he was running towards something instead of away. The clearing of the common drew closer and as he approached he slowed. Something was going on here. There were people everywhere but no fairground. He burst through the tree line and into the clear ground.

*　　*　　*　　*　　*

In thunder, lightning and rain the people stood and cast glances back and forth between the police with their trained guns and the Midnight Man sat upon his burned and charred perch. The police called for him to give himself up quietly but he said nothing. He merely smiled and shook his head. The wind stopped whistling around them, and even the rain hushed. Then Mr. Midnight stood up and laughed. He laughed out loud for all to hear, a sound like broken glass and steam train whistles that stop the blood in the dead of night. He laughed the sound that perspiration makes as it squeezes from every pore during your nightmares, and he laughed like the raging of hurricane winds tearing up houses and throwing cars.

Children rushed to his side, five of them in all, each with a darker shadow than most. The five crow boys made in his image ran to his side, surrounding him and shielding him with their innocent young frames.

317

He laughed again.

"You don't want to hurt this innocent young flesh do you?"

Somewhere in the crowd a woman screamed and feinted, recognising the boy, her son, where a human crow now stood. The crowd pressed but dared not move closer. The five boys smiled back, daring someone to shoot.

P.C. McRae looked at Martin, then at Victor Midnight, then at Martin again. Martin nodded. He could hear the thoughts, from inside. He could see the doubt.

"You see, " He said, "Do you see?"

McRae did not answer him; he turned his gaze back to the scene around the carousel and could not help but hold his breath.

* * * * *

Some people are just rotten to the very core, and others around them can almost smell the decay that has set in, as their soul turns bad. As Victor Midnight stood at the centre of the carousel, with the five crow boys around him he emitted such a terrible carrion odour that Gregory could not understand why nobody had ever noticed before. He had walked out of the trees into the common as naked as the day he was born but nobody noticed. All eyes were upon the scene ahead. He walked forward towards the police car and the burned carousel beyond. He could hear shouting from the police car, someone he once knew, someone else who knew the evil contained within this man they all watched. Gregory strolled past the police car and brushed past

318

P.C. McRae.

"Midnight, I'm going to eat your fucking heart, you inhuman piece of shit." He ran towards the calm figure, but did not get more than a few steps before he was dumped on his face. The crowd behind cheered, whether at his attempt to rid the planet of this man or at his arrest he was not sure. The two armed police guards who had pounced on him were attaching handcuffs to his twisted arms while Victor Midnight smiled down on him.

"Good evening Gregory, nice of you to join us."

He growled back and was kicked into submission by one of the armed police, snatching the growl away from him. They hoisted him to his feet and dragged him backwards towards the police car. P.C. McRae thought he had seen enough now.

"You are all weak." Victor Midnight was shouting, taunting them. "None of you will shoot." He stepped forwards, looking around him at the police surrounding him. "You are too afraid to shoot, too afraid of the consequences." Air pressed heavy on the crowd, the wind silenced itself.

"You are all weak, too weak to live with the fear of guilt."

He watched them, casting his gaze over each in turn until finally resting on one. A young officer. The boy, just turned man glared back through the one eye of his sight finder and kept the barrel of his rifle steady. Midnight stared him back in the face and smiled. He actually smiled. Before he knew it the index finger of his right hand had applied the necessary pressure. He held his breath for a moment. The bastard had smiled. He had deserved it. The rifle kicked silently against his shoulder, there would be a bruise there tomorrow. Then the silent air was split in two by the crack of rifle fire.

With one, two followed and then four, then eight and more. Countless tiny explosions in the dark and countless lethal missiles launched. The crowd pressed hands to ears as one, but none could look away. One thought among all as they watched the riffles go off, glad it's not me. It was not them who would be lying on the slab at the morgue, like it was not them being cut out of a car on the M6, but they had to look, to make sure. No, it's not me, thank God. Thank God it's you and not me.

Mr. Midnight stood in the centre of a rain of gunfire and smiled. Martin nodded.

"You can't hurt him," he shouted, "You don't understand what he is. He belongs to us now. We invited him here, so he has to stay with us." But nobody was listening to the mad boy in the car. Only Gregory heard him.

Martin looked as Gregory's face was thrown against the car window. Gregory looked back. I knew you once, his eyes said, and you knew me. But not any more. His eyes were wild and feral, darting from one place to another, not out of fear or submission, but out of the habits of a hunter. They ran with the visions of a thousand prey and a thousand meals. Martin understood. Gregory smiled back at him.

From behind, through the fog of gun smoke and under the cacophony of gunfire Mr. Midnight was calling him.

"Gregory, it is time for you to change again."

He could feel the pulling sensation in the pit of his stomach as

320

the wolf was dragged forwards, but the wolf was still asleep, exhausted.

"Don't listen Gregory, close your ears. He can't hurt you if you don't want him to."

But he could.

Gregory could feel the wolf stirring inside and he knew that he would always be this way. He knew that he would always be at the beck and call of people like Victor Midnight, unable to control his feelings. Tears leaped to his eyes and blurred the image of Martin's face, his one time friend.

We invited him here, so he has to stay with us.

Gregory looked back at the Midnight man, then at Martin again. Martin shook his head, he could see what was happening here.

"No Gregory, fight it, don't give in."

Gregory shook his head and placed one palm on the window of the car. Tears now filled his eyes, making the world beyond them swim, like a lazy summer dream. Only this was not summer, and it was no dream.

"Goodbye Martin."

We invited him here.

Before Martin could answer Gregory had turned around and stood upright, pushing the arresting police officers backwards and to the ground. He growled as he let the wolf show itself to the surface just enough. The people around the car backed away, and he pulled his hands free from the cuffs. The wolf did not want to go, but was too tired so could not resist. Not yet. Gregory pushed it back down. He turned again to face the

Midnight Man and this time smiled back.

The guns still trained on Mr. Midnight had one by one ceased firing, as they were having no effect. He was chuckling, but otherwise ignoring them. The crowd moaned as smoke began to clear, showing one child dead where a crow had once been and one injured, shot in the leg. The injured boy screamed and Mr. Midnight ignored his screams. The other three boys watched him with horror dawning on their faces, like the dawn of sunlight after a long winter night. Gregory marched forward through the smoke towards him, brushing off an attempt by P.C. McRae to get a hold on him again. P.C. McRae bounced off him, and was sent sprawling backwards against the car. Martin tried to open the door but could not. For the first time in his life all he could do was watch.

We invited him here, so he has to stay with us.

Gregory reached forward and snatched a loaded rifle from the first armed policeman who got in his way.

Mr. Midnight watched him and laughed.

Gregory breathed deeply, taking the night air into his lungs. He sniffed at the sky and flexed his fingers against the cool air. It was good to be alive. The tears had all but dried away now; his vision was swimming back into focus.

Mr. Midnight faced him, across the clearing that had developed between himself and the police.

"What do you think you are going to do with that you stupid boy? Haven't you been watching for the last ten minutes?"

Gregory pushed the butt of the rifle into the face of an on

rushing police officer, who was attempting to get the rifle back. He could feel trained guns on himself now, there was not much time.

We invited him here, so he has to stay with us.

"Suicides go to hell, right?"

Victor Midnight sneered. His eyes narrowed.

"You wouldn't dare."

Gregory dared.

He up ended the rifle and slid the end of the barrel under his own chin. The air tasted good today. The wind was fresh, and he could see and hear the birds in the trees waiting to come out. He would never be alone again.

"Come with me."

Victor Midnight howled, piercing the sky and the air with his frustration.

His face twisted into an inhuman snarl and he reached for the naked man with the rifle perched under his chin. Gregory smiled back and pulled the trigger.

*   *   *   *   *

Hannah sighed and tried to suppress a tear that would not be denied. It was beautiful here. They sat together and watched the sand blow across dunes, on and on forever. The desert heaved with a sadness she had never before felt. Something inside her cried out and another tear leaped to replace the first. Sylvia placed an arm around her shoulder.

"It's all right to cry." She said, so Hannah did.

*   *   *   *   *

The gunshot echoed around the common, back and forth like the lament of a grieving animal hunting for a sympathetic ear. As the crowd watched Gregory slump to the floor in front of Victor Midnight, the top of his head sprayed up into the sky like a glorious bloody fountain. Victor Midnight howled, then he pleaded. The crowd backed away, the police officers backed away. The crow boys disappeared, blending with the crowd, leaving one of their number dead and another helpless among the charred remains of the carousel. The helpless one called for help, but nobody would listen. The wind began to pick up again, then change direction, it seemed to be blowing upwards.

P.C. McRae watched the scene with growing repulsion. Victor Midnight's shadow was uncurling to it's full height and width. It stood behind and around him, nine feet tall, and six feet wide. McRae looked from side to side, to see if there were any birds nearby, but could not see any, although he could swear that the shadow this man cast had wings. Great feathered and ragged wings, like a huge crow. The air blew upwards and clouds gathered overhead, sweeping in from all directions. It seemed as though the storm was collapsing in on itself, and Victor Midnight was screaming now, as though it was taking him with it. The crowd ran.

They ran in all directions and P.C. McRae thought it best to follow suit. He jumped into the driver's seat of the car and started the engine. As he drove away he watched the scene behind in his rear view mirror. The clouds gathered overhead and swept downwards, turning the hurricane inside out. What had been the calm centre was now a raging battleground for the elements and the outside had become calm. The storm was caving in, turning on itself with Victor Midnight at the centre. He watched just long enough to see the man's shadow ripped from him like a piece of loose clothing and then his body torn apart.

That was enough. P.C. McRae drove on and did not look back. Only the scream of the winds fighting over the remains of Victor Midnight's body reminded him of what he was driving away from. Finally, as the police car pulled away from the common gates and into the road leading to Seahaven the winds groaned and creaked, lifting the charred carousel high up into the night sky. The wood splintered and was gone, folding in on itself with a deafening crunch.

Martin Phillips was not in the car, but P.C. McRae secretly thought that did not matter anyway. He thought that they would see no more murders in Seahaven, and hoped that the boy had got away safely. All he wanted to do now was to go home.

*   *   *   *   *

Clouds dissipated slowly, ushered on by a gentle breeze and the clocks of Seahaven turned as they had always done. Four o'clock in the morning came and went, with people gathered in the streets below the common. The ground where the carousel had stood seemed to be ripping itself free and spiraling skywards into the nothingness beyond.

By the turn of five o'clock in the morning the sun peered tentatively over the horizon, as though to check if the coast was clear and the people of Seahaven, still out of their beds, with no beds to go to, breathed a heavy sigh. Rusty orange seeped through the greyness of the sky and finally the night was pushed aside. The night, it seemed, was over.

It had been a long night, with a storm. The murderer of Seahaven had been caught and was in police custody, they would say. And if anyone were to ask then the answer would be yes. Yes, they had just had the worst storm in their history, but that was bad luck. In a week or so the shops would be open as usual.

*   *   *   *   *

Help arrived in the guise of the fire department and a unit of the armed forces from a nearby barracks that morning at a quarter past seven. None of them could believe the devastation they were witness to. The town square had been reduced to rubble, a huge crater where the Town Hall and the police station should have been. The locals said it was a lightning strike. A weird accident, very unfortunate. Most of the houses and shops around the high street had been burned down in a large fire, and other

326

buildings were severely damaged and would have to be condemned. Of all of the fishing vessels in the fire only one remained intact. The greatest shock of all, however, was the devastation that the storm itself had caused. The gale force winds had leveled a good half of the town, spreading the debris in a seventeen mile radius. This place was likely to have an insurance claim to make any insurance company chief executive reach for his bottle of Valium. The East Harbour was turned into a refuge for those who were left homeless by the fire and the storm, but many had chosen to leave town already and seek the shelter of friends or relatives elsewhere. Some preferred to move to hotels in other towns rather than stay.

*   *   *   *   *

Four days later it rained red bricks and wooden splinters in the former Soviet Union somewhere, and trees fell from the sky in Alaska. Robert McRae watched all of this on the nine o'clock news at his brother's house in Edinburgh. He switched the television off. There was no point in dwelling on it. It was just a freak storm and nothing more. The darkness had merely been an overcast sky, which they should have seen as a warning that the storm was coming. Witches, and demons? Werewolves? There were no such things he would say. Don't be ridiculous.
Robert McRae nevertheless chose to leave town and travel three hundred and thirty miles to his brother's house rather than stay in Seahaven any more. He thought about retiring from the force

and opening up a café here in Inverness. A twenty four hour café where the lights were always on. He smiled at his brother and sister in law who were watching him warily from across the room.

"Are you all right? " Asked his brother.

Outside distant thunder rolled slowly towards them.

"Yes, I'm fine." Robert McRae answered, "Are the doors and windows locked?"

Epilogue: After the Storm.
2019

Sylvia and Hannah watched through a window from the café in which they sat, keeping a careful eye on the figure walking up the street below.

"He's done well to get this far." Sylvia spoke finally.

Hannah smiled warmly at her, "Surely you're not going soft already."

She shook her head, "No, I think we should make him wait a while longer, and see what he discovers on his own before we interfere."

Hannah nodded, and took another bite out of her watermelon. This place was so beautiful, and the desert, she had never seen anything like it. It was so wonderful and sad that it made her cry every time they went out there. Is this what it had been like for Sylvia all those years? Had she felt this strongly? Seen so much without trying?

Sylvia nodded, "Yes."

Her eyes sparkled with new life. Hannah looked around to see if anyone else was looking at them. She was now certain that Sylvia was the most beautiful creature in the world. Ezekiel purred softly, pressing his nose against the window, allowing Hannah to stroke the soft fur behind his ears. Sylvia sighed and looked out of the window at Martin, searching in the streets below. He moved easily among the people here, gliding in and out of them, talking to them in a dialect, which was indistinguishable from the locals. She realised that he would catch up with them before long, and she would have to keep her promise and show him what he was looking for, the way she had shown Hannah. She looked at Hannah from the corner of her eye, being careful not to let her see her watching. She was beautiful. It was good to have a companion, not to be eaten by the sadness every time she looked in a mirror. They could both now be together as long as they cared to live for. Now that Hannah had accepted the change herself they could be together forever.

Hannah leaned forward, "And I would not have it any other way Sylvia, even if forever is a long time."

Sylvia looked around at her again, watching the glitter in her eyes and the glow in her face. "Why Hannah, I do believe you just read my mind."

It suddenly struck her as she looked upon the face of the person she loved more than she had ever loved anyone, that whatever happened to them now they would be happy. Hannah threw her arms around her neck in the crowded café and they kissed.

*　　　*　　　*　　　*

"What you want is what I've got." he said, eyes aflame with dreams. A thousand sunsets in the left, a thousand sunrises in the right. Horses snorted at the front of his wagon, grunted in their

330

darkness, blinkered from the crowd.

He pulled a pale, dust worn sheet from the wagon's top, and let it slip down into the dust below. Onto the ground where feet had trod, and would tread again. The sheet settled. All eyes looked up.

V. J. MIDNIGHT

And below . . .

SUPPLIER

The man turned to the crowd, his grin as wide as oceans, teeth wide cliffs holding back the tide.

"That's me." He called to all who would hear him.

"Victor Midnight at your service."

His arms swept, and the crowd gathered.

Bottles and jars lined his road dusty shelves. Elixirs and tonics. Some clear, some blue, a rainbow hue.

All glitter and summer rain. All lustrous in the light of a thousand eager faces.

What are they?

What does he sell?

What shall I buy?

The voices whispered, to their darker selves. Secret voices, secret thoughts.

"What you require I can provide."

Mr. Midnight smiled, the sea at its darkest hour, murky and treacherous, concealing unknown treasures in immeasurable depths, and tipping his tall black hat bowed his head.

Silver hair flowed from where the hat had been, catching the sunlight, turning it cold. Then he was upright again, the hat in place, pacing, eyeing the crowd.

I wonder if he has a cold remedy?

A cure for cancer?

And aphrodisiac?

I wonder if . . .

Murmurs rising silently within. Everyone is still, no one breathes, lest he catch that breath and sell it back, or to someone else.

To own someone's breath, what is in that? Their soul?

Mr. Midnight's eyes twinkle, far off stars now, distant suns, alien heat.

His gloved hand reaches and a bottle comes.

Magician's trick.

"A cure for all ailments." Says he.

"Come up here, " he beckons the crowd.

"Try it and see."

How often has he plied his trade?

How many years?

First one approaches, a woman alone,

then three. Then nine, and on.

He smiles and takes their money,

in return for his liquid gold.

Tonic for cash.

Something new for something old.

And tonic is not all.

"Bargains galore, the likes of which you never saw." He cries.

Knives that never need sharpening.

Cups which just refuse to break.

A liqueur that tingles on the tongue. All of these and yet more to come.

The only charge is twenty shillings, for each and every one.

And if, just if you need something more,

"Just come around to the back door."

He would say, with sunset eyes and starry smile.

"I can get you what you want, but it may take a while."

All day he sold his wares,

but this day there had been no

unusual requests.

Plates and forks, and carving knives.

Tonics wines and spirits, yes

but no eternal lives?

Not one.

Nor children.

Nor wealth.

Nor happiness.

Nor age (usually a child's request).

So with the setting of the sun Mr. Midnight covered the sign.

How often?

How many years?

Mr. Midnight sighed and packed. No dreams to sell in this dreary town. No one to believe in his carnival eyes.

Yes, but how many years?

He pulled himself up, upon the chariot's seat, prepared to leave for another place, another year. But would they buy from him? Would they trust his face? He who wondered in the roads and tracks, and the fields before them just to sell. He who is without age, for time is but his shadow.
Would they?

"Excuse me sir."
Mr. Midnight halted his arms, let loose the reins of his restless steeds.
"Excuse me sir." The voice called again.
He turned his head towards the sound of folly.
"I was wondering, " the boy said quietly. He shifted his stance, as though to transfer guilt from foot to foot.
He looked to the left and to the right,
To make certain they were alone.
No one in sight.
His cautious glances confirmed his wish.
Alone they were, for good or ill.
A solitary boy, with a man and his cart,

334

upon a solitary hill.

"An unusual request?" Mr. Midnight asked, stepping down from his perch.

His black coat fluttered in the breeze, feathered and ragged under the harvest sky.

The boy nodded, shuffled again. Embarrassed by his want?

Storm clouds boiled over the horizon, sweeping clear skies aside.

"Well." Mr. Midnight smiled, placing a long arm around the boy's shoulder and led him to the door.

The boy felt suddenly small, the world suddenly cruel.

"You had better come inside."

The end

Printed in Great Britain
by Amazon